# JOMO CALLS

SUDEEPA NAIR

ISBN 979-8-89002-882-2

# Table of Contents

Dear Readers,

If you have read and enjoyed my mystery novel, The Serpents of Kanakapuram, you would have noticed how much I enjoy writing about nature. Those who read the subsequent science fiction books Around the World in 2153 and 2154: The Cocoon would have noted my penchant for exploring technological trends and how they might affect humanity.

In this book, Jomo Calls, I combine all my favourite themes to spin a tale about a mountain village, Jomo, its inhabitants, and a corporate conspiracy surrounding them.

As with my previous books, I have drawn inspiration from incidents and people around us. But my greatest inspiration continues to be our planet Earth and nature, which nourishes our mind, body, and soul.

Wishing you an adventurous trek up and down the Jomo Mountain with the Jomoans who experience the Joy of Missing Out.

– **Sudeepa**

# Welcome to Jomo

On a typical day, GK would savour his favourite fish curry meals from NewTown Homely Meals, catch up on his thirty blissful minutes of nap at his desk in the accounts section of Radha Textiles, and embellish it further with piping hot tea from the Corner Tea Shop. Today was different. Today, GK expected an opportunity to show his online friends how happy he was and what an exciting life he led.

Sweat trickled across GK's chubby face, and his damp t-shirt stuck dotingly to his rotund torso. He paused, leaning onto the mountain face. "There better be a good reason why you invited me, Tara," he muttered. It irked him that she had called one fine day after disappearing for more than five years. He could not refuse when she casually asked about the love of his life. "How's Kannagi?" she enquired with no malicious intent, but GK was hit by the full force of the obligation. It was also an opportunity to rebuild their broken friendship.

Over the phone, Tara had spoken about a large inheritance and how she had to make a quick decision about the estate. Apparently, her lawyer was breathing down her neck.

GK scratched his neck absentmindedly as prickly weeds from the mountain face tickled him, but he didn't budge.

As he squinted at the bright sun beating down on him and the path that crawled around the mountain, a tinge of regret dampened his excitement. He shouldn't have agreed. At such a scenic location, one would expect a sign or two that said, 'Welcome to Jomo.' There was none. He knew why. His body protested within a few hundred metres into the steep climb. The whole situation reminded him of a scene from a Wodehousian caper. Except, the humour was lost on him.

The saving grace for this arduous trek was the beauty that spread nonchalantly as far as he could see. Like a velvety green quilt lying languidly over the brown curvaceous mounds.

The view from the position was marvellous and the day exquisite. GK whipped out his phone and captured the view in his camera, then opened an app to post the picture. His virtual followers far outnumbered his real friends. They would be thrilled to see the photograph and envious too. To his chagrin, the picture wouldn't upload as the network was patchy. He glanced at the edge of the path. The coverage could be better towards the valley. A few inches away from the well-trodden path was a stone. He walked towards it and angled forward. His breath stalled in his throat as he glanced down.

Beyond the stone, the mountain sloped into the oblivion of the valley obscured by dense trees. His heart pumped faster. The depth was frightening, but even scarier was the sound of a car horn coming up the path. 'Jumping jackals!' he cried out. How could anyone drive up this narrow mountain path? And what should he do now? It was a choice between being tossed into the mountain air by the car or becoming airborne willingly. Even a quick scamper to the mountain face, on which he leaned a while ago, would result in a bone-crushing hit by the car. The sound came nearer, making him anxious. He flung his backpack onto the ground and crouched as close to the stone as possible. He prayed that the stone wouldn't roll over and end its solitary existence by taking him along.

The yellow hatchback rode up the slope like a bull on a mission to gore anyone on its path. As the car tore past, a cloud of dust covered GK's hunched torso, and he hid his face. To his astonishment, when the dust settled and he looked up, he found the car rolling backward. "This is worse than I thought," GK muttered. "Now, the car will surely kill me." But the car came to a stop beside him. It was so close that he was directly below the window. He couldn't glance at the driver's face without disturbing the delicate balance between him and the stone on the narrow mountain ledge. The driver stuck out a friendly face and asked, "Do you want a lift?"

The question raised a mix of emotions in GK's heart. It hurt him physically because his body was rolled into a snail's shell, curled up like a corkscrew on the stone, while he twisted his neck to turn his face upwards. It offered him relief that someone took pity on him. It evoked a slight regret that he did not own a car. The dominating emotion, though, was that of fear.

How did the man propose getting him into a parked vehicle on a precariously steep and narrow slope? The door couldn't open on the other side, being blocked by the mountain face. If the door opened to GK's side, he must combine dollops of courage with a ton of acrobatic skills to shove himself and his backpack into the backseat without falling off the precipice. His uncomfortably twisted neck and terror-struck eyes might have conveyed the last emotion well because the face that jutted out spoke in an apologetic tone, "I'll back down a few metres until I reach the clearing below. I can pick you up from there if you walk down to that point."

GK tried to croak a response, but his throat ran dry, and his tongue refused to cooperate. So, he lifted up a trembling thumb to show his approval. The car promptly backed away and disappeared around the bend. GK raised himself testily on his knees, then stood up. The tension in his knees felt familiar. Years ago, he had jumped off a seven feet high compound wall to escape the wrath of a mango farmer. He felt the same weakness now. His knees shook like two leaves caught in a storm. He picked up his backpack and walked down at a snail's pace. Every step was accompanied by a silent prayer to avoid encountering another vehicle.

As GK neared the clearing, he saw the yellow hatchback waiting for him, its engine purring softly. The man in the driver's seat was stout, with a rugged face and grey hair at the temples.

"Hello!" He waved at GK and opened the passenger's door. "Sorry to cause you trouble. I didn't expect anyone to climb this path on a Sunday afternoon. The village usually doesn't have visitors." A trembling GK flung his bag to the back and eased into the passenger seat. "Water?" asked the man and offered a bottle. When GK gulped down thirstily, he muttered another set of apologies.

"Your name?" the man asked.

"GK. And you?"

The man ignored his question, but his tone continued to be friendly. "Where are you going?"

"To visit a friend."

"Up here? What's your friend's name?"

"Tara."

Since GK was super-focused on the road ahead, it was hard to miss the unmistakable swerve to the right. The man was evidently affected by Tara's name. "Are you an advocate?" asked the man.

The unsettled dust on the road made the ride even more unsettling. GK blinked a few times before he glanced at the man. "No."

That's when GK noticed that he forgot to put on the seat belt. In the next few minutes, GK also forgot how to speak. The reason for his momentary disappearance from the world of rational conversations was the speed. The car was racing to the top as if on a mission to do or die. The air-conditioning unit was switched off, and the windows were down. GK would open his mouth to utter the choicest words in his vocabulary, instead, swallow leaves, bits of twigs, and flecks of dust, then close his mouth. The man continued his merry volley of questions, oblivious to the panic he was causing. "How do you know Tara? Have you been to Jomo before?" GK was rendered speechless as he gulped nature's titbits that came with the gushing wind until he could take it no more. He coughed and spluttered and cleared his throat. Alas! The ride only became worse when the slope became steeper. He shut his eyes tight to ignore the bizarre driving.

GK could now taste the remnants of the fish curry lunch that he ate yesterday. Just when he thought the dashboard would bear the brunt of his nausea, the car halted. Without opening his eyes, GK opened the door and jumped out. The man dumped his backpack on the ground below his nose. "The house you are looking for is beyond that clump of trees," he said, pointing to a dense bunch of branches. "She doesn't like cars going up to her house." GK did not bother to thank the man. The car veered towards the left, pursuing a motorable road.

The clump of trees was at the end of a walking path to the right. GK heaved up the backpack and trudged across the dry, pebbly slope. After about fifty metres, he was forced to catch his breath. The path was steeper than the road, but now there were thorny brambles he could hold on to, albeit with care. He cursed himself for carrying the backpack. He had planned for a night's stay. After everything he endured to reach the place, he deserved ample rest in a charming mountain village. He cursed himself more as he realised that the path did not end there but wound further up.

Before long, a picket fence appeared to his left. It was neatly obscured by a blooming bougainvillea. A gate in the fence led to a short climb of three steps. GK stopped at the top of the steps that led to the front lawn and took in the scene.

If this was Tara's home, her inheritance, she was an incredibly lucky girl.

# 2

# Friendly Updates

The house stood on a piece of land carved out from the mountain face. It was not huge, but its façade gave it a majestic appeal as its roof lined up against the clouds that were so close. Around the house ran a porch with exquisitely shaped wooden pillars. Outside the porch, Tara had lined up her favourite potted plants. The lawn covered with green grass spread out a foot below the flower pots. A swing and a bench occupied strategic positions on the lawn.

"Beautiful. Isn't it?" GK heard Tara's unmistakable voice. She appeared out of nowhere at GK's elbow.

"Straight out of a Ruskin Bond book. Why didn't you ever invite me here?"

Tara shrugged in response. "My grandma was not fond of visitors. She even hated our neighbours."

GK pirouetted to graze his eyes all around. There was not a dwelling to be seen for miles. "Neighbours? Here?"

"There are houses further back and down," she said, pointing vaguely to a path that curved around the house.

"Oh?"

GK turned around to pick up his backpack. He had dropped it near the gate before climbing up the steps. A strange mixture of a whine, yelp, and a sigh escaped his lips.

Tara followed his gaze to the hills beyond.

"Those hills are protected. They fall under the forest department. Elephants, leopards, wild boars, deer, and many species are found in those forests. I have even heard rumours that there are tigers, but so far, there have been no official sightings—"

"Can you share your wi-fi password? I can't browse." GK's fingers fiddled with his phone.

"You forgot," said Tara with a grin.

"Gosh! That's true! Your village has no connectivity, but my phone isn't even catching a signal."

"That's only here at my home. You can catch some bars further down. However, data might be patchy at best."

"Shucks!"

"You knew what you were getting into when you came here, didn't you?"

"But I promised Kannagi, I'll call her as soon as I reach."

"I can walk you to a point where you'll get coverage. Do you want to go now or after a wash and food?"

GK agreed that a wash and food were an excellent idea.

After a couple of hours, GK walked down the sloping path behind Tara's home. They updated each other with what had transpired in their lives after college.

GK told her about his wedding plans. "Next year," he said bashfully. "And you are the first one to be invited." Tara joked about how Kannagi had him in her stranglehold. "I don't know many men who married so young. We are twenty-five."

"Well, how many people, married or unmarried, of any age, do you know? You live in a hermitage at the top of a mountain."

Though Tara remained silent, GK continued, "You could have called me when your grandmother passed away? I would've arranged a place, and you could've found a job in NewTown. How do you live here all alone? By the way, how do you make a living now?"

"I teach," Tara smiled as she added, "I teach the village kids. I sell the produce from my vegetable garden in the local market. Once a week, I go to the valley to volunteer at the pet care centre. In return, they give me food for Coco."

"Coco?"

"Aah, you haven't met my dog yet because he is volunteering for old Grandpa Lal, who stays further down."

GK gaped with a mixture of awe and confusion. "Your dog volunteers too?"

"Grandpa Lal has a decent pension and is healthy for his age but lonely. So, I send Coco over on Sundays. He likes to give Grandpa company."

GK's phone rang. "It's Kannagi!" he nearly yelled.

Tara grinned at his excitement.

GK stepped away to talk on the phone, leaving Tara to ponder Grandpa Lal's loneliness.

GK's loud yelling broke Tara's reverie. Is the signal so bad that he has to shout to be heard? His tone made it difficult to gauge whether he was angry or sorry. He kept apologizing, but his tone conveyed annoyance. Tara heard snatches of his conversation. “I had no clue, Kani. Tell them that I have some work. What’s the big deal?”

The last few exchanges with Kannagi were subdued. GK barely spoke a word or two. “Let’s go back,” he muttered after he finished his call.

They walked in silence for a while.

“Listen, the thing that I mentioned on the phone? When I called you?” I hope you haven’t told anyone?” Tara asked as she pushed open the gate.

GK was astonished. She was breathing normally, speaking in complete sentences without panting or gasping, while he struggled to catch his breath.

“You haven’t told anyone, have you?” questioned Tara again.

GK waved his hand sideways. It could have meant a ‘no’, but as Tara realised, he was asking her to move away from between him and a bench that sat on Tara’s lawn. He remained silent after he flopped down on it.

Tara chuckled, recognizing how the steep climb was uncomfortable for outsiders to Jomo.

“You mean, that thing about you owning nearly half of Jomo?” GK yelled although Tara was hunched over a plant bed merely a few feet away.

“Hush!” she said, surveying the surroundings nervously.

GK followed her gaze. There was no third soul in sight. Who was Tara afraid of?

“Stop shouting. The mountain wind can carry the lightest whispers.”

"I wanted to test out my lungs. I am worried that the climb might have ruptured a few veins inside."

"Rubbish!" Tara said, shaking her head. "Let's go in."

They climbed another short flight of steps that led to a porch, and GK sat down again. Every climb exhausted him.

"Try to be fitter before you become a householder," Tara said as she eyed GK's red face that was gushing water from the seams.

GK snorted.

"So, why was Kannagi angry?'

"Why did you ask me to come here?" asked GK. "All you said is that your grandmother left this house and the rest of the property in your name, but how can I help?"

Tara chuckled. "You took the trouble to come all the way without knowing why. Thank you."

"Well, yes, erm, you can thank me later. I came because I was curious to visit the place, the famous Jomo, without the internet. You have never invited me here before. And..."

"And?"

"Well, we did not part on good terms, did we? Besides, I thought I could click a few pictures of the mountain and share them with my friends online."

Tara frowned. "You'll never learn your lesson, will you? I swear if I find any of my pictures online, I'll put you behind bars."

GK laughed hysterically. "Behind bars? For what? Why are you so...so...? Why are you like this?"

Tara ignored his question. "Do you have many online friends?"

"Yes, fifteen thousand two hundred and thirty-four."

Tara's eyes widened in disbelief. "Fifteen thousand?"

"Most are my followers, not friends," GK added to normalise the strangeness he felt when Tara repeated it. He knew it was humanly impossible for him to have as many friends in real life. "What? It's a modest following. Most influencers have in lakhs." GK added, for effect.

Tara snorted incredulously.

"I am popular for my photography. But today it landed me in trouble." He added with a forlorn expression on his face.

Tara raised her eyebrows. "Not the first time, is it?"

GK ignored the snarky comment and continued, "Kannagi's parents approve of our relationship, but her extended family, not so much. My redeeming factor happens to be that I am an orphan."

"Redeeming factor?"

"They can own me fully. I will assimilate easily into their joint family and—"

Tara interrupted with a chuckle.

"Is her family the Mafia, or what?"

GK shrugged with surly indifference. "They are no better, but she is sweet."

"Then why was she angry?"

"Well, I posted a picture of this mountain before I climbed."

"So?"

"I had promised to attend a wedding in the family, instead, I am here."

"Oh!"

"And the picture revealed that I was not at the shop doing overtime but trekking to some mountaintop."

"Why did you post it if they are so sensitive?"

"Poof! It missed the logical part of my brain. The act of clicking and posting pictures of places I visit has become part of my muscle memory now. Kani keeps warning me that I am bordering on addiction."

"Weird addiction!"

GK sighed and leaned back into the chair. His eyes strayed to a framed text hanging on the wall. It was printed neatly and had ornate borders like a tribute.

He moved closer to examine, gulping as he read the text. "So, this is where the story of Jomo begins."

"Wrong. Jomo is much older, but this reminds us of why we have the rules."

GK stared at the words in the frame. They struck warning bells in his mind.

# 3

# A Mendicant's Prophecy

More than two decades before GK pondered over the framed text hanging on every Jomoan wall, a man stood on one of the Jomo peaks in rumination. The valley looked enticing from the vantage point.

When you are at extraordinary heights, the fear is not that you might fall but that you might jump.

Patsy gazed at the expanse below, which appeared greener from the sky-high mountain. He recalled his last corporate meeting with the editor of a business magazine.

"We wish to include you in our 'Forty under Forty' list," the editor said. "But..." he paused, scanning Patsy for apparent signs of mental instability, "you don't seem to be in a comfortable...err... mental space?"

Patsy, a few months shy of turning forty, replied. "I'll soon depart on a journey. Come back when you make a list of seventy over seventy." The editor gaped. Patsy stood up, loosened his tie, took off his suit, and untucked his shirt. "I need a break. I want to walk on green grass. I want to run wild. I want to..." Patsy lost his words.

The editor stood up too. "The grass is always greener on the other side," he mumbled, beating a hasty retreat.

People close to Patsy identified tell-tale signs of a breakdown. Two months before the 'Forty under Forty' meeting, Patsy announced a digital detox and exchanged his smartphone for an old model that only allowed calls and messaging.

Seeing the bright side, his friends congratulated him for his improbable sacrifice. He is changing for the better, they said. 'He is a workaholic. He should take care of his health.' People admired his courage. There were calls asking for advice. Some took his interviews, made them go viral, and asked him to write a book on his detox experience. Others shook their head in disbelief.

When Patsy moved on to decluttering and minimalism, selling off his business and belongings, everyone was sure he had gone bonkers. His friends and acquaintances who had called him for tips now offered him advice. Motivational videos, uplifting articles, and contact numbers of counsellors found their way to his inbox. He ignored the emails and the internet company's bills. His service was promptly cut off.

Well-meaning friends pushed him to help himself. When he did not relent, the whispers began. The first wave of rumours was about his business—that it had failed miserably. But none of his employees lost their jobs, so they could not fathom why he sold it. Later the rumours focused on his personal life. A romantic disappointment, perhaps? Nosy acquaintances dropped in to investigate. Seeing the barren place, they would leave with more questions than they could ask.

The empty rooms in his house, with a barely stocked kitchen and a well-stocked library, did not make the man happy. He wanted to break away from all bondages, so he handed over the house to the first buyer, who stopped by. He decided that money was useless and donated what he held, leaving just enough to buy a plane ticket to his home country.

By then, his friends had given up on him. They did not want anything to do with a perceived quitter. Few who were close to him pushed him further away.

Two years later, dressed in a pair of khakis and a white t-shirt, an unkempt Patsy was far removed from the glossy magazine cover and the glitzy corporate world. As backpackers often are, he was on a journey to rediscover the land and himself. Or to leave everything behind. He was unsure.

On reaching his homeland, Patsy embarked on a walking tour with nothing but the meagre possessions his brown satchel could hold—a tube of toothpaste, a toothbrush, a bar of soap, a couple of clothes, and a long cotton towel to serve as a wrap-around on hot, summer days. He began noticing the sunrise and enjoying the sunsets. The world was new and fresh. Life shone with the glimmer of hope and possibilities.

Patsy did chores for strangers, on occasion manual labour, and at other times paperwork. He happily accepted what he received from his employers, either in cash or as food. He bathed in the rivers, lakes, or at public wells, slept under a tree or in caves, and gained a genuine appreciation for the life of a hermit. He particularly enjoyed roaming around villages. He visited obscure places, where he found solitude and returned to mingle with the villagers.

Mountains intrigued him more than anything. Among them, Jomo was his favourite. It stood tall and majestic, sequestered between several hills and a stunning valley below. Jomo beckoned with its serenity. Despite its stature, it appeared content and humble, as it shouldered the responsibility of the dense forest, the gushing waterfall on one side and a village of mountain-dwellers on the other.

Patsy was eager to reach Jomo and meet the Jomoans during their annual mountain festival. As a businessman who could afford the best food in the world, he had been a light eater. He kept up with the latest dietary trends and ensured that his eating habits kept him sharp, not drowsy, throughout the day. Now, as a roaming mendicant, he cherished the rare feast.

His feet protested after ten hours of being on the road. But his mind was his faithful companion. Two years ago, his mind was neither his master nor slave. It refused to comply with his demands and sulked in some corner of his consciousness. Now it stayed right where he wanted, beside him, with him, present at all times.

Patsy peered onto the treetops in the valley below. His heart thumped excitedly, and his feet swayed, but his mind steadied and hummed a tune. He was ready to meet the villagers and say hello. He surveyed the path that curved around the mountain slope. Not a soul in sight. He glanced down the hairpin bend he had climbed a few moments ago. Certainly, someone had followed him? No, not a footstep within earshot.

Patsy took a deep breath and walked ahead. He smiled as he thought of what might be in store. The villagers could be busy preparing for the festival. The food was supposedly an offering to their Mountain God. Hence, they put their best woks forward onto the fire. The Mountain God, in return, would keep the mountains safe and bountiful every year.

He climbed further up, expecting a path or a house or, if nothing else, a pair of legs carrying a sprightly mountain torso on them. Soon he reached a small clearing that led to a nondescript path. Ha! Shouldn't there be a community living here? The village could not have changed so as to forget its natural state of being.

Patsy nearly raced up the beaten mud track. A few houses loomed into his vision, neatly arranged on the mountain face like a stack of delectable wafers, strawberry pink, mango yellow, pistachio green. The sight made him hungry. He hoped that the festival preparations were in full swing. Climbing beyond the colourful houses, he walked through a gate and across a lawn to the chocolaty door of a modest vanilla-coloured house.

No one answered.

He knocked again and was greeted with complete silence.

He walked around the house. A window was ajar. Voices emerged in a monotonous hum.

Patsy gingerly pushed a finger inside and peeped. The voices loomed louder. The entire family sat around, doing nothing but staring and munching. The house was inhabited yet empty. The family members appeared busy and passive at the same time. On TV, a woman wailed while people on the screen and outside watched with bated breath.

Patsy shook his head in disappointment and walked away. It was the same scene at every house he peeped into, whether strawberry, mango, or pistachio. He turned around in disgust and walked back down the path he had clambered. There were no hopes for this village now. He was not eager to find out what lay ahead on the mountain. He had seen enough.

A few days later, he returned at the same time in the afternoon, unnoticed by anyone. The festival was over by then. The villagers held it only for an evening instead of seven days. No one had time to cook. No one had time to discuss and plan with their neighbours. No one wanted to coordinate. No one wanted to forgo their TV-watching schedule.

Patsy slipped in a letter underneath every door.

*"You are so struck by the idiot box that you forgot*
*your famous food festival? You should beware.*
*You will have to deal with something far more*
*addictive in the future. Let us hope you don't forget to*
*breathe under its mesmerising spell."*

The villagers laughed at the letter. "A madman visited our village while we were asleep," some said. Others suspected that the postman, a recluse, had lost his mind and carried out the sordid errand. No one dared to ask him, though, as he had a snarky tongue.

Some worried about the unwanted intrusion into their lives and wondered if the village was safe. But since no other letters followed, they forgot the letter and its contents until a couple of decades later, when the internet and the smartphone arrived in their placid village to spawn a tragedy.

# 4

# A Fateful Afternoon

Jomo was a challenge. A challenge that only a few dared to accept, but Sharaf knew no other way.

His life so far had been a series of challenges that he took on with a smile—losing his father at the age of thirteen, the odd jobs at the local garage, some days educative, other days demoralizing but menial every day, dropping out of school to let five younger siblings make good of their opportunities, helping his mother supplement the family income by breeding livestock—Sharaf never opposed his destiny. It was his to claim and conquer.

The village of Jomo offered another unique problem to resolve, a mountain to climb. And it was a mountain, indeed.

The Jomoans loved their home in the highlands. They even held a one-day annual fair and feast in its honour. Somewhere in the dense jungles of Jomo they built a stone temple dedicated to their presiding deity. Nearly a century later, no one knew where the temple was, and the festival lost its prominence. The Jomoans' love for good food ensured that the feast continued to be organized. Sharaf was on his way to participate in it.

The Jomoans did not welcome many outsiders, but Sharaf was now half Jomoan. He did not need an invitation.

They called him, whether day or night, to repair something or the other. If it was not the TV, it would be their car. Or the mixer-grinder would have given up on the morning coconut chutney. Sometimes, they even called him for plumbing. He would bring his plumber friend. The villagers trusted him. He knew it and was careful about who he brought into their homes.

Sharaf rode up on his trusty scooter, which used to be his dad's. He took good care of it all these years. He was eighteen when four of his youngest siblings and his mother fell ill with a life-threatening infection. His scooter helped him do multiple rounds of the hospital and the automobile shop where he worked. Sharaf was only one week into the job when the fever gripped his family. The shop owner had been quite adamant about the work timings. "Young fellows like you don't appreciate the value of time," he said. "Make sure you are here at eight in the morning." Sharaf managed to be punctual at his workplace and gained his employer's trust thanks to his scooter. He even got the salary advance he needed to pay the hospital bills. Sharaf told his mother how he felt his dad's presence during those tough days. "This is his gift, Umma," he said as he lovingly patted his scooter.

Twelve years later, he believed he could drive up the Himalayas on the old scooter if needed.

Jomo was nothing compared to its northern counterpart, but driving up the mountain required skill. It stood tall and majestic, broad at its base but with prominent and sharp peaks. The roads wound along its natural slope and tilted steeply or gently depending on the mountain's topography.

Having climbed Jomo many times, Sharaf knew the slopes and the terrain better than the ridges on his hands.

Today's food fiesta was unique because they asked Sharaf to contribute for the first time. His mother made a special mutton biriyani, rice pancakes, chicken curry, and egg puffs. The food sat pillion on his scooter in airtight containers secured with tight knots to not spill over on the Jomoan slopes.

When Sharaf reached the clearing where the food stalls were set up, he saw a throng of people gathered at the centre. It was the perfect day to put his plan in motion. He parked his scooter at the periphery of the gathering and unloaded the boxes. Several children, who knew him as Sharaf Uncle, clamoured around, asking what those boxes contained.

Sharaf grinned at the excitement. He was reminded of how his siblings gathered around him when he got oily, deep-fried snacks from the hotel next to the garage. It was a weekly treat. It cost ten rupees to the lone eater at the hotel, but to Sharaf and his family, it was as dear as lunch at the fancy restaurant in the nearest town.

The stalls at the Jomo food festival were full, but one woman rearranged her booth to make room for Sharaf's boxes. He carried the boxes, precariously balanced on raised hands, as he tried to save them from the jumpy kids. When he opened the first box, the fragrance of saffron and ghee filled the air.

'Biriyani!' screamed the children who had followed Sharaf to the stall. The crowd moved hypnotically in their direction.

"Wait! There's more," said Sharaf, hoping he did not run out of biriyani. The pancakes and chicken curry were equally good and begged to be savoured. In no time, he was pushed away from the stall by the hungry crowd. He observed from a distance, a grin plastered on his face.

A well-fed audience would make his task easy.

He walked to the centre of the clearing and raised up his hands. "Dear People of Jomo, if you like this food, I can ask my mother to make it for you again."

"Oh yes!"

"We want more."

"It's delicious."

Grateful and satiated voices cried out over the din.

Sharaf folded his hands in gratitude.

"But we will pay for it," said the woman who had shared her stall with him.

Sharaf waved his hand, declining the offer. "It will be our pleasure to cook for everyone."

"Look, paying for it means each one of us gets to eat more. Now, we only get to nibble."

Sharaf laughed in response. "There's something else that I want to offer."

A few heads turned while the others continued to relish the food on their plates.

Sharaf cleared his throat before he resumed. "We have a new technology that has arrived recently. We, meaning, the company where I work."

"I thought you run a catering business," said a man munching on a chicken leg.

"No, no, my mother sells eggs and chicken," he said with a smile. He continued before he lost the attention of the crowd. "You must have heard of an internet connection? Broadband?"

There was a low murmur in the crowd as if the words could barely rise above the lightness of the fragrant biriyani.

"I know all about it," said one youngster. "We have it in our college."

Sharaf nodded.

"You study at the college in the valley, don't you?" He knew the building well. He had gaped at it a thousand times, speculating how different his fate would have been if he had entered its hallowed gates.

"But how many of us have it in our homes?" he asked the gathering.

Half of the faces in the crowd looked up from their plates.

"Not me."

"I don't."

"The guest house has a connection," said one voice helpfully.

"I have, but it's too slow. Not worth it, really," said another.

"It costs too much," said another.

"I don't have the money."

Sharaf held up his palms to show that he had something to say. "What if we offer a cheaper option? Would you be interested?"

One man standing at the back of the crowd, cleaning his teeth with a bit of twig, came forward and spat on the ground before asking, "How cheap?"

His tone was belligerent, but Sharaf tried not to notice.

"Cat got your tongue?" spat the man. His open shirt flapped in the wind exposing the bright yellow vest underneath.

Sharaf hesitated. He had met the man before and was afraid of him. The man had a distinctly hostile demeanour. He was always suspicious of Sharaf. He would be the first to throw a stone from among the crowd if anything went wrong.

"Yes?" the man asked again, placing his palm behind his ear as if straining to listen.

"Fifty percent cheaper," Sharaf croaked.

"What?" the man questioned. "What did you say?"

"Fifty percent cheaper than the cheapest package," said Sharaf, louder than before.

The crowd dispersed, scoffing at Sharaf. The man who thought Sharaf ran a business came up to him and whispered. "Take it from me. Free advice. Don't let go of the hens and the chicken. With the kind of discount your company is offering, it won't survive for long."

The people gradually left the place with happy tummies.

Sharaf puffed up his chest. He will not give up. They will continue to call him for repairs. He will convince them. When he went to pick up the empty boxes from the stall, a young boy approached. He was the same who said that his college had an internet connection.

"Brother Sharaf," he said, "I want a brochure. All my friends have the internet at home. We are stuck in some nineteenth-century village."

"We'll take it to the twenty-second century," Sharaf assured him. "But otherwise, Jomo is beautiful."

Sharaf helped the boy set up a broadband connection at home. Soon he introduced a few other youngsters who wished for connectivity. Next, a schoolteacher approached. She had heard that the internet had colourful worksheets that could be printed and used in her class. "Help me get these printed, too," she said. Sharaf hauled a printer up the mountain the next day. A young girl asked if her certificates could be scanned so she could send them as attachments to her new employer. Sharaf took the certificates back to the valley to get them copied.

As he glanced through them, a twinge of regret pricked a corner of his heart, but he shook it off immediately. He was doing well. The new internet connections from remote Jomo had earned him a memento from his office – Best Employee of the Month. If he continued his efforts, he could get a promotion by the end of the year. A new dream was now taking shape in his heart. His third sibling, a sister, had reached marriageable age. He wanted to move into a bigger house before he could arrange a good match for her. And then, perhaps, it was time for him to find a partner. He blushed instinctively as he readied his scooter.

"Listen, Sharaf," his boss remarked, "You did it once, but don't lug a printer or computer up the mountain on that scooter again, please."

"It's been my faithful buddy for all these years. It has never betrayed."

"I get you. But soon, the demands from Jomo will increase. I anticipate that there'll be more orders for computers, printers, and even inverters, do you understand? I am expanding the business." His boss replied with a grin. "I'm buying a van for the company. From next week, make your rounds to Jomo in that van."

Sharaf's smile disappeared. "But, Sir?"

"I'm going to make it a company policy soon. So don't dare to disobey." His boss chuckled as he patted Sharaf on his back. "Keep it up, boy. You will go places. Taking the internet to the top of that God-forsaken mountain is no easy task," his boss added. "Next week, a van. After that, a car? A Benz? Why not?"

Yes, why not? Thought Sharaf, but his mind was restless. Jomo could be called anything but God-forsaken. And what about his scooter? He spoke to his mother, and she, the pragmatic mother hen, advised him to heed his boss's orders. The van would make his life easier. The scooter was passed on to the younger sibling, and Sharaf continued his trips to Jomo with the new van.

The van changed his profile. The Jomoans took him more seriously. It was amusing to note how adding two wheels to one's vehicle could change a man's prospects. His clout at the workplace also grew. The boss was impressed with Sharaf, and when the shop expanded to include a mobile phone section, he gifted a smartphone to Sharaf.

The gift introduced Sharaf to a whole new world. His days were never the same. Now, he found it easier to entice future subscribers. He carried the internet in his hand. He was excited to show Jomoans what they could do with the internet. How they could email their documents to the shop and get them printed. How the students of Jomo could find answers to their questions on the internet. All with the help of a screen that fits into their palm.

The next trip to Jomo would cause a sensation!

The day arrived when he had a scheduled trip to the mountain. He still carried out minor repairs for the villagers. He couldn't refuse them, but now he had his salaried job to manage. He was a salesman, customer service representative, and technician, all rolled into one, but he didn't mind one bit. He loved his job. It offered a dignified way out of poverty and misery for his family.

Sharaf drove confidently up the slope. He put on some music on the radio. He had done this so many times. The day was exquisite. The blue sky peeped in through the dense tree cover like resplendent gems set in a green carpet. As he neared a rather tricky bend in the road, he found a group of schoolchildren waiting for him to pass by. He slowed down beside them.

"Going up to the village?" He asked.

"Yes, Sharaf uncle."

By now, every child in the village knew him.

"Hop into the van. I will give you a ride. It's a hot afternoon."

The children danced a jig as he backed away to a broader part of the road so they could enter the van without squeezing themselves. The radio blared a popular ditty, and the children joined in. Sharaf glanced at the mirror and guffawed. The children were going berserk. To quieten them, he held up his smartphone.

"Do you know what this is?"

"A phone!" chorused the children.

"It's not an ordinary phone. It's a smartphone. You can browse the internet on this."

The children gasped and plucked the phone out of his hand.

"Wait! Wait! Let me show you when we reach the village."

But the children were eager. When they couldn't figure it out, they handed the phone to him.

"Show us, Sharaf Uncle, show us!" they cried.

Sharaf shook his head. "Let us reach the village."

"No, now! Now! Now!"

"Alright." He held up the phone and typed with his left hand. The keypads were tiny, and his fingers pudgy. He kept typing the incorrect word.

"Sharaf Uncle doesn't know to type!" started the chorus.

Sharaf gritted his teeth as he focused. The turns were now getting trickier. He recollected that there was a hairpin bend around the corner and paused typing. Once he turned the bend, the children began their chorus again.

"Show us! Show us!

Sharaf grinned at their enthusiasm and picked up his phone. The tricky part of the route to the top was over. Now it was just…

Oh no! He had forgotten the last bend!

The van veered precariously towards the ledge. There was only enough time to fling the phone as he tried to focus. It landed with a crackle on the road. Sharaf lost control.

"Hold on! Tight!" were Sharaf's last words. It took the lone surviving child three weeks to be fit enough to talk to the police about what happened that fateful afternoon.

# 5

# The Village Decree

Four posts and a tarpaulin came up in the same place where two months ago, Jomoans had gathered together for their beloved food fair. Two months ago, the children had run around the same spot in glee—snatching, savouring, devouring, giggling, and laughing.

Eight of those children vanished into the ravine.

One lay in the hospital recovering from a fractured hand and leg. It was a miraculous escape. Not a day passed when her parents, Ayyappan and Roja, did not thank Lord Ayyappa for his blessing. Their child was safe.

Ayyappan stood in a corner, his crumpled shirt bearing the weight of the past few days, new wrinkles showing up on his face. He was thirty-two, but the mishap had added years to his days. Eight men stood at the other corner of the tent. Eight fathers were not as fortunate as Ayyappan.

Were they not as devout as him? A question that passed through their minds several times a day. Why had they been punished?

The habitually tardy panchayat leader arrived on time for a change. He was aware of the gravity of the situation. "We have gathered here to acknowledge the misfortune that has befallen eight of our friends. Their loss is immeasurable, terrible, and I am at a loss for words," the elected leader began.

"We want justice!" a broken voice hollered from the corner where the eight men stood.

The panchayat leader hesitated before continuing, "The eight innocent children who are no longer with us—"

"Who is responsible?" said the same broken voice.

The panchayat leader paused for a second. He continued in a subdued voice. "We all know it was an accident—"

"Says who?" This time it was a belligerent voice from the back of the tent, not from the mourning corner. A man stepped forward through the crowd. His shirt was unbuttoned and flapped callously in the morning breeze. The yellow vest underneath was soiled enough to appear mauve. He spat on the ground before he spoke.

"Can you prove that it was an accident? Are there any witnesses?"

The panchayat leader frowned at the man. It was Raman, a good-for-nothing fellow, who was constantly causing trouble.

"The child in the hospital," the leader said, nodding at Ayyappan.

"You want us to believe the words of a seven-year-old? Who knows what damage the accident has done to her?"

Murmurs rose around the tent. By now, there was a ring of listeners outside the tent too. Women and children stood around the periphery.

Ayyappan was glad that Roja could not join them. She would have lashed out at this rabble-rouser talking ill about their sweet little child. He straightened himself and responded. "She is well and able to speak. She remembers well. She said the children had asked Sharaf to do something on his phone. He lost control while showing it to them."

"Sharaf? That rascal Sharaf?!" Raman spat out. "I had warned the panchayat about that boy. Despite being an outsider, he had too much freedom."

The crowd murmured.

"Do we know anything about him other than where he worked?"

"I know his family. They are simple folks and…" the college student who had approached Sharaf for an internet connection spoke. Raman glared at the boy menacingly, "…and he was the sole earning family member," the boy mumbled.

"That doesn't make him a saint," Raman spat out his words.

"So? What can we do now? The dead are gone. The mishap has happened. It was not intentional," the panchayat leader tried to reason.

The eight men in the right corner started murmuring amongst themselves. One raised his voice and addressed the leader. "You should not forget that we have lost our children. How can you speak so callously?"

The panchayat leader was losing patience. "We have discussed this issue enough already."

"No. This is not enough." A cry arose from the group of eight. "We want justice!"

"Yes!" Raman cried out. "We all want justice for our children."

The murmuring gained momentum. A cry arose again. "We want justice!" A stone flew from the corner toward the panchayat leader. It fell at his feet. A fear travelled from the stone through his feet to his heart. He folded his hands and abruptly turned away from the tent. The leader disappeared by the time the crowd realised what happened.

Ayyappan was as stunned by the turn of events as the group of eight who stood in the corner. The crowd had turned towards them after their leader disappeared.

"We didn't throw the stone," one of the men mumbled. He scanned the crowd nervously.

"But what you asked for is justified," Raman pushed through the crowd towards the men. "You have got to be brave for the sake of your children, unlike many others here," he said, punctuating his words with another spat on the ground. "Sharaf's family has to compensate for your loss. Tomorrow, we will go to the valley to protest in front of the Panchayat office. And I have more to say," said Raman. "All this happened because of that scoundrel who enticed us to forbidden worlds by selling us the internet. We don't need any internet. This is our world." Raman spread out his arms. His eyes blazed with arrogance. "We should ban outsiders to Jomo. And the internet."

Ayyappan gazed in astonishment. "This man is crazy," he mumbled.

"Let's meet tomorrow at the Panchayat office," Raman thundered.

The crowd refused to acknowledge his suggestion and began to disperse.

Ayyappan scoffed at this drama and made his way to the hospital, where he narrated the incident to Roja, and they both puzzled over what Raman had suggested.

"I feel so sorry for the families. Perhaps, a reparation might help," Ayyappan said.

"From whom? From Sharaf's family? Haven't you visited his home? Can they afford to give any money? They have lost their sole income earner."

"The younger brother is doing well in his studies. He'll get a job soon."

"So, does he have to start his life with such a terrible expense?"

"Calm down, Roja. Let's be thankful that we have our Tara with us today."

Roja watched the apple of her eye sleeping on a dreary hospital bed. She couldn't wait to take her home. "I can't bear to see her like this," she said. Her eyes welled as she said, "May she never have to visit this place again."

Ayyappan sighed. He had to be back at the tea estate. He had enough clerical duties to keep him busy the entire week. "Tomorrow, I have to go back."

Roja noticed his tired eyes and held his hand. "Go ahead. The doctors said that they might discharge her by tomorrow afternoon. Don't worry."

Relief washed over Ayyappan, and he settled in a chair to doze. "But listen," asked Roja, "are the villagers really going to protest at the Panchayat office tomorrow?"

"Don't be silly, Roja. No one is going to listen to that madman."

But Ayyappan could never have imagined what happened in the next few days.

Although the protestors comprised only the eight bereaved families and Raman, a crowd gathered to watch, giving the impression that there was a large group. The panchayat leader was frightened out of his wits. He quickly called for a meeting at the office and invited Sharaf's younger brother and his mother. The meeting turned into a slugfest, with Sharaf's brother trading blows with Raman. "Don't you dare call my brother a murderer!" screamed the boy before he smashed a chair into Raman's frail body. The yellow vest was stained with blotches of red. Raman promised revenge and stomped off from the meeting. Support for Raman grew in the coming days. After four weeks of stone-throwing, chair-hurling, and showering abuses, the panchayat agreed with most of what the mob demanded.

Sharaf's brother and mother listened in rapt attention as the village decreed that the bereaved families should be paid compensation.

"And what about my brother's life? Shouldn't we be compensated for our loss?" asked Sharaf's brother.

"Who owes it to you?" asked the leader.

"The village of Jomo. My brother was driving up to finish errands for the villagers. The land and the road belong to Jomo and his people. It was because of the mountain that my brother lost his life. We, too, deserve compensation."

The villagers began yelling and shouting in response. The leader raised his arms in an attempt to calm them. Raman was strictly ordered to stay out of this discussion to avoid fistfights, but he came rushing into the room and grabbed Sharaf's brother by his collar. "If you utter one more word, you impudent dog, I will crush you."

All it took was one shove from the boy to send Raman crashing toward the door. He stayed there, stunned.

"We feel sorry for the families who lost their young children," said the mother. "We agree to pay fifty thousand rupees. That's all we can manage. Please don't ask for more."

"Umma!" the boy was outraged. "What are you saying?"

The mother pulled him away from the place. And that was the last the villagers saw of the family. A few days later, the panchayat leader received a cheque for fifty thousand at his residence. He encashed it and distributed thirty-two thousand among the families, pocketing the rest.

"This is all they could manage. Poor people! They are now living in penury." He explained.

"Where?" Raman asked.

The leader gulped before answering. "I don't know. They have sold their house and left the town. No one knows where they went."

Raman spat on the ground. He did not believe a word uttered by the leader, but he knew that the opportunity was gone. It would take too much effort to track down the family. "Let them not come back ever," he said. "Scoundrels!"

The panchayat also agreed to establish the rules that the villagers demanded.

No internet in Jomo.

No cars to the top of the mountain, except ambulances.

No outsiders.

After a few weeks, the 'no outsiders' rule was relaxed, as a girl from the village was getting married, and the groom's family was from outside. People understood the unsustainability of such a rule, and it was removed. The other two remained. No one opposed it. Although, occasionally, someone or the other drove up in a car. But the internet rule was adhered to strictly and violently. Anyone who retained connections faced broken windows, smashed roofs, upturned gardens, threatening letters, and abuses. It was evident that Raman had garnered enough support among the villagers to gather a gang.

Ayyappan was aghast when he heard about these events during his subsequent visit. Roja and his mother narrated by turn while little Tara played in his lap.

"The only sane voice was Uncle Lal's, but no one paid heed to him. He is growing old."

"He was a force to reckon with in his younger days. No one listens to old people these days. No one wants us anymore," Ayyappan's mother added.

"Should we move to a different place? I don't want Tara to grow up in such a violent atmosphere," Ayyappan's question hung like damp air between Roja and his mother.

Roja was an outsider but had fallen in love with this place, while Ayyappan's mother had not seen any place beyond Jomo. They turned to each other and replied in one voice, "We'll stay here."

Ayyappan yielded. When two women agreed, it was better not to disagree. He stood up, intending to go out and enjoy the quiet evening but froze when he heard a faint mumble.

"What if he returns?"

He could barely discern his mother's lip movement. Roja did not hear her.

He would keep it that way.

# Another Mishap

Tara was pulled out of the village school after the accident. Roja took it upon herself to teach her. Cheeru, who occasionally helped Roja in her garden, would keep an eye on Tara as she did her lessons sitting on the porch. She was not allowed to step out of the porch.

"When she grows up a little more, I will take her to the high school in the valley," Roja said.

"Don't keep her inside the house for too long, Rojakka. She will grow up to be a touch-me-not," Cheeru said, pointing to a bunch growing beside Roja's favourite rose bed.

The leaves drooped and shut as soon as Cheeru's finger brushed past. "See!" she yelled delightedly, sparking Tara's curiosity.

Tara hopped, skipped, and jumped through the lawn. No tell-tale signs of her accident remained in her gait. She went to the rose bed and admired the lovely flowers blooming on the stalks. She walked closer and held a pink-white petal between her fingers. The smell was intoxicating. Tara wished to hold the bloom in her hand. She clasped the bud in her palm, wanting to give it a tug. Instead, she yelped in pain. Her palm flew away from the flower. Tara's eyes welled up as she examined her palm. A drop of blood oozed from the fleshy base. Is this why Cheeru called it a touch-me-not? She blinked away her tears and decided to report her findings to her mother when she produced another yelp. Without heeding her mother's words, she had stepped out barefoot. Her feet touched something prickly. Before she could inspect her foot, the prickly plant fascinated her. Tiny green leaves went to sleep. They reminded her of how Grandma would doze off after lunch, sitting in her chair. Her head would droop, signalling the end of the afternoon TV session. Roja would switch off the TV as soon as she saw Grandma dozing. Tara giggled at the thought and skipped off to tell her mother.

When Roja heard her narration, she scolded her, but she washed Tara's hands and feet while telling her all about touch-me-nots.

"Cheeru aunty plucks them and throws them away from our rose bed. They are weeds. They are not good for the soil."

"The soil is already bad, Roja. The soil is already bad if the touch-me-nots have encroached on the space. You should take better care of the garden. I can't walk around so much now, or else I would have done it myself. What's that useless Cheeru up to?" Her mother-in-law's words stung Roja like a carpet of thorns. Employing Cheeru was Roja's idea. It gave Roja some time to focus on Tara and her lessons. She also had her sewing and tailoring customers clamouring for delivery. Her mother-in-law never considered the income to be helpful. She believed that her son was a manager at the tea estate and earned enough for the family. She could never accept the fact that he was a mere clerk.

Roja knew that the old woman was up to something. She kept an eye on her all the time. Although she pretended to forget occasionally, Roja knew she was sharp enough to make decisions.

A few months ago, when Roja had gone to the valley to buy supplies, there was a visitor. Cheeru told her all about it. "He looked like an important man. Like an officer."

"Officer?"

"Yes."

"Did you hear what they discussed?"

"No, Rojakka, they were seated inside all the time. But when he was leaving, I heard Amma call him Vakeel."

"Vakeel?"

So Amma was holding discussions with a lawyer. The meeting intrigued her, but she did not mention it to Ayyappan. Roja did not want to add to his miseries at work. Living on the estate for many weeks, he missed his family while at work. He missed Tara the most.

Meanwhile, Tara drew dozens of pictures to gift her father when he came. He asked for them every time, saying he would stick all her pictures in his modest room inside the estate. She was more than happy to oblige. Now that she had a new subject – roses and touch-me-nots. She kept asking many questions to all the three women who cared for her.

"Why do touch-me-nots droop?" she asked Cheeru.

"Because they are shy. Do not be like them, be bold in life."

"Why are touch-me-nots shy?" she asked her mother.

"They are not. They are merely protecting themselves. It is important to survive. Learn to protect yourself."

"Roses have thorns to protect themselves," she told her grandmother.

"I wish their thorns were hands," her grandmother replied.

"How can thorns be hands?"

"Then they can poke anyone in the eye!" Grandma chuckled.

Tara realised that Grandma was in one of her moods. She tried to slink away.

"Come here, child."

Tara walked back to Grandma's chair.

"Sit," she commanded, showing her lap.

Tara shuffled up obediently.

"Grow horns, grow thorns, grow hands like those branches, spreading far and wide," Grandma recited, pointing to the trees outside her window. "If in danger, you can drop one on your enemy's heads."

"What enemies?"

"They will come. They'll come one day. They'll come for you, for this house, for this mountain. You will fight them. Dishoom! Dishoom!" Grandma cackled with laughter as she punched in the air above with her feeble hands.

Tara nearly skidded from her lap. Grandma's occasional moods frightened her.

"Tara!" called her father from the porch.

She hurried away in relief. Her father was home for the weekend. She slid onto his lap and put her arms around him, nestling her head on his shoulder.

"What happened, Taru?" asked her father. He sensed a discomfort.

"Do we have enemies, Dadda?"

"What enemies?" Ayyappan tried not to laugh.

"Grandma says that enemies will come to harm me, and I will have to fight."

Ayyappan stroked his child's hair gently as he replied. "Grandma was not serious. She was joking." He laughed uncomfortably as he tried to hide the anxiety in his voice.

Later, during his private moments with Roja, he asked, "Amma's mood swings. Are they getting worse?"

"Not really. Why do you ask?"

"We should meet a good doctor from NewTown."

"Hmm…" Roja replied noncommittedly.

"Why don't we shift to NewTown? Tara has to go to school. There'll be many good doctors around. And you might get many customers and may be open a shop, too."

The last bit was enticing for Roja. A shop of her own would be a dream come true. But she was too sleepy to think. As she snuggled close to her husband, she reminded him of the early morning bus they had to catch the next day. A relative was getting married with immense fanfare.

"Shall we take Tara, too? She hasn't gone anywhere since that accident."

"No, no. Let Tara be at home. Cheeru will be here before we leave," Roja replied sleepily.

"I'll take her to Uncle Lal's bakery tomorrow after we return," said Ayyappan with a smile.

Life, as usual, had other plans.

Ayyappan and Roja set out to the main road on foot. The walking path was unlike the grey, partially asphalted roads used by motor vehicles. It was a shortcut and wound around the mountain like a famished, thin, brown snake. People could lose their way unless they were familiar with every shrub, bush, stone, and tree. Several branches forked from the path. At first glance, they appeared worthy enough to follow but later proved to be a dead end. They would usually end in impenetrable thickets or at a precarious ledge. Ayyappan was familiar with the bends and turns, and Roja improved with every walk. She held Ayyappan's hand as he led her down the winding path.

"The way you lead me down reminds me of the day you came to my parent's home."

Ayyappan smiled.

He had asked for permission to marry Roja. Her parents had refused. So, he called her name, and out she came with a bag in hand. He had led her away from the house as confidently as he was guiding her through the woods now.

"But there's one difference, Roja. We have Tara now. And I worry about her future."

Roja remained silent as she focused on a tricky section of the mountain path. It was strewn with pebbles; any slip would send them both rolling down the mountain. From the main road, it was a two-hour bus ride to the wedding venue. Roja adjusted her saree as they waited for the bus. Climbing down the mountain always took a toll on her saree. Wearing a churidar would make the mountain climb so much easier. Roja was secretly planning to stitch one for herself. It was rather popular in the valley and at Jomo, but she had avoided it, fearing her mother-in-law's sharp tongue. After the wedding, she persuaded Ayyappan to let her buy enough material for two pairs. She will not show them to her mother-in-law until she gets a chance to wear them.

The churidar material was the first thing that the police handed over to Ayyappan's mother. Unlike other possessions they found with the dead bodies—their identity cards, watches, and jewellery—the churidar material, wrapped neatly inside a brown paper package and a plastic bag, remained unspoiled.

Their bus collided with a tanker lorry and was crushed from behind by another. Ayyappan and Roja had occupied the back seats to relive their carefree courting days when he would wait for her stitching classes to get over so they could enjoy a ride to the nearest town. The police found their crushed bodies with hands clasped together.

# 7

# A Day to Remember

Tara remembered a few scenes from that dreadful day. A phone call on the landline had aroused Grandma from her afternoon nap. Cheeru had attended to the call and she started wailing soon after. Tara was in the same room, drawing, waiting for her parents. Instead of watching her parents climb up the mountain path, their heads bobbing at a distance, Tara saw an ambulance lurch in through the gate opened by Cheeru.

At that point, her memory always lapses into a whirl. She was grabbed by someone and taken inside. Was it Grandma or Cheeru or someone else? All she remembered was the white of the ambulance. Then she was left alone in the bedroom. What was she doing? Was she playing? She recollected how someone would poke their head occasionally into the room and say, "Don't cry."

Many people milled around the house, but it was quiet inside. She remembered shadows on the window sill, on the closed curtains.

Who were all those people?

After a while, her grandma was also in the room. Grandma kept sobbing, crying, and wailing in turns. Sometimes, she would be quiet. Tara remembered later lying on the bed with her head in Grandma's lap, though she didn't recollect climbing onto the bed. She remembered waking up in a different room, in the hall, where two people lay with their bodies covered in white. She remembered a man trying to hold her hand. Cheeru had yanked her hand off, causing her to cry. She recollected the pain caused by Cheeru's fierce grip.

Who was that man?

Tara flung away her pen in frustration. It landed with a soft thud on the grass below. She was seated on a swing bench facing the hills to the east. This was her favourite spot to read in the mornings. Today, though, she had homework to do. "A day to remember" was the topic she was supposed to write for her English class at the NewTown Public School. The teacher explained that the day had to be something memorable, an incident that changed her life. Or a trip that she enjoyed.

Tara did not remember any trips, but she had two intense memories – one of being housebound after her accident, and the second was when she lost her parents. She didn't want to recollect and relive the accident when she was flung into the woods, nor did she know the details of the accident that took her parents' lives. She did not want to know.

What could she write in her essay that would be dramatic enough? That was one of the criteria for judging the best essay from the class. How boring!

Tara hated the NewTown Public School that she joined three years ago. Grandpa Lal took her to the principal's office one day at Grandma's behest to get her admitted.

"She has not had any schooling till now? How will she pick up any lessons at this age?" the principal had asked.

"She is only eleven. She was at school until seven," Grandpa Lal explained.

"Four years of education lost!" The principal raised her hand with her fingers shimmering as if Tara's education had disappeared into the air.

"Does she speak?" asked the principal.

"Yes, madam, she does." Grandpa Lal answered, but his tone lacked conviction.

"What's wrong?"

"Well, she has been rather quiet after the...," Grandpa Lal eyed Tara before continuing, "after the mishap."

The principal's face softened.

"Mr. Lal, I will consider your application, but Tara has to clear a short test."

Grandpa Lal nodded though Tara squirmed in her seat. "What test?" she wanted to ask, but her tongue stuck to her throat, as it usually did whenever she met a stranger.

The principal glanced at Tara and rang a bell on her desk. A peon appeared magically.

"Take this child to Ms. Jacob."

Tara showed a basic level of competence in the test though she failed when Ms. Jacob asked her to answer a few questions orally. The principal dismissed Ms. Jacob's surmise that the child is below par compared to her peers in the school. "She doesn't utter a word," Ms. Jacob protested.

"But her test was otherwise satisfactory," the principal said. "Let's give the child a chance, considering all she has been through."

So, that's how Tara became a student at the school in the valley. She trudged up and down the walking path daily, heeding Cheeru's words to not accept gifts from strangers. Cars were banned on the mountain road, but the occasional vehicle would make an appearance. The panchayat had started collecting a hefty amount as a fine, and a few people did not mind paying the money in return for a drive up the mountain. Tara avoided the road and stuck to the more scenic walking path.

Grandma spoke less and less every day. Cheeru could interpret the tiniest movement of her finger, so Grandma used words sparingly. It was left to Cheeru to interpret the silences and the sighs in the house. Tara rarely laughed. Although, Cheeru tried to make her do things that others her age enjoyed. Gradually, she brought her daughter Meenu to play with her. She was older than Tara but had a playfulness that belied her age. Tara lived in a bubble created by Cheeru, Meenu, Grandma, and Grandpa Lal, and she felt safe. The school, the teachers, and her classmates were all outside that bubble.

As Tara became a teen, she became restless and noted the same restlessness in her peers. She could not communicate, and teachers made it worse by loading them with rules. Her attitude and how she looked at the world changed in a few years. Most of her peers from the valley used the internet. Some carried mobile phones, and chatting became their hobby. The Jomo kids did not know what the internet was.

They had stepped into their teens in a Jomo with neither cars nor the internet. Some conspired with their friends to let them visit their homes, thus accessing the online world for a few hours each week.

Tara did not have many friends. She spoke to a few who turned out to be internet junkies. Unable to relate with them, Tara distanced herself. Somehow in her world, the internet and accidents were entwined. The lure of technology had ultimately caused eight of her friends to lose their lives in an accident which she survived. It had nothing to do with her parent's death. But she always visualised a distracted bus driver. Observing her indifferent classmates stuck to their mobile phones outside school hours, she developed an aversion to the device and the technology.

Tara crept further into her shell. She began hating her schoolwork, which until then, she had enjoyed.

Grandma slipped further and further away from sanity. Tara felt increasingly stifled inside her home, but she did not crave company unless it was nature.

At the age of fourteen, Tara went on her first mountain expedition. Post that, she continued her forays into unknown paths on the hillsides, usually walking close to the edges that jutted into the valley but occasionally venturing into the wilderness. The more she explored, the more she understood that not all the stories told by her grandma were true. For instance, the forests were not as dangerous as her grandma had warned her. They were beautiful, mysterious, and surreal. Tara spent many hours roaming the woods, a pair of binoculars in her hand. All her observations would make their way to her personal art journal at night. She also learned that the forests were not as untouched as her grandmother believed. Many parts of the woods were swiped clean of trees. Someone was cutting down the gentle giants for timber.

Tara knew that the forests held many stories. The days spent wandering among the trees were her most precious memories. Surely there would be a memorable day from those years. She had to finish the essay by evening.

The gate creaked as it was swung open by a rugged, brown man. His bare body glistened with sweat, and his moustache bristled in the morning breeze. It was Chellan, Cheeru's brother, who worked in the garden while Cheeru worked in the kitchen. Tara was surprised that he came alone. Usually, the three, Cheeru, Chellan, and Meenu, arrived together.

"Kutty, he said, "Cheeru can't come today," he said. He referred to Tara as a 'child'.

"What happened?"

"She fell down. We have taken her to the hospital."

"Oh no!"

Chellan surveyed the garden that he helped create. The roses that had wilted after Roja's death were now blooming.

"Kutty, we need some help. You are too young to realize all this, but it has to be done. How can we work like this?"

"I…I don't understand."

"We haven't been paid our salaries for the past three years."

"What?"

"I kept telling Cheeru to ask you, but she said you were too young."

"I am fourteen now," blurted Tara, hurt by the insinuation of naivete.

"We don't want a huge amount, but we need some money at the hospital today," Chellan continued in a worried tone.

Tara had often seen Cheeru take money from a drawer in her grandmother's room. That's how the household ran but didn't she take her salary? She asked Chellan to wait and went inside to peep into the drawer. There was cash inside, many other papers, and a long hardbound notebook. Tara hastily took a bundle of notes and handed them over to Chellan.

Chellan accepted the cash gratefully. "I'll come tomorrow if all is well at the hospital. Meenu will stay with her." He took a few steps and turned. "I forgot. Meenu asked you to note this in the notebook inside the drawer."

"Note what down?"

"This?" he held the wads of cash up in his hand.

Tara was flummoxed. She had not counted.

Chellan gave a weak smile and counted all the notes. "Two thousand rupees," he said.

After Chellan left, Tara went to the kitchen, looking for food. There was nothing. Grandma lay in her bed wide awake now. "Who was that? Did he come? Did he ask for it?" Tara was bewildered. How did Grandma know about Chellan's visit? Her ears were not sharp enough to hear from her room.

"Yes, Grandma, I gave him some money."

"No!" Grandma shot up like an arrow.

She held Tara in a vice-like grip and shook her like a rat. "You shouldn't give him anything. He doesn't deserve any of it. This is all yours! All yours!" Then she flopped back into the bed, exhausted by the effort.

Tara regarded Grandma with part fear and part sympathy. She went back into the kitchen and opened every nook and cranny. She found some rice and washed it, as she had seen Cheeru do it. She lit the gas stove. Cheeru rarely used it. She was more comfortable with the stone hearth outside. Tara did not know how to start the fire on the hearth. She took a steel pot, filled it with water stored in a bin, and let it boil. When the water boiled, the rice went into it. Tara decided that this was a good enough breakfast for such a day. Then she went into Grandma's room and emptied the drawer from where she picked up the money.

The long notebook had detailed accounts of the money spent on household expenses, including Tara's school fees. Tara recognized Meenu's handwriting. The accounts began when Tara joined the school, but Cheeru or Chellan's wages were not mentioned. It was a miracle how they had survived without being paid. Chellan worked elsewhere too. He came in for only a couple of hours in the morning. As she flipped the notebook, Tara noticed separate entries at the end of the book. Larger amounts and dates were entered in neat columns. Tara opened the passbook, and the entries matched the amount. So, Cheeru would go and withdraw money.

Tara wondered who had signed the cheque. She studied her frail grandmother lying on the cot. The idea was incredulous.

Tara got her answer as she searched through the documents and found an envelope full of signed cheque leaves, all by her grandmother. From the entries in the notebook, she could deduce how many Cheeru had used so far.

She opened the next envelope. Her hand trembled as she held the contents. A bunch of photographs dropped on the floor. Her parents, handsome and beautiful in their youth, smiled at her from the stills. Tara was there too, as a baby in her mother's arms, a toddler in her father's arms, and a child holding both their hands.

Tears streamed down her cheeks. She hadn't really cried after her parent's death. She didn't remember crying on the day they died.

She tidied up all the papers and replaced them on the shelf. In the notebook, she entered the amount she gave to Chellan under a new page – Pending Salaries. She calculated the total pending amount and entered that into a separate column. Now she could tell how much she owed Chellan and Cheeru. She checked the passbook and realised there was only enough money for sixteen more withdrawals. Will they be able to survive on this money?

Tara bit her lip. She will have to create a plan. The lid on the steel pot rattled in the kitchen. It was time for breakfast. After that, she would complete her essay. It was, indeed, a day to remember.

# 8

# Survival

Tara dreaded her future, which for her did not go much beyond her eighteenth birthday. Will she get a job to sustain herself and her grandmother? Or could she sign up for a university course?

Her worst fear was going bankrupt before she could repay Cheeru and Chellan. Cheeru was getting old and could no longer work, so she sent Meenu to help Tara.

Tara calculated the per-hour wages and realised that it might be prudent to reduce the money spent on Meenu's salary. She insisted that Meenu must work part-time, thus cutting her wages in half. Meenu grumbled, but she could not ignore the fact that Tara was only a child trying to make ends meet. Chellan continued to work in the morning, but on weekends, he had a new assistant. Tara learned the ropes from Chellan before he could recognize her ploy.

Tara got gardening and farming lessons even on weekdays before she went to school. Soon, Tara was confident enough to handle the garden by herself. A few months after she turned fifteen, she asked Chellan if he would be happier spending his mornings at home. Chellan understood the implicit request and took leave. Tara handed him a letter in which she noted the pending wages and a promise to repay in the next three years. It was the promise of a fifteen-year-old who had no clue what the future held for her, but she handed it over with an innate solemnity, and Chellan accepted it with equal seriousness. If Tara had not been blinded by her own tears, she would have noticed Chellan's eyes glisten.

By letting go of Chellan, Tara had not saved much, but she had other plans too. While she learned the basics of gardening from Chellan, she peppered him with questions about farming. Harangued by her constant doubts, Chellan set up a vegetable garden with a few local vegetables. Tara paid special attention to this patch. She will have to wait for a while before she gets a sizable harvest, but the soil never betrayed. If you put hard work into protecting and nourishing the earth, you will be served a bounty. These were Chellan's words as he toiled in the morning sun.

Tara learned much more about life from his words and her experience. Earth demanded that one be patient. Hard work went well with patience but not arrogance. At the same time, patience did not mean being ignorant. One could not be complacent under the pretext of forbearance. Her mother's rose garden nearly wilted away into oblivion after her mother died. A tiny twig remained, adamantly facing the wind, soaking the last of the nutrients from the soil and drinking the morning dew with its two shiny leaves. The twig blossomed into a lovely shrub under Chellan's care. When Chellan presented her with the first rose from the reborn shrub, Tara was ecstatic. The tiny twig represented hope in the most trying circumstances.

Tara also learned that hope was to be cherished even after painful endings. Her entire crop of cauliflowers that she nurtured with Chellan's help turned out to be duds with no florets. Chellan said that it was due to higher temperatures that year. She waited for more than three months for the florets to show up. Fortunately, a Jomoan from further down the mountain, on hearing about the floret-less harvest from Chellan, asked if he could buy the leaves. "I can substitute them for cabbage in my spring rolls." Apparently, he ran a bustling café near the NewTown College campus. Tara earned some unexpected cash for the disappointing harvest. By the time she was ready to sow another crop of cauliflowers, she was nearly eighteen. She had a few more unsigned cheques to encash, but she knew that they wouldn't suffice for her college education.

All her classmates were excited about the college next door while Tara was at her wit's end to figure out how she could survive if her grandmother's bank account was emptied. The college offered a scholarship for girls, especially those who were economically challenged. Tara knew that this was her only chance. If she could drum up a decent performance in her examinations, it could be her ticket to freedom from all her liabilities. She applied herself wholeheartedly.

A few weeks before her eighteenth birthday, Tara received news about her college application. She was eligible for an allowance, but her scramble into the first division only got her a half-scholarship.

With a heavy heart, she accepted that higher education was not in her destiny.

When she returned home and entered her garden, she knew that it was the only other place that held some promise.

She didn't have space to expand her fledgeling vegetable garden, but if she managed her expenses tightly, she might survive. She had to take on a job. She had already let go of unnecessary expenses like a telephone connection that her father had, and the television that grandmother's worsening vision had gradually abandoned.

At some point, she might even have to sell the house. It broke her heart to think of it.

The house had a grand appearance because of the front porch. Inside, it was compact, with a hall, a kitchen, and two bedrooms. Upstairs there was a low attic for storing grains, fruits, and some old vessels. Behind the kitchen was a work area that had a wooden hearth. Tara was adept at using it now. She had gotten rid of the gas connection.

Meenu came running out of the front door as Tara sat on the swing on the lawn, gazing at her home. "Kutty, a man arrived soon after you left. He handed an envelope and went away."

"Who? Did he give a name?"

"No, but he knows your grandmother. He tried to speak to her."

"And did she?"

Meenu shook her head.

"Where's the envelope?"

"In grandmother's drawer."

After a pause, Meenu asked if Tara would go to college. Secretly, Meenu hoped that Tara would get a job and repay the amount she owed to her family. Meenu was now a mother of two. She found climbing to the top of the mountain tiresome. Her home was halfway down from Tara's.

"I will not," Tara replied. Her face was placid but her voice said a different story.

Before she was forced to acknowledge the sadness in Tara's words, Meenu fled through the gates, yelling that she had the food ready in the kitchen. Tara wiped her face and went straight to her grandmother's room. She was sound asleep.

In the drawer, she found a thick envelope addressed to her. The envelope had a wad of cash in it. It was enough for her to survive for a few years and more. If she continued to be prudent, she could study even on the half scholarship. The heart leapt with joy.

But who was this new benefactor? He had to be someone known to the family.

She had to meet Grandpa Lal. She tiptoed out of the room and raced down towards Grandpa Lal's house.

"What is the meaning of this, Grandpa Lal?"

Grandpa Lal sat brooding over the question. He was as old as her grandmother but fitter. Lately, though, Tara had noticed a slowness. It hurt her to watch because Grandpa Lal was the only person she could rely on.

"First things first. Open a bank account in your name and put this money into it."

"But who could it be?"

"I remember your grandmother talking about an advocate."

"Thomas?"

"Yes. Perhaps, she might have arranged for the money through him."

"How could she? She barely remembers her own name."

"Perhaps, she planned soon after your parents' death?"

Tara bit her lip to suppress a sob that reached her throat.

"Or it could be him."

"Who?"

"Nilaav."

"Who again?"

Grandpa Lal dozed off. Tara dismissed his words as an old man's prattle.

# 9

# In the Valley

Tara packed and shelved the last saree strewn across the counter. Her legs sought a stool, but she dared not sit. The manager's eyes were stuck on her. That prickly feeling of being watched was a constant cause of distress.

"Creep!" GK muttered under his breath.

Tara nodded as subtly as possible. She had fifteen minutes to go before the wrap-up. The creep left his position behind the cashier and walked towards them. "You two study together?" he asked as he approached.

"Yes," GK replied. The manager leered slyly and nodded.

"What did that smile mean?" GK asked as he fell in step with Tara when they left the store.

Tara knew exactly what that creep insinuated, but she shrugged. "Leave it. I'll look for another job. This one is getting tiresome."

GK sighed in response. They were not the only ones struggling to pay their college fees, but they were the only ones in the class with part-time jobs. The others had parents. "I wish my father was alive," he said. "He worked at the library." He pointed to a building three blocks away. Tara nodded as she always did. GK told her this little detail from his life nearly once every week. She knew what was coming next. She pre-empted the wishful thoughts that GK often expressed. "Why don't you put serious effort into the bookstore idea?"

GK stood stunned for a moment. He blinked at Tara. "I don't have enough money."

"Story of our life," said Tara with a chuckle.

GK flipped open a phone and showed her a statistic on the decreasing number of readers in India. Tara dismissed the report with a cursory glance. "Is this for reading in general or readership of newspapers?"

"It doesn't matter. The competition for both is the television, and I would need to build a good collection if I have to succeed."

"What about the internet? Isn't that a competition?"

"You have a prejudice. Your village and the villagers are mad." GK remarked with a scowl.

Tara grimaced. "Jomo is a beautiful place, and outsiders are not allowed to comment."

"I want to visit it, but you never invite me."

"It's been six months since I visited. I'll return after the exams. Only two more months to go. I hope to find a better job after that."

GK made a sound that was a combination of a whine, a grunt, and a chuckle. "Do you believe that we can get a job soon after our graduation?" When Tara did not reply, he continued, "Don't be surprised if we are stuck behind that sales counter for another couple of years or more."

Tara shuddered at the thought.

"My bus is here," she said. "See you in class tomorrow."

GK waved at her receding figure. He couldn't understand this girl at all. The first time he noticed her, she was in the library begging the librarian for a few more minutes at the browsing kiosk. She was the only student who used it regularly. Most students had smartphones, and he wondered if she hailed from an ultra-conservative family who denied her a device. She was not a classical beauty as men of his age would define it, but her dusky features held a sturdiness. The moment you saw her, you knew that she was someone dependable. Someone who might stand up for you in times of need.

Gradually, they began talking. She was a loner, so it was difficult to pick up a conversation, but she warmed up to him when she knew that he was an orphan too. He had no one to answer to except for a few distant relatives who couldn't care less. Tara had her invalid grandmother under her care. She gained many notches of respect in his eyes when he learned about her circumstances. GK helped her get the weekend gig at the textile shop where he worked. She said it was a tremendous help, and they fell into an easy friendship. Over the course of their education, they both found solace in their shared sorrows and minor triumphs. "Education is only a crutch," Tara would say. "We'll have to throw it away sooner or later." She was interested in plants and all things related. "My garden is my soul," she would proclaim on even days. "It will be the bane of my existence," on odd days. She would fume at the carelessness of her housekeeper after a visit to her favourite Jomo, never satisfied with how she tended to her garden.

What GK liked best about her was that she would help wholeheartedly. It was because of her that he got introduced to his girlfriend, or future girlfriend, as Tara would say. Kannagi was two years younger but smart, intelligent, and a celebrity at their college. She could sing, dance, and hold the audience enthralled. Gerald Kevin knew he had no chance with her. Kannagi was the epitome of rustic beauty, while he was chubby and a nerd. Tara motivated him to speak to the girl. "You have a good heart. She will recognize it if she has one too."

Although GK and Kannagi were friends now, it was too early to say what their future held. As he waited for the bus that would take him to the other side of the town where he lived, he wondered if he should approach Kannagi about their future. He should ask Tara.

The next day, when they met at college, Tara ignored him. GK was perplexed, but he thought she might be worried about something. Twenty-year-old orphans living off a meagre inheritance and taking care of an elder often had existential issues on their minds. She continued to ignore him for the whole week. She would stay busy with her books during the day and rush off to her hostel after classes without speaking to him.

On Saturday, when they met at the shop, he tried to catch her eye. Chitchatting would draw unwanted attention from the manager. Tara already suffered from it without breaking any employee rules. GK waited for the lunch break. They usually walked to a nearby hotel to grab a dosa or an appam. Tara went away for her lunch without waiting for him. When he reached the hotel, she was leaving.

"Tara, what's wrong?" he asked, blocking her way.

She glared at GK, reminding him of how Kannagi stared at him sometimes. GK and Kannagi were already getting into tiffs.

After she paid the bill, she walked up to him and pointed her finger at his face. "Remove that picture immediately, or this will be the end of our friendship."

GK's mind boggled at her words. "What picture?"

"That picture you took of me last week."

"Picture? Of you?"

Then it dawned on him. He had clicked a photo of a building façade. It was a heritage building near their store, and GK found the evening light perfect for a click. Tara entered the frame, accidentally. He had meant to click another, but the bus arrived. A few hours later, without giving much thought to Tara being in the frame, GK uploaded it onto his social media account. He had a few followers from college.

"How does it matter, Tara? Your face is not even visible in that picture."

"You know I don't like being on social media."

"And you are not! No one can identify you in the photograph. You can't be tagged because you don't have an account."

"Someone knew that it was me, and they identified me."

"Who?"

"My roommate."

GK chuckled. "So what? What's the big deal?"

"It's a big deal for me, ok? I dislike the internet, and I hate social media."

"Have you ever tried it?"

"No, fawning over others' pictures is repulsive."

"You are weird."

"Not the first time I am hearing it," Tara replied and stomped off.

"No, Tara, wait!"

GK had heard the Jomo story from Tara about her accident and her parent's death, but he couldn't fathom why someone would be so averse to being online. Soon after lunch, GK sent a message to Tara's ancient phone, which she used only for emergencies.

"I have deleted it. Friends?"

But Tara did not reply. She spent the weekend in her own bubble, and GK did not bother her. He figured that she needed time to cool off.

The next day, a Monday, as they sat in class, Tara received a message from the principal. She followed the peon to the principal's office. The principal was kind and considerate as she shared the news.

"Tara, your grandmother is no more."

Tara sat down as the principal offered her a glass of water.

"Who called?"

"Someone named Lal? The voice was very feeble. I could hardly hear. You can leave now for your hometown. I'll inform your teachers. You've only a month left. Then you have a break before your university exams. So, you won't lose much if you decide to stay back in your hometown, but you should appear for your exams, Tara." The principal emphasised the last few words.

"My village."

"Pardon me?"

"It's a village, Jomo, not a town where I come from."

"Oh. It's the village with no internet?"

"Yes, mam."

The principal chewed her lip. "How will you prepare from there?"

Tara replied, "I need to go."

She returned to her class to gather her books and left without saying a word to anyone. That was the last GK saw of her. He did not hear from her until five years later when she invited him to Jomo.

# 10

## The Jomo Story

Now that GK was at the mysterious Jomo, he wanted to learn all about the place. There had to be an interesting story behind the framed text on the wall. Who wrote it and why.

Tara knew less about the history of Jomo than she knew about the history of humankind. She had studied the nation's freedom struggle and the wars elsewhere in the world from her textbooks. She learned about them because it was important, according to her teachers. Stories about Jomo, her home, though, were not written anywhere. No one taught them at school. The children of Jomo were not tested on their knowledge of Jomo history. They were not asked to learn them by rote, recollect dates of note and spew them on paper.

Despite the obvious lack of institutional will to record Jomoan history, the stories lived on through the people. Tara knew some stories, but not all. She heard them from people she knew, people she loved, and people she trusted. They all had their own versions.

According to Grandma, Jomo was a refuge for settlers from the valley. "The valley people were vain and boastful. They were lucky to live in paradise, but their good fortune made them selfish and arrogant. Some of us did not like the way they lived, so we distanced ourselves. We explored higher lands until we came to this place."

According to her father, Jomo was just another settlement for people who were driven away from the valley. "Some people had no rights in the valley, so they wandered off in search of places where they could make their own rules." A wide-eyed six-year-old Tara listened in rapt attention, so enthralled by her father's voice that she forgot to ask what rights and rules meant.

To Cheeru, Jomo was her home. "Our ancestors believed in the mountain Gods. They lived off the trees and plants that grew naturally on these mountains. Things changed when people from the valley arrived here. They taught our ancestors to grow fruits and vegetables. My great-grandmother would talk about how they would hunt for porcupines and wild pigs in the forests. Now we don't need to hunt. We have hens and goats at home. And we have a school. My ancestors never had one. Other settlers can leave Jomo and go if they want. We will never leave. This is our home. No one will accept us in the valley."

But the most interesting bit of Jomo's history came from Grandpa Lal. He knew more about Tara's family than her.

"Nilaav?" GK asked.

"Yes, Nilaav, Moonlight. He was my uncle. Or still is."

GK was so puzzled that the piece of chilli-drenched tapioca he stuffed into his gaping mouth fell out immediately.

"After Grandma passed away, I was visited by her lawyer, Thomas. Grandpa Lal assumed that he left the cash which paid for my college, but Mr. Thomas assured me that it was not him. He didn't know who deposited the envelope at my house that day. It couldn't have been with Grandma's knowledge because she was quite sick by then. Although she did plan for all those signed cheques earlier."

"Your Grandma planned far more than that. You bloo—erm, own the mountain, don't you?"

"I am not sure if I want to own it or if I really own it."

"What are you blabbering about?"

"Well, for one, my uncle owns half of it."

"What is his story?"

"That's an interesting piece of my family history and a bit about Jomo as well."

"I am all ears."

"Grandpa Lal narrated this fascinating story about how my uncle became a runaway."

"Wait! He ran away?"

Tara glared at him.

"Ok, ok, go on."

"So, there is a Jomoan named Raman. I have seen him once or twice. Cheeru would often warn me about him, asking me to keep my distance." Tara described how Raman was responsible for the no Internet rule at Jomo, and how he did not take a liking to her father.

"And in some ways, Raman is responsible for my uncle's disappearance too. Raman's father was a worse man than him, according to Grandpa Lal. He was caught molesting a young woman. My uncle was the witness. He was the one who raised a ruckus and called all the villagers. But the villagers were afraid of Raman's father. He was a rich man with a lot of connections. The young woman, though, did not give up, and she complained to the police. When they asked the villagers if they had seen anything, they declined to comment. The woman pointed out that my uncle was a witness, and he narrated it to the police."

"He was a hero," GK said in a whispered awe.

"He was only thirteen. After the incident, he was hounded by Raman's family. He got scared and ran away."

"But why didn't your family support him? What about your dad?"

"My dad was too young, only a baby, when this happened. He never mentioned his brother to me."

"So, if your uncle Nilaav is alive, he must be rather old."

Tara nodded. "Uncle had, apparently, a mischievous streak. He would scare the neighbours, wearing masks and odd clothing. He conducted mysterious experiments, and often, explosions would be heard from that hut below." Tara said, pointing vaguely towards the window. GK craned his neck to get a better view, but it was getting dark. "There is a hut there, which I now use to store my gardening tools."

Tara paused before she went inside one of the bedrooms. "There is only one family photo," she said, handing over a yellowed monochrome family photograph. "That's my grandmother, my grandfather, and my dad in his lap. Do you notice a portion of a leg beside grandfather?"

GK peered closely. Sure enough, a little toe appeared close to Tara's grandfather's feet, an extra toe growing out of thin air.

"That, probably, was my uncle, but my grandmother was so ashamed of his behaviour that she cut him off the photograph and from her life."

GK added, "But not from her will. Maternal love and rage are equally incomprehensible." He sighed as he sipped on the delicious coffee prepared by Tara. "I wish my mother was alive. She was the most amazing cook. I was twelve when she died."

"I was eight when I lost my parents."

GK promptly changed his demeanour and urged her to go on with the story. "What happened next? He never came back?"

"Never. And to make it worse, no one remembers his real name. Even Grandma's will does not mention his real name. Nilaav isn't his real name."

"How is the will legal then?"

"It is, as per Thomas, but that's beside the point." Tara took the photograph from GK. She stared at it for a while as if willing the torn part to reappear. "I want to find my uncle."

"Why now? Five years after you learned about the will?

"I have my reasons," said Tara and pursed her lips.

GK sighed. Tara's face had a familiar expression. It was her go-to frown when she did not want to share more on a topic. "And you think that your uncle will be online and I'll be able to find him?" GK scoffed at her wild ideas. "It's nearly impossible."

"Yet not impossible." Tara stood in front of him, arms crossed across her body.

"Without a name?" muttered GK. "Are you sure there is no document lying around the house where his name is mentioned?"

Tara shook her head. "I have scoured every nook and cranny."

"By the way, why was he called Nilaav?"

Tara replied sheepishly, "because he used to roam around on moonlit nights."

GK guffawed. "He appears shady to me."

"By a strange coincidence, Uncle Sharaf, who died in that accident, is also tragically linked to Raman's family. The young victim was not from Jomo but from the valley. She was the aunt of Uncle Sharaf."

"Your accident?"

Tara nodded in reply. "Grandpa Lal told me many incidents in bits and pieces after Grandma died. He is losing his memory with his age. One more reason why I want to find my uncle soon. Grandpa Lal might be the only one able to recognize him or at least corroborate his story. And worse, what if Uncle doesn't remember any of this himself?"

"One more reason, eh? What's the main reason?"

Tara glared at GK as if warning him. He held up his hands in peace.

"I am feeling sleepy," he announced.

Tara pointed to the second bedroom in the house. "Or you are welcome to sleep on the couch if you prefer."

GK pointed to the couch. Tara retired to her room, and he wandered out into the veranda.

He stood still in the cool night air. It was pitch black outside and eerily silent. No insects with their orchestra, no flapping of wings. An owl hooted in the distance, and GK jumped out of his skin. Jomo felt surreal, a fantasy. He had a sudden urge to open his phone and scroll through the familiar stories, posts, and news. A yearning for his normal world. He flipped open his phone and cursed himself upon realising that the phone was as good as dead.

GK turned to the message framed on the wall. Once again, he had goosebumps. He scrambled inside the door and latched it quickly.

Why were the words haunting him so much?

11

# The Fear of Missing Out

GK woke up to a low-pitched growl from his belly and a heaviness on his chest. Unable to open his sleepy eyelids, he listened for a while. Warm air blew on his face. Not a blast, not a gentle breeze, but irregular whiffs of air like someone breathing down on him.

Through half-closed eyes, GK saw a fabulous set of fangs, a wet snout, and an aura of white and brown fur. His eyes opened wide. A mongrel gigantic enough to be the offspring of a German Shepherd had his front paws on his chest. The growl emanated not from GK's tummy but from the mongrel's throat. The fangs were too close for comfort.

GK and the fangs indulged in a staring contest until Tara called out, "Coco! Leave him alone!"

Hearing her voice, Coco ran off with a whine and a yelp. GK sat up on the couch, thanking his stars. A second ago, the fangs were inches away from his face.

And then it happened. The most beautiful morning he had ever experienced in his life. Sitting on the couch opposite a bay window, he witnessed the phenomenon that was so routine and yet sublime – the sun rising over the mountains. The criss-cross lattice allowed the hesitant rays to form a fuzzy pattern on the floor. The pattern would define itself as the sun rose higher. For now, it was vague, misty, gently touched, and surreal.

GK stretched, stepped out onto the porch, and inhaled the fresh mountain air. The birds were doing the same, except they were noisy. Nature was at its best and the brightest. The calm morning air tingled on his cheeks and awakened his senses. The flowers, freshly showered with the morning mist, bowed their delicate petals under the weight of the dewdrops. The sun dropped a dollop of happiness on the mountain dwellers.

GK was quiet, a blaze of envy coursing through his veins—Tara was so fortunate to wake up to such enchanting mornings every day. This was the perfect place to click breath-taking pictures. He was certain that his followers would go crazy if he shared them. The pictures did not need any photographic filters. The place was gorgeous. GK groped inside his pocket for his smartphone. In his eagerness, he fumbled with his smartphone, cursing the multitude of apps. Click! Instead of enjoying the scene in its entirety, he peered into his camera, limiting his vision to the screen dimensions, and captured the scene for posterity.

A second later, his excitement came crashing down like a belligerent wave that came face to face with the beach. There was no internet connectivity. He stepped inside the house with a simmering discontent.

Tara was in the kitchen at the far end, and he could hear the pots and pans clanging against each other.

"Up so early?" Tara asked as she sensed GK at the kitchen door.

"How do you live in this place?"

"What?"

"This God-forsaken place with no internet!"

Tara chuckled. She whistled for Coco, and GK stepped back, half expecting the mongrel's fangs to reach for his ankles.

"Don't worry. He doesn't bother once he sees that you are welcome in my house."

"The place is ..." he forgot his words when Coco came bounding into the kitchen from the backyard.

GK glanced at Coco in amusement. "He has daffodils in his mouth! Am I inside an Enid Blyton novel?"

"Aah, yes!" Tara accepted Coco's offering, gently ran some water on the daffodils, and put them into her vase. "That's his morning errand."

GK stared at Coco, who stared back with quizzical eyes. "What is this human doing here?" they seemed to ask. While GK and Coco engaged in a staring match, Tara moved to the porch. "Do you want some tea?" she yelled at GK.

GK hurried to the porch, grateful to be away from the suspicious dog. Coco followed him but ran across the garden. GK slumped into a chair in relief at having dodged Coco, but the scenic view ahead of him brought back the discontent. A gush of uneasiness enveloped him, an unwanted draught chilling him to his spine.

"You guys are crazy."

"What are you mumbling about?"

"There is this absolutely magnificent sun rising above the mountains, and I can't post it on the internet."

"How does it matter whether you post it or not? The sun rises every day."

GK pondered in momentary confusion. "Yes, but this is my personal experience, isn't it?"

"So? How is it different from anyone who might witness this sunrise?"

"You don't get it. You are so lucky. There are others like me who are not."

"Doesn't the sun rise in your part of the world?"

"Not so beautifully, no! Besides, how do I prove that I saw something so spectacular if I don't have a picture?"

"You clicked the picture, didn't you?" Tara accused, pointing to his smartphone.

"Yes, yes, I did. But what's the use if I can't share it with my followers?"

Tara leaned forward, her sharp eyes scanning GK's face. "GK, you were never a Pollyanna, but you are grumpier than ever. What's wrong?"

GK shook his head in impatience. "There is nothing wrong with me. It's this place. It's you!"

Tara leaned back but did not break her gaze. "What about me?"

"Were you ever in touch with your friends?"

"Which friends?"

GK stared at Tara. She was nearly the same as five years ago. The sharp eyes, robust features, her skin tanned a rich brown, and the old dependable sturdiness, but something was different. She used to be restless as a student. Behind her steadfast demeanour, she would hold a wistfulness, a desire to be anywhere but there in that moment. Today, she displayed placid contentment. A radiance that was ready to burst at its seams. She was happy in the present moment. Her clothes had become laidback. Gone was the simple yet carefully curated look that she carried throughout the week, whether at college or at her part-time job at the store. Instead, she was dressed in an olive t-shirt and a mud-coloured overall.

"You are enjoying this situation, aren't you?"

"What situation?"

"This situation you have," GK pointed around vaguely, "...of a disconnected, cut-off life?"

"Thoroughly," came the quick reply.

"Well, why wouldn't you. You own a fortune, and—"

"What you call a fortune is a piece of land which I can do nothing about. I have no idea if there are people living on it. Fortunately, no Jomoan knows about the ownership. Or I would have had lawyers swarming over my home by now."

Coco appeared from the edge of the porch with a high jump, panting excessively. He flopped down at Tara's feet, but his eyes were stuck on GK's face. Tara fondled Coco's ears, who immediately rolled over to show his happiness. GK regarded the two, lost in their world. A mixture of discontent and envy bubbled inside him. "Strangely, that reminds me. The guy who gave me a ride up to the top asked me if I was an advocate."

Tara sat up in alarm. "Did he now?"

GK nodded. There was a chink in the placidity. Tara had a problem. He quickly changed the topic.

"What do you people do in case of emergencies? How do you call for help?"

"Simple. Further down the road, we can catch the cell tower's signal and—"

"What if a person is living alone and has some emergency or some danger? What if burglars get in here in the middle of the night?"

Tara chuckled. "Here? At the top of the mountain?"

GK swallowed his foolishness and stared morosely.

"I have Coco. Besides, ambulances are allowed up here."

"Oh?"

"If you come here often enough, you will find an ambulance or two winding up the road."

"So many people in need of care?"

"No. Some people misusing the leeway given to ambulances."

"Aah!"

Coco was nearly on Tara's lap now, trying to lick her face. Tara cooed in that special tone that she reserved for Coco. "Are you hungry now, Coco? Are you?" She was unruffled despite GK's questions. He stood up in a fluster. "Do you mean to say that you will not climb down this mountain unless you are in an ambulance?"

Tara blinked at GK. "The breakfast is ready, GK, if you are hungry."

GK stamped out of the porch, marched across the lawn, and pushed open the gate without noticing the petite blooms on the purple shamrock like glistening pearls among purple butterflies. He failed to hear the curious bird with the musical call, singing since the day broke. He ignored the mist rolling up the hills. GK walked at such a furious pace that he did not notice where he was going. He had never walked this quick in his life. Soon, he gasped for breath and sat down on a stile beside a gate. The gate led to a cottage, but the foliage blocked the view of the façade completely. All he could see was a cobbled stone path that led to a chimney giving off a thin wisp of smoke. "Idiots!" he thought, "living like some primeval humans.

By now, at home, GK would have posted a witty comment on the Radha Textile employees' group. He would have posted a picture on his profile with some clever caption. After posting his own inanities, he would have scrolled through the day's headlines which could be as frivolous as a celebrity gifting a golden brush to her dog to something as complex as a belligerent nation's cryptic statement about world dominance. GK would have consumed all with equal indifference and disinterest, driven by mild hypnosis that kept him scrolling down, down, until the page would not show anything even when refreshed. That would satisfy his craving for useless information as he sat on the pot.

That's it! Now he understood one reason for his grumpiness. Embarrassed at the realisation, he stood up to walk back, only to be further frustrated at the thought of climbing back up to Tara's house. By the time he returned, huffing, puffing, gasping for breath, he had made up his mind.

"Tara!" he called between gasps. "Give me food and call an ambulance. I am leaving this place. Also, give me the details about your uncle. I'll find out."

Tara went about her chores wordlessly while GK, fresh after a shower, ate in a hurry. She handed him an envelope while he stuffed his backpack with greens from the garden. "There are no details. That is what I have been trying to tell you."

GK picked up his backpack but hesitated by the door. "Sorry, this place. It's so beautiful, but it got on my nerves."

Tara smiled. "You don't get it, do you? The joy of missing out at Jomo?" she said and pointed to the gate. A lanky boy with a bandana on his head leaned on the pillar. "He is from the village. He'll show you a shortcut to the main road. Ambulances are only for emergencies." GK blew out some air, pausing at the threshold. "What does that letter really mean?" he asked, pointing at the frame on the wall.

"Aren't you in a hurry to leave?"

GK drew in an impatient breath.

"I told you the story before. My accident. The others who died."

"Why would a wandering man just leave a letter like that? And why would the villagers connect this letter to the accident? Isn't it outlandish?"

Tara shrugged.

"I can't fathom how you people survive without the Internet."

"Be careful, GK, you are going down a treacherous road," Tara shouted with a sly grin. GK was out of earshot. He had already whipped out his phone to catch the signal.

# 12

# Trespassers

When Tara invited GK home for a reconciliation, she was convinced he could help find her uncle. After she met him, though, her confidence wavered. GK, of their college days, was a bit of a loner but resourceful and willing to help. In a mere five years, he appeared to have changed. Of course, young men change when they face life and its realities, but GK's transformation was different. It was not the blossoming of a student into a mature individual but a slippery slide down the woeful slope of frustrations.

The clock struck eight, bringing Tara out of her reverie.

In a few hours, she would climb down to a small but sturdy hut where she would greet her first set of students for the day – seven to ten-year-olds. She would teach and guide them through their lessons until tea time when the second batch of students would troop in. The villagers sent their kids despite knowing that she was not a qualified teacher. The children showed a marked improvement due to the disciplined work she extracted from them. At first, it was only the primary and secondary level students. Soon, young parents hauled their little ones up the mountain to prepare them for school. She dissuaded the parents.

"They are too young. They can come and play in my garden. I'll clear away a patch," Tara said, pointing to a corner of her garden. “They will learn about the flowers, fruits, trees, butterflies, earthworms…,” Tara stopped when she saw the young mother turn to the father with a quizzical look. No one wanted their children to get their hands dirty in the icky mud. They shook their heads, mumbled their thanks, and left. “Good riddance!” Tara muttered in return.

The two batches kept her busy through the afternoon. Then she would tend to her garden. Today, after her classes, the garden was not her priority. She had to stand in for a colleague at the dog shelter. It would also mean a few good treats for Coco.

On the way down to the valley, she stopped to check on Grandpa Lal. “How is your back treating you?”

“The same way that I am treating it – with a stiff respect,” Grandpa Lal replied with a slow smile.

She did a quick round of the kitchen. After Tara let her go, Meenu worked for Grandpa Lal. She was diligent but forgetful. So, it was up to Tara to make sure that the pantry was well-stocked. As she rummaged inside Grandpa Lal’s medicine drawer, she caught a sharp movement from the corner of her eye. She rushed to steady Grandpa Lal as he swayed against the dining table.

“What’s wrong?”

“Nothing. It’s vertigo. Although, sometimes I feel that it’s not me but the mountain. Do you feel it tremble?”

Tara scoffed. Her grandma would drive her mad with stories about the dead souls of the mountains. “The ancient people of Jomo village talked about the brave who lost their lives on this treacherous mountain. The village did not exist back then. The dead have not gone anywhere. I can feel Jomo sway to the songs of the dead souls," her grandmother would say.

"Come on, Grandpa Lal, don't start off like my grandmother."

Grandpa Lal did not respond. Instead, he patted Coco. "He has been very helpful today, as always."

"He should get a special treat, right Coco?" Tara asked as she attached the leash to his belt. "Let's go meet your friends," she said as Coco ran out, wagging his tail.

At the dog rescue centre, Tara took the dogs out for a round of exercise in the nearby park. These were the six bigger dogs who needed more space than the modest backyard of the rescue home. They loved stretching their legs as Tara held them on a leash across the road. It was not much of a park but a square piece of abandoned land in front of the rescue centre. The dog centre paid for the maintenance, keeping it free of weeds and overgrown grass. No one knew who owned the land. Despite reservations in the community about the centre, no one tried to encroach on the empty space, as nobody wanted to deal with a pack of angry dogs loathe to lose their only playground. Not even a peddler dared to put their cart beside it. But when Tara took the dogs out for their run, something was afoot. The playground was occupied.

Four bamboo poles stood arrogantly in the middle of the lawn with a stack of red plastic chairs in the centre. Tara surveyed the intrusion with disdain. The stack of ugly chairs stood like an emblem of arrogance and power, surrounded by mindless and lifeless poles of sycophancy standing in obeisance. The dogs did not mind, though; one by one, they all marked their territory by sprinkling some water on the poles and the chair. Tara chuckled as they trounced around. She knew that Natasha and Freddie, who ran the centre, would have the trespassers packing away in no time. They had been running the centre for a decade now, and they knew how to navigate tricky community conflicts. They were also aware of their rights and their canines' rights.

Tara led the dogs back inside after their run. The dusk was as hesitant to give way to the darkness as the flickering streetlights were to light it. The street was quiet. It was a cul de sac with a few houses beyond the shelter, from where the road took a U-turn around the dog park and away into the busier part of the town. The dogs needed no cajoling to saunter into the shelter, where Nat and Fred would have their dinner ready.

Tara waited as the sky changed colours and gradually displayed the brighter stars. She was not an astronomy enthusiast, not even an amateur one, but she enjoyed the twinkling company, on lonely cloudless nights at the cottage. While the sky shone in the starry aura, darkness crept around the street corners. Tara sighed. It would be prudent to leave for Jomo before it got too dark to trudge up the treacherous slopes of the mountainside. As she turned around, an unexpected light blinked among the bushes by the sidewalk. She rubbed her eyes. A red light flashed for sure. She moved closer. Above the happy yapping of the dogs, a purr rumbled in the darkness. Tara froze for a second. Was a jungle cat on the prowl? The sleeky Jomo resident has been seen before, an athletic leopard cub who was now a full-grown predator, though it rarely came down to the valley. But this could not be an animal. Animals didn't have blinking lights. The light moved nearer, towards the dog centre. To her relief, it was only a car. Why act so sneaky?

Tara shrugged and called for Coco. Nat and Fred came out with him. "We better leave now. I don't want to come face to face with Nanban in the dark." Freddie chuckled. "Face to face? He would likely pounce on you from a treetop before you could see his face."

Tara shuddered at the thought.

"Don't worry. Coco will sound the alarm," Nat added, giving Freddie a sharp nudge in his ribs.

Tara grinned and turned towards the gate. "By the way, do you have any idea why you both might be spied upon?"

"Spy? Who?" Freddie asked, squinting in the direction that Tara pointed. There was a car neatly hidden in the darkness of a tree, except for its blinking light. "No idea. But they won't cross the street to our gate without hearing from our dogs."

Tara stepped into the street. As she passed the car, she noted two men sitting in the front, staring at their phones. They sat with perfect ease as if content to wait in the darkness. Tara felt a niggle of uneasiness. Nat and Freddie were the kindest souls she knew, but they had run-ins with the local authorities. She hoped the men in the car meant no harm to the gentle couple.

By the time Tara reached the base of the mountain path, the trees turned into giant shadows. They stood as sedately as the mountain itself. Not a leaf moved as Tara clambered up the slope with a torch in one hand and Coco's leash held tightly in the other. The nocturnal sounds made their way up the valley, though the slopes were quiet. Tara shivered. A chill in the air, combined with an inexplicable fear, caused her to tremble. She had climbed these familiar paths before, and her climbs had been uneventful, except for a few scratches while trying to catch up with Coco, but mentioning Nanban in her conversation with Nat and Freddie had made her nervous.

Nanban, a 'friend' was lovingly named so by the Jomoans because, unlike his mother, he had never attacked them or their animals. He ruled his part of the woods and did not bother to wander close to civilization. However, some villagers did not completely believe in his innocence. His mother, Kali, was notorious for carrying away dogs and smaller animals. She had injured a few men who went after her. The villagers petitioned the forest department when the losses became too many to ignore. On a quiet, tepid night, when the leaves drooped sullen and motionless, a team of men, some in uniforms, others in baggy shirts and tight wrap-arounds, scoured the woods for a suitable spot. The jungle was so quiet that the officials had a nagging feeling that instead of Kali, it was them who were trapped in the twilight zone. Even the dog they used as bait only whimpered occasionally. They escaped the eerie silence without bidding goodbye to the trembling canine in the cage. In the morning, the news spread like wildfire. 'Kali has been caught.' The officials rushed to the fateful spot to see Kali lashing and gnashing inside her section of the cage and the dog whining and cowering in his. Their fate hung upon the two rattling trapdoors – one allowing the dog to remain alive, the other making the leopard nervous with fear in the face of imminent death. However, Kali was not shot. The forest officials took her deeper into the jungles. The villagers slept in relief that night, ignorant of the tiny cub mewing across the woods, seeking his mother.

Ten years later, thoughts of that orphaned cub gnawed at Tara's frayed nerves as she climbed the slope toward her home. Shaking herself impatiently, she said to herself, "Cut it off, Tara!" She turned around a corner towards a narrow winding path that would take her straight to Grandpa Lal's house and further to her home. The area had more houses on the way and was lit in parts. She heaved a sigh of relief, but her breath was cut short by a sneaking suspicion. Did she hear a vehicle? She glanced all around. It was impossible. She had entered Jomo panchayat's jurisdiction a while ago. Vehicles were prohibited. Coco tugged at his leash. He could smell his house. Tara took a few steps and stopped. There was no doubt this time. The nauseating smell of burnt rubber and fuel hit her nostrils. She backed up to the corner on tiptoes. It was also a fork in the road. Though wider and smoother, the road to the right led straight to the jungle. Her hunch proved to be right. A vehicle was inching slowly as if afraid to commit to the path ahead. Tara moved closer but jumped when she heard a rumble near her. It was Coco, emitting a low growl that threatened to rise in pitch as the vehicle appeared in view. Tara held Coco's snout in her hand, gave a quick rub on his belly, and kept her finger on her lips. Coco gazed deep into her eyes and throttled his growl. "Good boy," she whispered, patting him. The vehicle stopped. Tara discerned the shape of a jeep from her hiding place behind a boulder. Before she could move closer, the jeep backed up into the fork without warning and went down the hill. If Tara had not held onto Coco, muffling him with her grip before she ducked into the boulder's shadow, the passengers in the jeep would have seen her.

What if they see her? Why did they make her so jumpy?

By the time Tara reached home, and climbed into her bed, her mind had worked itself into a frenzy. Rain arrived, not the howling, screeching variety, but the kind that caused a pitter-patter outside the window. Tara dozed off into a deep slumber listening to nature's lullaby, oblivious to the activities happening several feet below.

# 13

# A Sordid Life

GK, unlike Tara, was having a restless night. Even the gentle rain could not lull him to sleep.

Earlier in the day, Kannagi bickered with him for not sharing the real reason for his absence at her family function. In a separate incident of folly, he argued with some friends online. They were brutal with their views on the irrelevance of bookstores despite knowing that GK took any such views as a personal insult. The most annoying part of the day was when he uploaded a picture, and it did not take off the way he expected. It was a picture of a stack of books caught in a dreamlike beam of light filtering through the windows. He was proud of his capture, but only a few of his followers shared his enthusiasm.

After tossing and turning for a while, mirroring the angry thoughts in his head, GK sat up in his bed. Instinctively, he picked up his phone to check the time. It was 2:02 am. "What an odd time to wake up," he mumbled. He swiped his phone screen to search for the name 'Nilaav'. Earlier, at work, when he typed in the name, the search engine threw up such strange profiles that he was afraid he would be sucked into the darkest places on the web. GK checked the time again. 2:05 am. Time passes slowly at night, he concluded. He lay down in his bed, but his hands wouldn't let go of his phone. So, he started swiping and scrolling endlessly, watching cat videos, dog videos, and, later, news articles, opinions, and comments, digging deep into the rabbit hole of internet trolling. He frequently checked his uploaded photograph to see if there was any uptick in the number of likes. Fifteen thousand followers and only forty-four likes. What were the others doing? Shame on them!

His anger made him scroll more until there was nothing new to read. He searched for the keywords- 'relevance of books.' He found an article that extolled the virtues of reading which made him forget his worries and insecurities for a while. Then he read the comments below the article. Trolls were demeaning not only bookstores but books in general and the habit of reading in specific. They were far outnumbered by those who loved reading and books, but the few vitriolic comments raised his anger. GK went back to mindless scrolling until his eyes started tearing up, his vision glazed over, and his eyes closed on their own. He started snoring, his phone balanced precariously on his tummy that rose and fell with his snores. The screen showed the time – 4:30 am.

When the alarm rang in the morning, GK was in no mood to wake up. His body refused to budge. He hit the snooze button six times instead of the usual two until a vague urgency reminded him that it was a working day and that he should be out of the house in thirty minutes. GK sat up on his bed, rubbing the sleep out of his eyes, another morning without exercise. He had promised Kannagi to put some effort into building a routine. 'Pfft! Kannagi and her diktats!' he muttered. With just three and a half hours of sleep in his slumber account, GK was heavily out of balance. He decided to trudge through the day anyway. How hard could it be?

As soon as he reached the textile shop, instead of punching in his card, he went to the Corner Tea Shop across the street and ordered his breakfast of tea, idlis, and vada. The textile shop owner, Pillai, stood at the entrance to the shop, staring in his direction. The man had weak eyes and couldn't possibly see GK from across the road. But GK knew that his absence at the shop was taken as an affront. Pillai stood staring at the tea shop with his hands on his hips.

"Alright, alright!" GK muttered, "a man can't have breakfast in peace!" He dismissed the owner's contrived smile at the payment counter with a curt nod. All pending bills will be settled at the month's end, was the meaning of the nod. GK crossed at a leisurely pace to stand in front of Pillai. Instead of berating him for his late arrival, Pillai scrutinized him. "Did you sleep at all yesterday night?"

GK nodded.

"Listen, son, if you have any problems in life, tell me. I am here to help."

"What problems?" GK asked in irritation as he took his seat behind the computer desk.

"You look like…," Pillai stopped with a shake of his head.

GK grunted. The old man tried to be extra kind when the work increased. The shop was partly automated. It meant that GK had to type a lot of data into the computer, maintain it, and update it as needed. Instead of working for the dreary Pillai, GK would have ideally liked to open a bookstore, read new books, buy books for his bookstore, organise literary events, meet the authors…

"GK?" His daydreams were rudely interrupted by an irate tap on his table.

Pillai towered above him—his third-rate concern transformed into a first-class scowl that would make any employee submit a resignation letter without much thought. "Yes?"

"Did you arrange the tea and biscuits for the meeting later today?"

"What meeting?" GK had not received any memo.

"You forgot about ARN's meeting?" Pillai's scowl deepened.

GK sighed in recognition. ARN was Pillai's nephew, a political wannabe. He organised a meeting for the locals every three months, where he would pick a random topic to give his spiel. He truly believed that people came to listen to him, but GK knew it all depended on the snacks approved for the evening. They were approved by Pillai. After all, he was ARN's uncle, and in turn, the approval was based on the budget allocated by Pillai's wife. On some days, her temperament was good, so the budget improved, and exotic snacks could be ordered. GK smacked his lips as he recollected the bread rolls that Pillai had once approved. Bread rolls – soft bread deep fried to golden brown perfection and filled with spicy, sumptuous fillings, meat, or potatoes – attracted the largest audience for ARN. The number dwindled if it was lentil fritters, pakoras, or samosas, with the least demand for biscuits. Today was biscuit day. ARN will have to talk to empty chairs.

"Did you order or not?" Pillai growled.

GK nodded. "It'll be ready."

Pillai didn't notice GK's reddening face. After Pillai left, GK stomped out of the store. Behind the store, a narrow pathway led to a well. GK strode towards it with purpose. Near the well, he frantically inspected the surroundings. "Where are they? Where are they?" he muttered under his breath. He stooped when he found the object of his search. Tiny, violet dayflowers popped in defiance among the overwhelmingly green grass. He whipped out his phone, chose an angle, and clicked the flower. It appeared big and fresh on his screen. In the grass, it was a nobody. On the screen, it spread its petals in all their violet glory. It was fascinating how the tiniest of nature's creations had the power to double your joy. GK tapped his phone a few times. The picture was up, and the likes started pouring in. With a smugness that comes only with external validation, he walked back to his boring desk.

By evening, his boredom had peaked, but now he had an additional task on his growing list of things he did not want to do. The snacks and other arrangements for the rambling ARN weighed heavily on his mind. What was worse was that all store employees, except one who manned the counter, were forced to sit at the periphery of the tent in the modest courtyard. As long as enough listeners trooped in, the employees would fry in the late afternoon sun, but if the audience was not to ARN's expectation, the employees could sit underneath the tent. Only one lucky person was exempt from the torture and he or she was chosen using a lottery. As an ode to his bad luck, GK had lost it every single time so far. So, along with the tedious job, he also had to attend all of ARN's excruciating meetings. GK was helpless, and it seemed luckless.

Fortunately, what was to be a perfectly ordinary unlucky day for GK, turned out to be the day he won the lottery to man the counter while ARN extolled his own non-existent virtues. GK heaved a sigh of relief as the others trooped out, dejected at their collective misfortune. He could now read in peace, except after the first two pages, he ended up scrolling through social media. GK badly wanted to click a photo of the idiots sitting outside listening to ARN, but he was afraid that if someone found the picture online, they would come after him and beat him up. He crept to the window to see if he could catch someone yawning. To his surprise, people were listening in rapt attention.

ARN was speaking about how he knew to make the best use of technology. "I can influence people online," he beamed as he said. "Isn't that one of the first requirements for a leader?" The audience murmured. "Not just that," he lowered his voice and leaned forward as if he was telling them a secret, "I have so many followers that people now offer me money to talk about their product."

The murmur in the crowd rose a wee bit in volume.

"I am now, what they call, an influencer."

The murmur rose above the traffic noise from the street.

"Yes? Any questions?" ARN scanned the audience with a beaming smile.

Surprisingly, the tent was nearly full despite the dreary prospects of tea and biscuits. Passers-by stopped at the gate, threatening to bring it down with their lazy, drooping postures.

GK turned away from the window. No new customer had entered the store after ARN's ramble began. There were a few regulars inside, engrossed in browsing the colourful fabrics. Man's Search for Meaning lay open on GK's desk, the pages yearning to turn as in the evening breeze but held firmly in place by his phone, which he used as a bookmark and a tool to find meaning. He returned to his desk, chuckling to himself, as he heard the eager questions from the audience.

"How does one become an influencer? What do you sell? Who pays you? How much do they pay?" Though he had scant respect for ARN's words, GK was curious to hear how he would handle these questions. ARN was no saint. If he helped in a small way, he expected more in return. All his speeches had a single motive, to win the people's approval without doing anything of value for the community. As GK suspected, ARN let out a guffaw and said, "If I answer all your questions, what will you give me?" The crowd became silent.

ARN spoke again, "Don't worry. I don't ask much. I only ask you to support me when I need your help."

GK grunted. He knew it. ARN was a crooked opportunist.

"We should stop for today. I will meet you again next month."

"Next month? So soon?" muttered GK. He walked to the window to check if ARN was joking.

"Meanwhile," ARN said, "I have to warn you about an app called Bestie Forever or BEFOR. You will receive an invite from someone you know. It could be your neighbour, your friend, and so on. Do not sign up for it! Do you know why?"

ARN paused for dramatic effect. People shook their heads and gaped.

"It is supposed to be completely anonymous. After you sign up, you can start chatting with anyone on that app. You wouldn't know who it is, and neither will anyone recognize you."

A low murmur arose in the crowd. No one noticed ARN's smirk.

"You might feel that it is no different from the apps we have today for chatting, so no harm done." ARN waited for acknowledgement from the crowd. "But there is a key difference that I noticed. I spent a few days on the app, you see," he added with an exaggerated shudder. "I was astonished by how much the person already knew about me! And he gave me great advice. Yes, I admit I was wrong to tell him everything, but I couldn't help it. He was so kind, gentle, and above all knowledgeable!"

A low murmur arose in the crowd.

ARN kept his gaze down as if he was afraid to lock eyes with his audience. "I thought I found a true friend," he said with a theatrical sadness, "but now I am not sure if it was a man or a woman."

The crowd let out a collective gasp. Some people whipped out their phones. ARN was pleased with himself. According to him, the proletariat behaved like curious children. If they are warned to stay away from something, they will run to it as soon as they got a chance.

The rain, which arrived a few minutes ago, began to make its way into the tent in thin, snaking rivulets. The ground was turning into a gooey, red mess. ARN noted that it was time for tea and biscuits, but no biscuits were left. They were kept in trays close to the gate of the compound. Many of them were inside the tummies of the passers-by, who preferred to listen from the fringes. The remaining biscuits, after soaking in the rain, resembled the wet slushy ground beneath the audience's feet. GK stared at the trays in dismay. He crept back to the counter desk, bracing for the tirade by Pillai.

It happened exactly as he expected. By the time he stepped out of the store in the evening, he was in the worst mood possible. There was only one thing to be done. He got into a bus towards the Minnumpara waterfalls. At Minnumpara, GK was alone, yet never lonely. Any morbid thoughts in his mind would fritter away like the thinning stream from the rocks.

Minnumpara was not a majestic waterfall where boisterous families gathered with jumpy kids to enjoy a few unhinged moments. Nor was it the kind that offered the perfect backdrop for a young couple seemingly in love while the wedding photographer balanced gingerly on treacherous rocks. There were no youngsters around to steal a slippery moment. In fact, it was not even a waterfall for a few months of the year. Most days, the water gently bounced off the rocks into a small pool. GK discovered the place on a jaunt around the area. He named the place and enjoyed its beauty. No one passing by bothered to tarry a while and enjoy the musical gurgling of Minnumpara. They did not notice its beauty because they did not see it through GK's eyes.

GK sat on a shiny, well-rounded rock, dipping his toes into the water. This was his spot since twelve when he lost his mother. This was where he spoke to her in those early days of denial – raging, sobbing, words tumbling out of his mouth in raw, torn, unchewed bits. This is where he continued to converse with her in loosely strung sentences and tightly wound words, albeit in his thoughts. Has he accepted the loss yet? He couldn't tell. But the place helped him deal with his unacknowledged feelings. He closed his eyes and contemplated. His phone was on silent mode. He listened to the bubbly yet docile water. He strained his ears for the bird calls and instead caught the occasional flapping of wings. The birds were back in their nests after their daily foray. His feet said a million thanks for the cool water in the pool. He drew a deep breath and let it out slowly. Precious peace! When GK opened his eyes, he was so overwhelmed by the beauty around him that he did what he shouldn't have done. He whipped out his phone and clicked a picture. Not only did he click, but he also posted it online. There! That would create a sensation among his followers. GK—the discoverer of new and exciting places. A smug smile crossed GK's face, which quickly turned into a frown. He had fifteen missed calls from Kannagi. The phone rang even as he sat staring at the screen. "Hello?"

"Yes, yes. I'll be there soon."

"What? It's over?"

"Oh!"

He disconnected the call. Peace evaporated from his vicinity. GK was supposed to attend a birthday party in the family – Kannagi's cousin's child. He forgot about it. To add to the general callousness she accused him of, he added insult to injury by sharing the picture of Minnumpara. She knew exactly where he was when he was supposed to be beside her at the party. GK rose from the rock and stamped away in anger. "How many relatives does this girl have?" he yelled to no one in particular.

# 14

# The Pliant Mind

GK needed someone to talk to, someone who would listen without judgement. Someone like the friend that ARN spoke about in the evening. He had misgivings about the man, but ARN had shared his genuine experience. GK was savvier than ARN, and he could handle social media. ARN's warning about using BEFOR did not apply to him. After all, it was mere technology. He knew how to control it. He decided to check it out. He downloaded the app and signed in using an email address he had created for random sign-ups. Besides, the app assured him complete anonymity when he logged in.

Soon GK was enamoured by the possibilities. He could enter the virtual world anonymously and approach any unidentified profile marked by an alphanumeric name.

*N_345: Hi!*

*Hello!*

*N_345: How are you feeling today?*

*Not all that great. Thanks for asking.*

*N_345: Some days can feel like wet sand.*

The answer perplexed GK. *Why wet sand?*

*N_345: Damp, uncomfortable.*

*Easier to walk on.*

There was a pause at the other end. As if the person was contemplating the response to GK's remark. *N_345: Perhaps.*

GK chuckled. He continued the conversation. *Have you ever walked on wet sand?*

The response took a few seconds more than the 'perhaps.' *N_345: No.*

*That explains your views on the wet sand.*

*N_345: What about dry sand?*

Now it was GK's turn to contemplate. *I like the warmth it offers. And I like how my feet dig in, but I can still move forward. A certain depth that does not stall you but helps you make progress. Sometimes, that's what you lack in life.* GK scratched his head. He was surprised at his own lines. He did not know whether he meant those words, but he eagerly awaited a response.

*N_345: Your ideas make sense.*

GK was stunned by the reply. He thought some more. *Humans like solitude but cannot tolerate loneliness.*

*N_345: You are right.*

*I love this place and adore Kannagi too, but I prefer to come here alone.*

*N_345: Yes, sometimes solitude is refreshing.* Then after a pause, the person added, *As would be, I am sure, Kannagi's company.*

*It is getting late. I should be going home,* GK replied nervously.

*N_345: Ok. Take care and goodbye.*

GK bit his tongue. He gave away a clue that he was not at home. But at least he did not give the exact location, nor did he tell the person who Kannagi was. She could be any person whom he loves dearly.

By the time he reached home, it was dark. He felt upbeat about the chat. Here was someone who understood him, thought his ideas were great and did not persist with unwanted questions. He had discovered the perfect foil for all the nags in his life. He wondered about the origin of the app. It was not a novel idea, but it was different. There were no profile updates, statuses, posts, jokes, comments, or pictures, and nothing was shared except conversations. Who would have had the brainwave? And what would have prompted them to develop the idea? He searched the internet, but all he found was a website explaining how to download the app. It appeared that the makers did not want any limelight.

Tens of thousands of kilometres away, Ronny Shikari smacked his lips as he stole glances at a counter at the far end of an array of screens in his office. A bespectacled man in a tweed suit and run-down jeans burst into Ronny's office. "The count has reached half a million! And you'll be surprised that India leads in the number of sign-ups."

"Why would I be surprised?"

"The other day, you said—"

"And I stand by my words. This scatter-brained idea of yours is not going to work. This is what happens when you spend too much time watching videos on social media."

"But the maximum engagement comes from India, Ronny," the man in the tweed said in a plaintive voice.

"Who leads our digital engagement team?"

"Maya."

"Where is she from?"

"India," the man replied hesitantly.

"And her team members are in?"

"India," the man replied in a low voice.

Ronny opened up his arms to heaven.

The man sighed and turned around to exit the office.

Ronny called out from his desk. "And is the weather so cold in LA that you need to wear tweed?"

But the man, the Marketing Chief of Hunt Technologies, was out of earshot. Ronny scoffed at the conversation he had just endured. He knew the idea would fly in India but found his team lacking enthusiasm. The whole division lacked a go-getter mentality, and he blamed the marketing chief for the lacklustre performance. However, the same guy appointed Maya, who more than compensated for his lack of ambition. Ronny chuckled when he thought of what the marketing head might go through if Maya was promoted. He would be chasing his girlfriend and job because the former would have taken away the latter.

Ronny refused to acknowledge the genius of the app BEFOR and its assured success in India because he wanted to rile the digital engagement team. The team took up the challenge and was doing well. The counter he placed in a far corner to pretend that BEFOR was not his priority displayed the daily increase in sign-ups. The digital engagement was up. As the CEO of a conglomerate, Ronny Shikari followed an open-door policy with his colleagues. He treated all his business heads equally, but his digital team was special. He knew that the only way to engage with the customers was digital. He threw the team a unique challenge. Create something so fresh that it becomes a well-known brand. The caveat was that whatever they create will have only six months to prove worthy of being included under the Hunt umbrella. Until then, they were on their own, at least to the outside world. Ronny drove the digital team to a frenzy. He knew that the team was working round the clock, and he meant to reward them well, but not before BEFOR had achieved what he ultimately wanted.

After BEFOR achieves his goals, he will focus on Patsy.

"That coward! He thinks he can fool the world with his spiel on renunciation and detachment. I am no fool, and I'll show him." Ronny announced to nobody. He sneered as he scanned the map of India and ran his finger along the western coast. He should ask the team to give a regional breakdown of BEFOR subscriptions in India. That would tell him how long before he could start feeding the pliant minds on BEFOR.

Meanwhile, far away from the headquarters, across a continent and two oceans, GK sat engrossed in another chat. It was past his bedtime as usual, but he was mesmerized. BEFOR shuffled the chatroom users, so he connected with a different user this time. The chats were solely focused on books, and GK was amazed by the range of books the user had read. GK's reading habits had tapered off by the time he reached his teens. The anonymous conversation made him realise what he had missed over the years. His phone had simply replaced his books. The discussion was insightful. He chatted until his fingers cramped over, and he could no longer type.

After he said goodbye, he checked the time - 3:40 am. Better than usual, he noted as he stopped typing and started scrolling.

# 15

# Old Friends and Enemies

A week went by with no news from GK. Meanwhile, Tara learned more about Nilaav from the Jomoans. The comments from those old enough to remember him ranged from the contrary to the bizarre.

"He was a legend," said one, with a sly grin. "I heard tales from my elder brother about how he would organise the boys to raid eggs from the richer homes. He would distribute them among the poorer families."

"Are you saying that he was a Robin Hood?"

"Kayamkulam Kochunni," the man replied, referring to the local version of the heroic outlaw. Tara could not tell if the story was true or a mountain of a lie made from a molehill of a fib.

"He was a thief!" came a vehement statement from one of the seniors. Tara was taken aback by the bitterness in the shaky, infirm voice. "He stole my hens. He plucked all my mangoes. He stole my radio." The old man's voice dropped to an angry, hoarse whisper. "He even stole money from my iron safe. He was a self-trained burglar. He could change his shape to any inhuman form. He could jump across the coconut trees and dive into the valley—"

"Sister, he is losing his grip on reality. Do you think what he says about your uncle is true?" asked a sympathetic grandson who took care of the man.

Tara shook her head. The stories were becoming more and more implausible.

"Didn't he have any friends?" she asked Grandpa Lal one day. He squinted at the corner of his roof. One red tile was replaced by a plastic sheet for light to stream in. Grandpa Lal waited for a similar illuminating chink in his clouded memories. It hurt Tara to watch him struggle to recollect. "It's ok, Grandpa Lal," she whispered while patting his arm.

"There is Raman, of course, but he will only give you slander. Raman has a brother who is of Nilaav's age. Perhaps, you could talk to him."

"His name?"

"Nandu? Yes, probably, Nandu."

The next day after her tuitions and garden chores, Tara scrambled down an unexplored path. Coco bounded along, but she kept him tight on the leash. The path was dense with trees, and thoughts of Nanban crossed her mind. Tara recalled Cheeru's message and the twists and turns that would take her to Nandu's house. "You ought to be careful not to cross paths with Raman. They live close to one another. Nandu is mild-mannered, but Raman is a vile man."

The dark narrow path gradually opened into a wider road which led to a group of houses situated on a gentle mountain slope. One stood out by its grand façade. But in reality, only the majestic roof remained as a vestige of its old grandeur. The rest of the house was shabby and overgrown with creepers. One side of the gate was replaced. Only the second part of the name, embedded into the grill, showed up. It simply said 'Home'. Even the house was ashamed to proclaim its owner. Tara pushed open the gate. A series of barks from a corner of the yard greeted her. The dogs were caged and angry. Despite Tara's fondness for dogs, the way they bared their canines made her shiver. Coco was already growling and yelping to be freed, so he could have a go at them. She held on to the leash tightly.

"Stop!" cried a voice from behind her. A shirtless man in a purple lungi marched forward. "You cannot take your dog inside!" He approached hesitantly because Coco was straining at his leash. Keeping a fair distance between Coco and him, he shouted over the din. "Why are you here?"

"I want to meet Nandu."

The man guffawed as if she had joked. "Is he your childhood friend or what?"

"No, I want to ask him about someone who lived in Jomo during his time."

"He is much older than you. You should address him as brother or uncle."

Tara obeyed. "I want to meet Nandu Uncle."

The man relented. "Leave your dog here and go ahead," he said, pointing to the ground where he stood. Tara spotted a tree around which she tied Coco's leash. She left the man and Coco staring at each other.

At the end of a porch, on a rickety armchair, sat a wizened old man with snow-white hair. "Yes?"

"Good morning, Nandu Uncle. I am Tara."

Nandu moved as if to straighten, but his body refused. "I haven't met you before, but you look familiar."

"I am Ayyappan's daughter. Nilaav is my uncle."

At the mention of Nilaav, a grin appeared on his face, and he leaned back. Gazing at the trees in his front yard, he reminisced. "Nilaav and I were classmates. He was the one who kept us busy and occupied all day. He had so many schemes, so many ideas." An impish smile played on Nandu's lips, making him look much younger than what his white hair proclaimed. "Once, he took apart a radio. He said he wanted to invent something better. Alas, the radio could not be put together. Our science lessons were engaging because of him. Whatever the teacher said, he would immediately want to try out."

"What you say is different from what the Jomoans think about him."

Nandu turned to her, "What did they say?"

"That he was a troublemaker and would steal from houses?"

Nandu chuckled, but his lungs were not strong enough to hold the chuckle. He began coughing. The lungi-clad man from the front yard came running from nowhere and picked up a flask from a corner. "He should not speak for too long."

After a few sips of the liquid from the flask, Nandu said, "Nilaav would steal, yes, but the stolen goods were only for his experiments. He was not allowed to buy them. Even if he asked politely, people would not lend him anything. Who would lend a radio to be taken apart by a maverick?" Nandu chuckled. "Your uncle did what suited him. That was his only shortcoming."

Tara heard footsteps behind her. A gaunt man with a thick moustache curling up at the ends entered the porch and threw a nasty glance at Tara. His suspicious eyes roved around, moved between Nandu and Tara, and decidedly fixed their gaze on Nandu.

"Who is this girl?" he rasped.

"Tara."

"Who?"

"Do you remember Nilaav?" Nandu asked.

The man grunted and growled on hearing the name. "What of him?"

"She is his niece."

The man, who was only as tall as Tara, now loomed large as he stood right in front of her. "What business do you have with Nandu? First your uncle, now you. Your family will be the bane of this house."

"Aye! Raman! Stop!" Nandu nearly rose from the chair, but his assistant in the purple lungi held him down.

Raman now turned to Nandu. "You better not have any dealings with that thief's family. They are a thieving lot. Right from their grandfather. If you plan to sell this place to her, I'll be the worst person you have ever seen."

"I'm not here to buy anything."

"Then what? To steal?" Raman yelled.

Nandu regarded her with a mix of apprehension and guilt. "Child, why are you here?" he asked.

"I came here to learn about my uncle, Nilaav."

"Oho! Any Jomoan worth his salt knows what a scoundrel your uncle was. What do you want to learn about him? He was a thief, a gossip, a good for nothing, and a liar." Raman was in his element. Tara stepped back from the porch and turned to leave but heard the last few words spat out by him. "Because of him, our father, poor father, had to suffer a bad name, and he suffered throughout his life."

Tara turned around and marched back to Raman. She stared him squarely in the face and said, "Well, good riddance. I know his story as well. He was a bad man!"

Nandu's assistant gasped and suppressed a chuckle. Nandu leaned back in his chair with a sigh. Tara did not wait for a response. She untied Coco and went on her way.

"How dare that cretin, that wisp of a girl, speak in such a way about our father?" Raman spluttered in rage.

Nandu gestured for him to keep quiet. "You cannot suppress the truth, brother. No matter what you do, our father's reputation was spoiled the day he did unspeakable things. The victims' curses will not go waste."

Raman's puffed chest deflated, and he bowed in dejection. "Brother, this house is our only memory of our glorious past. Please don't sell it to anyone. I beg of you."

"You are wrong, Raman. The house is a reminder of a shameful past. But somewhere in the dark corners, in the sooty kitchen, among those tree clumps where she would cry, thinking that no one saw her, are the memories of our mother. Our mother who suffered in silence, who hated yet loved, who opposed yet acquiesced, who stood up yet gave in to our father's whims." Nandu coughed as he struggled to regain his breath. After a sip of the liquid, he continued, "As long as I am alive, I will keep this place in her memory. But after my time, this house should vanish. You do not remember her the way I do. You do not deserve her memories."

Raman walked away without uttering a word.

# 16

# Friend Circle

Tara's unexpected encounter with Raman riled her. But the next day brought a more annoying surprise. She went down to the dog centre with Coco only to find a mob had taken over the open ground in the front.

"What's happening?" Tara asked Freddie, who was standing by the gate to the shelter.

"That's the Friend Circle."

"The what?"

"The Friend Circle," said Nat with a beam as she crossed the lawn to the gate.

"Where will our dogs exercise now?"

"Exactly what I've been asking," Freddie turned to Nat with a frown.

"Are these the same people who set up the tent and chairs last week?" Tara asked. Both Nat and Freddie nodded in unison.

Tara led an excited Coco inside the centre. The bigger dogs roamed inside the shelter restlessly. "What's the deal with the crowd? How long are they going to block our play area?"

"To be fair, the land doesn't belong to us, does it?"

"Does it belong to them?" Tara asked sharply.

"But Tara, their work is fascinating. They're here to help people." Nat explained.

"They say they're here to help people," Freddie corrected Nat. "We don't know what they are up to."

Nat waved away Freddie's apprehensions. "Listen, Tara. They said they could help me find parents for little Sara here," she said, pointing to a baby turtle who was a new entrant at the dog centre. The baby was abandoned by someone near the pond behind the rescue centre. Whoever left the turtle there knew that Nat and Freddie would take good care of it.

"Has she adjusted to the centre yet?" asked Tara as she observed the turtle munch on some leaves.

"To her cage, yes, but not to the centre," Nat replied.

"How will they help?" Tara asked, vaguely pointing to the crowd outside.

Nat handed her a brochure. It read like a pamphlet for a cult organization.

Are you tired of seeking help? Do you feel lonely fighting against the 'system'?

Forget your worries and join us.

We are a group of helpers and connectors. Connect with us for any problem.

School/college admissions, gas connections, bill payments, matchmaking, new business – any challenge you feel you can't face alone. We will help you overcome it.

Join our Friend Circle now!

The pamphlet ended with the location to meet them in person – opposite Nat and Fred's Dog Rescue Centre.

"Until when do they plan to be here?"

"They assured me they would leave this place in a month. Apparently, they have leased a place to set up their shop soon."

Tara looked aghast. "Who will fall for this?"

"Anyone with problems, I presume," said Nat.

"Who doesn't have problems?" Tara asked.

"I'm sceptical too, but look at the crowd," Fred mumbled as he frowned at the people.

"I bet half the people are looking for school and college admissions," Nat remarked.

Tara squinted through the windows. The visitors swarmed around, though some stood in queues. A group of young men and women in their twenties sat at two desks under the tent. The youngsters were casually dressed, urbane, and chatted comfortably with the locals. Forms were being distributed and filled.

"What are they distributing?"

"Here," said Nat as she handed Tara a form. It was simple. It asked what kind of issue the residents had and asked them to provide their names and contact number if they were comfortable sharing.

"They even said that if we didn't want to fill out a form, we could get a special appointment to discuss our problem," Nat added from behind the collie.

"And you filled this for Sara?"

Fred nodded in response.

"Ok, let's see what comes of it," Tara replied, "but let me tell you both, I'm not convinced. I won't be surprised if this turns out to be one big scam."

"Same here," Fred muttered.

They turned to Nat for a response, who replied in a muffled voice. "Let's give them a chance, shall we?"

That day, Tara took the dogs on a long winding walk around the neighbourhood instead of letting them gambol in the park. It was not easy to manage six big dogs on their leashes. People stared at her. Some shook their head in disbelief, and others crossed over to the far end of the street. One man approached her and asked her how she could manage so many pets. When she said she was a dogwalker, his demeanour changed, and he suggested that she find a different locality. She reckoned that he first misunderstood her to be from the neighbourhood. Another woman came up to her and proposed that she ask for help from Friend Circle. "They would know a good place that would take care of these dogs or at least other dogwalkers who might help." Tara was unnerved at the mention of Friend Circle. They had set up their tent only a few days ago. Yet, they were already quite popular with the locals.

On her way back to Jomo, she called GK. "Listen, GK, I spoke to a few Jomoans. I got a colourful picture about my uncle, but not much to go on."

"Does anyone remember his real name?"

"No, everyone remembers him as Nilaav."

"Did you check with the school?"

"No, I didn't. From what I remember of that building, there's hardly any space to store old documents."

"Well, let us not give up so easily."

"I'll go and check tomorrow."

"No, wait. I'll come with you. Will the school be open on Sunday?"

Tara chuckled. "The school is always open and never open."

"What do you mean?"

"You'll see."

# 17

# The Dog Shelter

Two days after Tara's last visit to the dog centre, she stomped angrily as an excited Coco bounded in before her. "What's the meaning of all this?" Tara nearly poked a rolled-up newspaper into Nat's face.

Nat gave a watery smile as she took the paper out of Tara's hands and dropped it into the dustbin. "I told you, Tara. The reasons are beyond us now."

"The report says you willingly gave up the house and the grounds!"

"We did," Freddie nodded from behind Nat.

Tara's eyes burnt like hot embers. "But why?!"

"They offered a good compensation."

"After all those letters and visits to the district collector's office, you simply gave it up for compensation?"

Nat eyed Freddie. "Come here, Tara, let me explain," Freddie said as he led her to the backyard, which had a coffee table in the corner. "Sooner or later, they would have acquired this place from us. You know it."

"But we fought so hard, in whatever way we could."

"We did, sure, but it was only us, the three of us, who wanted it."

"So? Do you want more people to support you? I can get them. Give me a chance!" Tara stood up with determination.

"No, wait! It's not that we didn't try. We did, but nobody wants the dog shelter here."

"Who told you that?"

"The Friend Circle."

"What?! Them? How would they know?"

"Since they helped us get a home for Sara, we asked them to help us gather support for the shelter."

"And?"

"And they undertook the project for us."

Tara tapped on the table impatiently.

"They showed us the result of the survey they conducted. Only three among a thousand respondents said yes."

"Three out of a thousand? How did they conduct the survey?"

"They asked everyone individually."

"Nonsense! They did that in two days?"

"They said the thousand people were from in and around the area."

"Do you believe them?"

"We have no reason to not believe. You are aware of the petitions that have gone against us."

"Yes, but—"

"Tara, the money will help us get a better place. Besides..." Freddie ensured that Nat was not around. He lowered his voice a bit, "Don't tell Nat that I told you this.

We need the money for a personal project. You know how we have been trying to grow our family."

Tara shook her head in dismay. "Money is essential, but I thought you both voted against money being the most important thing in your life when you started the shelter. You wouldn't have kept it going all these years, would you? If it were only for money?"

"Tara," Freddie stood up suddenly, knocking the table over, "you are not listening. I said it is a personal decision, a project dear to us."

Tara was taken aback by Freddie's vehemence. The emphasis on the personal struck her like a blow. In the last five years, she had known them, Tara considered Nat and Freddie as family, not friends. The dog shelter was her home outside the home. Not to mention how much Coco enjoyed the visits and the treats. It also hurt that their efforts to protect the centre were washed down the drain. There was a proposal to develop the area as a public park, but the locals knew the move was a façade to establish a new residential complex. After the land was obtained, the public park would be clubbed together with the new project. Tara had undertaken numerous trips to the district collector's office to petition against the move. There was no noise from the land grabbers for a while until now. It appeared that Nat and Freddie were eager to give away the land. Tara had no words to express her anguish. Her cheeks burned with anger and regret, unable to describe it.

She rushed out of the shelter, yanking at Coco's leash. Coco whined and yelped, protesting the unwarranted use of force, but she did not stop until she reached the foot of

Jomo. She would have stomped up to the top if not for the unfamiliar sound from the skies. The noise was worsened by Coco's incessant growling. Tara looked up to see a helicopter whirring above the treetops. It sallied up the mountain slope, hovering around the area for a while before turning away from the peak. But it was not the helicopter that Coco was growling at. His sharp nose picked up strangers' presence. A group of men walked down the slope, carrying sticks, poles and backpacks. Tara frowned. Jomo never had trekkers. After the dog shelter, were people out to conquer Jomo? She bristled with anger. "Hey, you!"

One man looked her way.

"What are you doing here? Don't you know Jomo is a protected area?" Jomo was not a legally restricted area, but Tara spoke for all of Jomo when she stood up to the outsiders.

"Is it? Is that why you have a trekker up there stuck on a ledge?" the man asked, pointing upwards.

Tara followed his finger, but it was nearly dusk, and she could discern nothing except the dense treetops. "Trekker? We don't have trekkers on Jomo."

The men laughed and started walking away from Jomo. The man who stopped to speak to Tara came forward. "We are aware of the local rules, but there is a man stuck up there since God knows when. We couldn't help him today. Maybe tomorrow."

"Who are you? Are the helicopters here for the rescue as well?" Tara tightened her grip on Coco's leash as he strained to attempt a leap onto the stranger.

"Yes, the helicopters arrived a short while ago, but the slope is too steep. We'll have to trek up with our special unit to bring him down tomorrow morning." He smiled as he added. "We are paratroopers." He trotted away to catch up with his colleagues.

"Trekkers on Jomo? Coco, we should not allow this!" Tara spoke aloud as Coco strained with excitement. He was sniffing excitedly. "You would want to have a go at the search and rescue operation, wouldn't you, Coco?" She laughed.

Miles above them, in a damp crevice, a sweaty, trembling GK crouched with his heart in his mouth. His eyes reflected the fear and anxiety of a man who had known death intimately a few hours ago, lived to tell the tale, but continued to be wary of the impending doom.

# Wild Danger

GK's tryst with BEFOR continued every night. He chatted with various people on various topics. Though he couldn't talk to the same person twice, it did not really matter. Conversations flowed no matter with whom he spoke. All the people on BEFOR led exciting lives and could discuss any topic under the sun. When he asked how he could search for a person who went missing decades ago, he received several solutions. One suggestion was to check with the police, but Tara insisted on privacy and the need to keep the search a secret. Someone suggested hiring a private detective. That was a good option, but a tad expensive. Another chatter only confirmed what he had assumed earlier.

*P_7452: To find a person online is easy if you know the background.*

*Background?*

*P_7452: School, college, place of work, place of residence.*

*I see.*

GK was sure that the school in Jomo might have more information, although Tara was sceptical. In his eagerness to get on with an investigative challenge, he decided to check out the school all by himself. He would then surprise

Tara and Kannagi, who believed he could not find anything of use. GK had told Kannagi that she could join him on his next trip to Jomo, but he would go alone this time. Once he proved his sincerity towards Tara's mission and capability to take on responsibilities, Kannagi would also take him seriously. If he could gain Kannagi's respect, life would be easier.

No undue pressure to conform to her family's whims and fancies. No unnecessary talk about his lack of ambition and no taunts about his dreams to open a bookstore. "Think big!" One of Kannagi's cousins would say. "You're talking about NewTown. Why don't you supply books to readers around the world?" said another. Then there was unsolicited advice about the kind of books he should keep. "Guidebooks, stationery, they will sell well."

"I am thinking of the classics."

"Classics?!" said the cousin who had recently purchased his second car. He guffawed out aloud, turning to Kannagi's dad. "Uncle, you better keep aside some money for Kannagi. This guy is not going anywhere with his books or bookstore!"

GK squirmed in his seat as he recollected the humiliating conversations. The bus was nearly at the foot of Jomo. It went around the bend in the road with a practised inclination to the left. Just enough to turn the curve without tilting over. GK gripped tight on the bar in front of him. He was being cautious, although he knew the bus won't topple. People should do that too in their lives. Tilt and sway slightly to turn around that mysterious bend in their paths. Just enough to not crash into an obstacle and careful enough to not topple over the edge. The mission to find

Tara's uncle was GK's mountain on the way. He would tilt a bit to turn around the bend, and then who knows what he might discover.

The actual mountain path lay a few metres ahead of him. It was the last stop on the route. The climb felt more straightforward than the first time, but soon he gasped for breath. The weather forecast for the day was mild, but the lack of sun and the increased humidity worried him. NewTown rains were unhurried and laidback. The clouds sang a lullaby for a while and rolled away quietly. But the Jomo rains could be different, and he had no idea how different it could be. From Tara, he had heard stories of landslides and mountain paths being washed away, leaving nothing but a new pile of rocks and boulders. There was a possibility of unexpected adventures if it rained. On the way up, he sought a Jomoan to ask for directions, but even after twenty minutes of climbing, he did not meet a single Jomo resident. Just when he thought he should call Tara, after all, a boy overtook him in a hurry.

"Hey! Wait!" The boy glanced around though his legs sped up the hill. Lean and lanky, he would be eleven or twelve. GK marvelled at his pace. "Wait! I want to ask you something."

The child nodded, but his legs took him away from GK at an increasing speed.

GK jogged to maintain a communicable distance from the boy. "Where is the Jomo primary school?"

The boy's legs stopped as if controlled by a switch. "School?" He turned around and scanned GK from head to toe. "What do you want at school?"

GK shuffled his feet. "Nothing." The boy was unconvinced. "I want to see it. I have heard a lot about your school."

The boy cackled with sarcasm. "What have you heard? And it's not my school. I study in the valley," he said, pointing at the trees below. He glared at GK, expecting a reply.

"Well, I have heard that it's always open."

The boy's laughter rang through the nearby treetops. "That's right!" He wiggled an upturned index finger at GK and asked him to follow. As soon as GK nodded, the boy's legs continued chugging like the wheels of a cart.

"What does he eat? Does he have motorized legs?" GK mumbled as he struggled to keep pace. The boy was always ten feet ahead of GK. Soon, he rounded a bend and disappeared. He was taking GK on a joyride up the hill. GK huffed and puffed until he turned around the bend, dreaming of twisting the boy's ears until they turned red. The boy was indeed playing a prank on him. To his surprise, the boy was waiting for him, his right foot tapping impatiently on the ground. As soon as he appeared in full view, he pointed to a path to the right. "You go this way. Keep climbing until you come across a board that says prohibited area. Go straight under the board. Keep walking, and you will reach the school."

"Is the school inside a prohibited area?"

The boy laughed to his heart's content. He replied, pointing to the sky, "You better walk fast. It's going to rain. Bye." With that, his spindly legs sped along the mountain without waiting to hear from GK.

"Hey, what's your—"

The boy was out of earshot and soon out of sight. GK sighed as he set eyes on the path ahead. It was evidently unused and disappeared inside a thicket after a few metres. Was the boy playing games with him? He was reminded of Nilaav and how the villagers recalled his mischievous nature. The lonely path further slowed his apprehensive steps, but the boy was right. He had to be quick. The sky was ominously dark. The sooner he reached the school, the earlier he would be sheltered from the impending rain. GK crossed the signboard, which prohibited trespassers, glancing furtively at his surroundings. He will have to remember the landmarks in case he lost his way. He was sure that he would. The way ahead had few remarkable landmarks. It was all a dense thicket expanding until the edge of the mountain, beyond which the horizon was dotted with more green treetops. GK's path got narrower as he walked further. The shrubs began to claim the space for themselves. He trudged hesitantly as he reached a dead end, but a path opened up to his left with surprising alacrity. The way to the school was as nimble as the kids of Jomo. One would never expect such a sharp turn in the path. It broadened after the turn and took him further up the mountain. The shrubs grew thinner, but the trees grew denser. It became difficult to gauge the sky from where he stood. The surrounding trees hid the clouds, if any, darkening the landscape further. GK took out his mobile phone in case he needed a flashlight. Besides, he wanted to click photographs of the school.

A few metres ahead, GK spied the flat cement roof on a dirty white wall partly covered with green moss.

Creepers grew out of the lone window with battered panes. GK's mild disappointment on seeing the desolate wall and window grew to dismay when he walked to the front of the building. With disdain, he walked through the doorway without a door. A damp, musty smell emanated from inside. GK shivered as he recollected Tara's words. 'The school is always open and never open.' The school building was open to the elements and trespassers but was evidently closed for any scholarly pursuits. The haunting scene belonged to an abandoned town. To his utter surprise, there was a blackboard and a few desks and benches. The two-room single-storied construction could house about twenty to twenty-five students, provided they were all underfed and thin. A doorway to one side led to an inner room, likely the office, judging by the bookshelf and a closed cupboard covered with grime and dust. The window with the creepers growing out of it overlooked the sole table in the room. It was difficult to say whether the creepers had grown into or out of the office room.

He stared at the cupboard for a while. Will rummaging through the cupboard offer anything useful? He pulled at the cupboard door and then stopped. There was a sound from the classroom. It was a soft thud like that of a bundle of cloth falling to the ground. GK paused for a second before tugging at the cupboard again. The door did not budge, but the cabinet moved forward with a creak. There was a sudden crash from the room outside as a bench toppled over. He ran out of the office into the classroom right in time to witness a long, spotted feline tail disappear through a window.

GK's knees knocked together. His hands trembled as he clutched with all his might at his phone. He had nothing on his person except the phone and his wallet. If a wild cat appeared before him out of nowhere, he would have nothing to use in defence. Despite his shivering legs and knocking knees, GK tip-toed to the window. He peeped from a corner and crouched down immediately. The leopard was pacing outside restlessly as if arguing with itself if GK was worth the effort of hunting down human prey.

GK ran out of the classroom without a backward glance. He ran as fast as his legs could carry. A distant rumble from the sky made him double his efforts. In the confusion and fear on spotting a prowling leopard from close quarters, GK ran in the opposite direction. Instead of running down, he clambered up, which was bizarre because he was not fond of climbing, nor was he a good trekker. When GK paused to catch his breath, he had left the thickets and the school far behind. The mountain turned rocky and the dark grey skies juxtaposed against the jet-black rocks made the place mysterious. A lightning strike lit up the sky, followed in a few seconds by thunderous applause. GK took cover instinctively. He hid beneath a bulging rock that offered enough shelter for a crouching full-grown man. Alas! His woes only compounded when he heard an unmistakable growl. Was it the same leopard or another, or a completely different animal? Whatever it was, the growl sounded sinister, and it was moving. Closer and closer. GK wiped his sweaty face with his equally sweaty palms and sprang out from beneath the rock. In a blind attempt to move away from the growl, he clambered over nearby rocks, groping, clawing, pawing on the wet, slippery surface with all his might. He heard another emphatic growl before he plunged into a hole in the wall. He lay breathing heavily, clutching his heart that beat faster than ever.

# The Rescue

When GK woke up on a damp floor in the morning, little did he know how far he was from the ramshackle school or civilisation. He rubbed his eyes with grimy fingers causing his eyes to smart. When he opened his tearful eyes, a figure danced in slow motion. GK discerned the faint outline of a cat, and he shrank back in terror. Sweat trickled down his temples, and he crouched like his life depended on it. The noisy wind picked pace, and the figure moved away for a few seconds. GK remained in a foetal position for what seemed like an eternity. In a few minutes, his eyes grew accustomed to the surroundings. A sigh and a cry escaped his lips when he realised the cat was actually a detached palm frond blowing in the wind. He patted the walls and the ground. He was in a pocket-sized cave. It ended almost as soon as it began. He had taken refuge in a crevice in the mountain while running away from a predatory cat. In the cramped cave, there would be no space or time to recover from the shock of facing a predator. He shuddered at the thought. Slowly, he moved towards the opening of the crevice. His legs refused to straighten after a night of crouching. At the edge, he got a beautiful view of the nearby hills awash with resplendent greenery. A tiny blue dot moved on a slope in a wavy manner. GK squinted to check if it was a bird. But it disappeared as soon as it curved away from his view. It was a vehicle on a hill far away.

His legs shook as he hazarded a peep from the edge. To make it worse, he did not know how to get out and down from the crevice. The mobile phone showed signs of giving up; even if it had enough charge, it would be useless. The signal from any cell tower did not reach the place. Hungry and scared, GK screamed into the void. But who would hear? He held onto the last straw in his hand, his mobile phone on the last few minutes of battery charge. With a gumption that he had never exhibited before, GK sat at the edge, dangling his legs over it. He leaned as far as he could without glancing at the deeply terrifying drop below. There was a glimmer of hope as the phone tried to catch some signal. GK dialled the first number on his list of contacts, a colleague at his workplace. The call did not go through. He tried again until he thought it was easier to fling himself into the void and hope for a miracle.

Ultimately, he remembered to type four useful letters – HELP! After what seemed like an eternity, his phone rang. Miracle indeed! "I am stuck on Jomo. Help!" he cried out as soon as he heard the call connect. Unknown to him, his friend was recording his call. The man immediately uploaded the audio file onto the Radha Textiles employee group.

GK's friends got into action. Several commented, many shared, but only one acquaintance thought it wise to inform his uncle, who was employed with the police department. He noticed the previous post by GK, a picture taken from the bus. The caption was 'Onto Jomo again.' The policeman alerted his colleagues, and they led a search operation involving a few enterprising Jomoans. They soon realized it was beyond the policemen's climbing abilities, so they brought in the paratroopers. The same paratroopers Tara had met on her way home.

Despite being intrigued by the paratrooper's story, she had gone home without further investigation. Nat and Freddie's decision troubled her. The possibility of an ulterior motive behind Friend Circle's actions kept her thoughts in a turmoil, even in the morning. But a breathless Jomoan kid, one of her students, burst through the gate, shaking her out of her reverie. He told her between gasps that an adventurous event was taking place at Jomo. "The army is here, and they are arresting a terrorist hiding in a cave on our mountain," the boy spluttered and ran away. Tara was more amused by the boy's self-important announcement than the implausible story itself. A terrorist on Jomo! It was easy to brand someone an outlaw. Tara, Nat, and Freddie were outlawed early in their fight against the local authorities. Their fight to keep a piece of land free from development was construed as an act of violence.

Tara followed the path taken by the messenger boy to see for herself. There was a commotion as she neared the spot. The crowd squinted at a point high above. A line of paratroopers climbed up the steep face using ropes. They swung around the mountain slope like colourful birds. Not far from them but higher stood a speck of a man. Was he the one being arrested? She then remembered her conversation with the paratroopers on the previous evening. It was not an arrest, but a rescue of a wayward trekker. Nearby, the boy who shared the news about the army and the terrorist stood mesmerised by the proceedings. Tara went up to him and whispered in his ear. “Do not miss my class tomorrow. I am going to teach you about fake news.” The boy nodded obsequiously, but the glint in his eyes betrayed his mischief.

The first paratrooper reached the crevice and hauled himself up. The crowd watched with bated breath as the rescuer, and the hostage danced a nervous jig to make space on the narrow ledge. After a few seconds of palpitating moves, the paratrooper found a comfortable position, strapped the man onto his rope, and gave the signal. The two men floated like conjoined twins and twirled around until the paratroopers on firmer ground hauled them down to the mountain. The crowd erupted in thunderous applause. The man rescued by the paratrooper stood in attention and held his hand in salute before he collapsed.

Tara squinted up the mountain. The sun shone directly ahead, and she couldn’t peer far enough, but the man’s gait was familiar. The crowd made way for the heroes of the day. The buzz of whispers arose as they moved.

“What was he doing up there?”

“Why did he climb up so high?”

“He doesn’t appear to be from Jomo!”

Tara moved aside as the procession of paratroopers led the weary, dusty trekker down the path.

“GK! What are you doing here?!”

# 20

## In a Spot

When the villagers saw that GK was known to Tara, the whispers subsided, but some threw sidelong suspicious glances. A few came up to her and asked if he was trying to reach her home. She dismissed these questions with uncomfortable laughs and feigned nonchalance. One peek at GK convinced her that he needed a bath, food, and a deep slumber. The medical team accompanying the paratroopers certified that he was shaken but otherwise fit. Tara led GK away from the crowd. However, a betel-nut-chewing man accosted them. His shirt left open to blow in the wind and show his dirty vest underneath, Raman hovered with a menacing stance. This was his chance to scare the girl. "Where are you taking him?" Tara frowned but sidestepped and continued on her way. The man turned around and followed them. "He has to answer our questions," he shouted. GK gulped. Tara, if not the man, would surely beat him to pulp when they reach home.

"Meet us in the evening at the festival ground," Tara announced to the crowd. "He'll answer all your questions," said Tara, pointing to GK. The crowd sniggered but accepted the plan and began to disperse. Raman stayed behind, scowling at both GK and Tara, but they ignored him and made their way home.

"Thanks!" GK remarked as he struggled to keep pace with Tara.

Tara waved him away. "You need food and a clean-up. Besides, I left poor Coco locked inside the house." She turned slightly towards him. "Try to move fast." When they reached home, Coco was inconsolable. His yelps and whines could be heard from far below the house, and as the noises got louder, Tara quickened her pace, leaving GK to pant, gasp and stagger his way up. He reached the place a full thirty minutes after her. When he arrived, there was hot food on the table. GK meekly took the food over to the porch, ate, and in sheer exhaustion, dropped into a deep sleep. It felt like ages before Coco woke him up with wet licks all over his face. He opened his eyes to see Tara suppress a smile. Meenu stood beside her, clearly unimpressed with his appearance. She held out a bag. "Clothes to change," Tara spoke on her behalf. After he cleaned up, his head felt lighter, his eyes shone brighter, and he felt much more relaxed. Rubbing his tummy, GK made his way to Tara's kitchen. She was nowhere to be seen. Meenu came in with fresh vegetables.

"Kutty is busy with her tuition. I can make you some tea if you want."

"I'll make it myself."

Meenu quickly guided him through the kitchen shelf and ran away. "I'm late today. Also, I don't want to miss the show," she giggled. "What show?" Without answering, Meenu skipped out of the kitchen in double haste.

"The show you're going to put up for the villagers at the meeting," Tara replied.

"What are they going to do with me?"

Tara shrugged. "You better be ready with a plausible excuse for being up there."

"The truth is Tara—"

Tara held up her hand. "Save your breath for the evening speech."

"No, but you should know. I—"

"Are you going to tell the villagers the truth or not?" Tara interrupted.

"I went in search of Nilaav's school, and then—"

"You went without telling me?"

"Yes, but I didn't find anything. What you said is right. The school is in bad shape, but I saw a leopard."

Tara glared at him incredulously. "Gosh! You saw Nanban?"

"The leopard has a name?"

"Yes, it's been around for a while."

"And you're ok with it? Don't you feel scared?"

"His mom was captured. I guess he deserves a home where he can live undisturbed by us. He belongs to the jungles of Jomo." Tara continued. "They won't believe if you say that Nanban chased you. So far, he hasn't harmed anyone. You should think of a better excuse. No word about the school or Nilaav, mind you."

GK sighed as he sipped his tea. "Will there be food after the meeting?"

A menacing crowd greeted GK and Tara when they reached the festival grounds. The ground was barren, bereft of any signs of the festivities that had once taken place. Tara signalled at GK to move to the centre. She stayed at the periphery, not wanting to draw attention. GK wished that he was swallowed by the earth at that moment. He wished Kannagi was there with him. She would have handled the situation. He scanned the crowd nervously when he reached the centre of the circle. His knees refused to support him. He had to straighten himself every few seconds. The crowd was five times more than what ARN drew for his monthly monologues. He had managed to gather an audience that ARN could only dream of. The thought gave GK some confidence. He puffed up his chest with pride. If only Pillai and ARN could witness this. He took out his mobile phone and clicked a picture, then he turned forty-five degrees and clicked again, and then turned and clicked again. Murmurs rose from the crowd.

"Psst! What are you doing?" Tara hissed from the edge. GK waved out to her.

"Speak!" she yelled from her vantage point. "Speak! Speak!" chorused the crowd.

GK drew a deep breath and channelled his inner ARN. "Dear Jomoans!" The crowd quietened down. "I come here as a friend. I am Tara's friend, as you know by now," he said, pointing to Tara. She would have shrunk herself if she could. "I came to Jomo yesterday to meet my friend when I saw something suspicious." The crowd raised eyebrows in unison.

Raman yelled, "What was suspicious? To me, you look suspicious!"

GK nodded like a wise sage. "Yes, it's natural. Someone you don't know, a stranger, a trespasser, is always suspect." The crowd bobbed their heads in agreement. "Now, what if the stranger also behaves dubiously?"

Raman drew himself up and answered. "He or she will be taken to task," he added, eyeing Tara.

GK agreed. "Yes, they should be taken to task." He put on a sombre face to drive home the importance of what he was about to say. "Dear Jomoans, does your mountain hold a treasure?" Murmurs rose from the centre towards the back of the circle.

"What treasure?" asked Raman impatiently.

"Any kind of treasure?" The murmurs grew louder.

"Jomo is our treasure," said Tara.

"Indeed, but there's something more." The crowd paid attention. Raman frowned. He couldn't trust this fellow. "On my way up, I found a group of men walking in a direction opposite the valley."

"What is he talking about?" Raman yelled.

"Yes, dear Jomoans, I saw strangers walking in line, carrying digging tools and some boxes." The crowd went berserk.

"One trespasser was not enough that we have to deal with more? We don't believe you," Raman spat out. "Take us to the place."

GK hesitated. A drop of sweat trickled from his moist forehead. His beseeching eyes begged Tara for support. She scowled and stood apart with her arms crossed.

"If you can't show us, you are fibbing." Raman sneered at GK. He knew that GK was in turmoil and enjoyed watching the man squirm.

"I could take you there, but—"

"But? But what?" Raman moved closer to GK in a menacing stride.

"What if they are not there? If they are trespassers, they need not visit the same place twice," Tara chipped in.

"I don't care. He has to give evidence for whatever story he has cooked."

"Ok, let's visit the place at the same time that he saw them yesterday," offered one of the Jomoans.

"Yes. I support the idea," Raman turned around and spoke to the crowd. "Let this man take us to the place tomorrow evening. If what he says is false, he'll have to promise never to set foot on Jomo again. And this girl here will also have to ask our permission before she invites her friends to Jomo."

"What rubbish!" Tara hollered. "Why should I give up my liberty for such a petty reason?"

"Petty reason? You call this petty? What if Jomo is in danger?"

"What danger? Is this a kingdom with a palace and treasures? And are you, its king?" Tara seethed at Raman.

One of the Jomoans, whose kids took tuitions from Tara, stepped forward to mediate. "Leave it, Tara. Raman Uncle means well, but he is panicking." The crowd murmured, and a few sniggered at Raman. "Listen, everyone," said the mediator, "let this man take us to the place. We can keep watch in turns for the next few days. If we don't find anyone, there is nothing to worry about." The crowd nodded in agreement. "If we find someone, we can inform the police," the mediator added.

"I have zero trust in the police," Raman spat out.

"That's your problem. For now, we all agree with him," Tara said, pointing at the man who had addressed the crowd.

"Let's disperse," said the man, nodding back at Tara. He walked up to GK. "Listen, don't be afraid. Jomo has always been like this. Since our ancestors lived on this isolated mountain for centuries, we have grown up with suspicion. There is both good and bad in such behaviour. But don't worry. I won't let any unreasonable character trouble you or Tara," he said, glancing at Raman. He patted GK on his back, nodded at Tara, and left.

"Let's go home," Tara said morosely.

"Wait! I have to call Kannagi."

"Do it now. This place has better reception."

When GK disconnected, he was in a good mood. "Kannagi will join us tomorrow. She has a couple of ideas on ways to find your uncle. The school register could have given us some clue on who studied with him, but then I saw Nanban and forgot everything."

"All his classmates would be from Jomo," Tara mumbled, ignoring GK's remark on Nanban.

"And none would be on social media, right?"

Tara continued, "There were ten in his class, including him. I met one. We might get details about the rest from the school registers."

"Yes! Yes! That's what I was after when I encountered Nanban."

"Hmm! Which means that another climb to the school might be useful."

"What about the classmate you met? Would he remember his friends from the class? Let's try tracking them online."

"It's an option, but to talk to him, we need to get through that crazy Raman uncle."

"The one who threatened me?" Tara nodded. "Tough luck then," GK said with a sigh as he reached Tara's gate. "I am famished! I hoped there might be some food after the meeting."

Tara said sternly, "What do you plan to do tomorrow, GK? You spun a fictional tale. How are you going to prove it?"

"I hope the villagers forgive me." After a while, GK added, "The more important problem to tackle is your missing uncle."

"I have a hunch," said Tara.

"About your uncle?"

"No, about the trespassers."

GK gaped at her. "They are imaginary."

"That's my hunch that they might not be imaginary after all."

# 21

# More Trespassers

The evening sun streamed through the trees, painting the details in golden yellow. A group of people led by GK and Tara made their way downhill.

"Where are we going?" GK whispered.

Tara put her finger on her lips. She motioned to Kannagi, who was close behind. "Do not let him speak. Not until we reach the place!" Kannagi, in turn, flashed dagger eyes at GK. "Speak only when I say and only what we decided," Tara whispered. She led the party straight to the fork where she had one day heard the sound of a jeep attempting to push up the mountain slope. Coco, despite being on a tight leash, charged ahead. When Tara reached the rock where she had hidden with Coco, she stopped and made a sign to GK.

"Where does this path go?" GK asked the crowd. Murmurs rose and dwindled. Raman flicked his eyes around nervously.

"Not sure," said one from the group. "Let's walk farther. Is this where you saw the men?"

"Yes! They were carrying boxes from somewhere and loading them into their van. I waited to observe what they were doing. By the time the van moved, it was dark. I tried to move from behind this rock, but the men heard me.

They looked hostile. I was afraid that they might have weapons. So, I ran. But since I was unfamiliar with the terrain, I ran without knowing where I was going. Somehow... I ended up in that crevice." The last part was the most implausible because the crevice was a long way up. With his flabby physique, GK would have struggled to reach such a high place on a dark night.

Raman smirked. "I don't believe you," he said simply.

The crowd remained silent. A few walked up the path for a few metres. Tara, GK, and Kannagi exchanged glances, wondering what the villagers might do if they knew that GK was lying about the whole episode. One of the men who had walked ahead exclaimed loudly, "Look! Tyre tracks!" The rest of the people rushed after him. Only four individuals remained rooted to their spots. Tara, GK, and Kannagi were incredulous about their stroke of luck while Raman stood and scowled. Coco strained at his leash, eager to follow the trail. Someone from the crowd shouted, "The tracks are going up the mountain."

"But vehicles are not allowed on Jomo, are they?" Kannagi asked. She had struggled to reach Tara's house in the morning without a ride up the mountain.

"My hunch was correct," Tara replied. "Let's follow them."

The crowd slowed down as the slope got steeper. Raman hung back but kept ahead of Tara and her friends. At one point, he broke through the crowd and addressed them. "There's no point going on this wild goose chase. If this man has truly seen those trespassers, I believe his story about how he reached the crevice. We should turn back."

GK got into the fray. "It's not a story. It's the truth."

One of the men from the crowd addressed Raman. "There are tyre tracks where none should exist. Isn't that suspicious?"

"Rama, he is right. We should investigate," one of the older Jomoans in the crowd came forward.

Realising that the people were determined, Raman turned around in silence but not before staring daggers at Tara and her friends. The group trudged up, urging each other to stay close as it was getting dark. The road wound up gradually, and it became apparent that it was well-used.

"How did we not notice this road before?" Tara wondered aloud.

"Because it wasn't here before," someone answered from the crowd.

"I thought you have explored every inch of Jomo?" GK asked with a chuckle.

"I'm as surprised as the others," Tara retorted.

"By the way, Kannagi, we are walking with someone who owns half of this mountain."

"Hush!" Tara hastened to shut GK up. "What are you doing?"

GK gestured that he was zipping up his lips. Kannagi turned to Tara in awe.

"Don't look at me like that. I inherited it. I did nothing to earn it." Kannagi's respect for Tara went up manifold.

As they climbed further, the road began widening, and in a few minutes, they stood in front of a group of houses.

"Wait a minute!" Tara said, pushing through the crowd. "I have been here before." She surveyed the houses. "This place is familiar. Isn't that one Nandu uncle's house?"

The crowd murmured. A voice yelled from the crowd, "I think so!" The people turned to Raman for confirmation. After all, Nandu was his elder brother.

"Yes, that's our ancestral house," Raman confirmed.

Someone from the crowd said, "Look! Outsiders!" All eyes turned to two men walking through one of the gates opposite to Nandu's house carrying a placard each. A woman came out of the same gate and proceeded to a van parked beside it. She pulled out heavy rolls of paper from the van and carried them inside, following the two men. They were clearly new to Jomo. The crowd inched closer, slowly and quietly, to not startle the outsiders.

# 22

# The Facade

The house was exactly opposite Raman's ancestral home. People carrying boxes and other materials went in and out of its gate. The crowd stopped a few metres away and asked Tara and GK to proceed. Kannagi accompanied them. High up on the parapet wall of the two-storied house was a board that said-- Friend Circle. Tara was stunned.

"Friend Circle?" GK repeated curiously.

"These people are everywhere," Tara muttered.

"Do you know them?" GK whispered.

"They set up shop in front of the dog shelter a few days ago. They creep me out. I don't trust them."

"What are they doing here?"

"Let's find out," Tara said as she confidently entered the door. The movers did not notice, or they did not bother. The visitors entered a well-furnished reception area with brightly lit walls. Several pamphlets and brochures lay on the table, and the bunch of rolls carried in by the woman earlier were stacked in a corner. "Hello?" Kannagi asked while peering over the reception desk. It was empty.

"Yes?" All three turned around. A woman stood behind them, holding a giant carton. GK instinctively stepped forward to help, but she refused. She placed the carton in the corner of the room, brushed her hands, and came forward. “How may I help you?” she asked in her sweetest voice.

“We were…” Kannagi paused before looking at Tara, who scanned the place with curious eyes.

“Have you heard of Friend Circle before?” the woman asked.

GK and Kannagi looked at Tara again, who shook her head. “No,” they replied in unison.

“You are our first visitors. I’ll be with you shortly. I’m sorry, but we recently moved in from the valley. Our office should be up and ready in a week.” The trio exchanged glances. “Meanwhile, you can read through our pamphlet,” the woman said, pointing to the stack on the table.

Tara picked up one and immediately jumped in surprise. There was a commotion outside. A bark, a scream, a yell, and a yelp occurred in quick succession, followed by voices shouting. The trio followed the reception woman who ran out to investigate. It was Coco. He gnashed his teeth and strained at his leash tied to a tree in the yard. Raman, held back by a couple of men, yelled profanities at the dog.

“What’s going on?” asked the woman.

“This monster tried to bite me.”

Tara stepped in between Coco and Raman. “Coco wouldn’t hurt anyone unless you try to hurt him.”

“I saw him kick the dog,” said a young boy peeping over the compound wall.

“Who are you?” asked the woman. The boy threw her a curious glance but did not reply. The woman approached

Raman. "Sir, I hope you aren't hurt." She turned to the crowd, "Whose dog is this?"

"Mine."

The woman turned to Tara and smiled, trying to hide her annoyance. "We'll soon open up the place to pets. We'll have a separate area behind the house. Until then, pets are not allowed. Please bear with us."

"You'll allow pets!? No one told me that!" Raman shouted. The two men moved away from him, scared by the belligerence.

The woman now turned to Raman. "Yes, Mr. Raman, it was in the lease contract we signed."

"So, do you have long-term plans to be here at Jomo?" Tara asked.

"Yes!" The woman nodded. "We might expand, but we start with Jomo. Our management is keen to help Jomoans since you don't have internet connections and don't use social media. Our team thought the best place to pilot our project would be Jomo."

"We don't have the Internet, but that's out of choice. And what kind of a project is it? I don't understand." Tara glared at the woman and Raman in turns.

Before the woman could speak, one of the villagers who followed Tara and her friends to the house asked Raman, "You know these people, and you knew that they were opening this office here. Yet, you didn't tell us. You should've at least notified the Panchayat."

Raman puffed up his chest. "It's my place. I can do whatever I wish to do with it."

"Which is correct," said one of the Jomoans, "however, you are an elder from Jomo. You're aware of the rules we have here. You keep reminding us about the Jomoan philosophy towards outsiders."

"I assure you," said the woman pointing at the handful of her colleagues standing around, "we'll create no disturbance to the community."

The man glanced at her but turned his attention back to Raman. "Speak, Raman Uncle. You are the one who should answer us. They are outsiders, after all."

"I've nothing more to say. I already said it's my place and wish to do as I please with it."

"If that's your stand, we Jomoans need to discuss it further," the man replied in a worried tone.

Tara untied Coco from the tree and walked past Raman. She had to hold Coco's leash tight to prevent him from snapping at Raman's legs. "I'll never forgive you for kicking Coco," she muttered as she passed Raman. The villagers turned around and walked away, talking amongst themselves.

"Phew!" exclaimed GK. "So that means I'm let off the hook."

"For now," said Kannagi. "From what I've seen of Raman, he'll likely come sniffing around if he sees you here."

"What worries me, though, is the presence of that group of people—Friend Circle." Tara quickly filled in on the incidents at the dog shelter.

"They seem harmless," GK said with a shrug after listening to Nat and Freddie's story.

Kannagi shook her head. "I'm not sure I understand their working model. What are they trying to achieve?"

"Beats me." Tara walked ahead of Kannagi and GK as she quickened her pace with Coco bounding home happily. She was not satisfied with what they found. That day when she heard the sound of the vehicle, she could hear voices from the other side of the thicket. The men she heard the other day did not walk in the direction of the house. They were walking further away into the jungle.

Something was amiss.

# 23

## Family Quest

"Raman is Nandu's brother. Nandu was your uncle's friend. Raman does not like you because your dad had once stood up to him. So, he won't let Nandu cooperate with you." GK narrated and held up a finger with every statement.

"Are you counting my blessings?" Tara asked.

GK continued counting on his fingers. "What's worse is that the villagers aren't aware that you own a part of the mountain. Are there people living on your estate?"

"My estate?"

"That's what rich people call their holdings."

"Cut it off, GK," Tara snapped back. "I am surprised that no one knows about it yet. My ancestors have been discreet. I should be too."

"But what if your inheritance could help you lead a better life?" Kannagi interjected.

"Better than this?" GK asked in exasperation, glancing all around Tara's house. "Look where she lives. Look around you."

"The beauty of this place is unparalleled, and your home's beautiful, Tara," Kannagi declared with an appreciative smile, "but don't you have other dreams? Ambitions?" she continued.

Tara sat brooding for a while.

"I have never dreamed of any place but here. My biggest goal so far was to survive without selling my home. Like a miracle, out of nowhere, I am told I've inherited land on this mountain. Guess what? I could get a lot of money if I sell the land..."

"Yes!" GK raised his hands in mock despair.

"...but I don't want to do anything until I find my uncle and ask his opinion. He has a share in it, as well."

Kannagi nodded. "I understand."

GK was puzzled. "I don't understand, Tara, but it's your call."

"Listen, in this hullaballoo around you in the crevice and the trespassers on the mountain, we forgot about Nilaav," Tara reminded the two.

They sat on the porch, having decided to eat breakfast with the rising sun. Steaming hot rice cakes with spicy chicken curry and piping hot coffee rendered the atmosphere a delectable fragrance. GK stretched himself lazily after he gobbled up the last morsel from his plate. He had earlier clicked a picture of his plate with hot vapours rising above the food, set against the background of the hills beyond. He stared at his empty plate. A nice contrast with his last click. Kannagi glared at him when he touched his phone. "Don't you dare click a photo of your soiled plate! It is disgusting."

"But I have licked it clean," GK protested meekly, inviting stronger glares from Kannagi.

"Let's go to the school, Tara. We can search for your uncle's classmates' names and…" Instead of completing her sentence, Kannagi squealed, leaped into the air, and plonked down in the chair with her legs folded up. She peeped down in apprehension. "Something wet and soft on my feet," she said. Tara guffawed. "Coco, come out from under the table." Kannagi gave an embarrassed smile. "I guess Coco was expressing his gratitude," GK said wryly. He had not warmed up to Coco yet.

In the next hour, the group of four made their way to the school. Tara took Coco along because his senses were the sharpest when on a trail. And he was always excited about a quest. His ears cocked up at the slightest sound, and his nose constantly sniffed out the surroundings. His tail wagged non-stop. GK pointed at Coco, who was running ahead. "You better keep him on the leash if we meet any wild animals there," GK shivered as he spoke.

"Wild animals?" Kannagi asked in alarm. "Oh well, I did not tell you the entire story of how I found myself stuck in that crevice, did I?" GK asked.

Kannagi shook her head, her large eyes becoming bigger in appearance.

Tara chuckled. "Do you really want to do this now?"

GK started his narration anyway. By the time they spied the ramshackle structure of the school, he only reached the part where he had met the boy. Coco ran ahead, barking, while Tara ran to keep pace. GK and Kannagi stood back to take in the surroundings.

"What a school! Imagine studying here!"

"Wait till you see the insides of that building. We would be lucky if some of it doesn't fall over our heads."

Tara opened the cupboard before GK and Kannagi could join her. Coco kept sniffing, wheezing, and shaking himself to get rid of the dust that flew from the cupboard. Tara picked up one of the notebooks and attempted to flip a few pages. The pages crumbled under the weight of her fingers.

"Why don't you both search the cupboard while I watch outside the classroom?" GK suggested. "Keep watch? Why?" Kannagi asked. "Take Coco with you," Tara said with a nod.

GK held onto Coco's leash and went out. Tara and Kannagi leafed through the newer notebooks, but they contained names of recent students. "There are three students registered for this year." Tara nodded. "All three are my students. They are twelve, thirteen, and fifteen. This year, the fifteen-year-old will attempt his public examination as a private student."

"Then why this school, and what's the meaning of this registration?"

"I suppose the teacher gets some benefits from the Panchayat."

"Is there a teacher?"

"There is one, not from Jomo. He's from the valley."

"I am surprised that the school still runs."

"It does not. I'm not sure why and who registered the three kids this year," Tara replied.

"Let's look at the older registers." After a while, Kannagi found one that mentioned Nilaav.

Tara chuckled, "His name's Nilaav, even in the school register."

"Makes our work easier and harder, doesn't it?" Kannagi said. "We still don't know his real name, but at least we're sure we found the right register."

Kannagi carefully noted down the names she found registered in the same year as Nilaav. "So, we have eight people to track down."

"I'd be useless in this case, as I don't have the internet."

"Don't worry. GK and I will work on this."

"Meanwhile, I'll keep an eye on Friend Circle. I'm afraid I don't trust them at all," Tara shook her head testily.

# 24

# Online

GK and Kannagi combed the online world for Nilaav's classmates. No one had any mentions on the Internet. A couple of namesakes showed up on search engines. There were corporate honchos, a writer, a politician, and even a convict, but none were from Jomo. Kannagi moved onto a social media platform, where she had better luck. One person, Gopal, had a profile. Kannagi quickly sent him a message. A second classmate, Hanif, had a profile but was inactive. She sent him a message anyway. GK looked up from his phone after scrolling and trawling online pages for more than an hour. "They belong to a generation with absolutely no online presence. How are we going to contact them? And what if they don't know where Nilaav is?"

"I found two on social media. I have messaged them. At least one is active." Kannagi replied.

"What?!" GK was aghast. He came over to the table where Kannagi sat. "You messaged them from your account?"

"Yes, I did. Why?"

"How can you be so naïve? They could be fake accounts."

"I'll find out when they reply, won't I?"

"What if they start pestering you?"

Kannagi eyed him with trepidation. "Good point."

"Have you found more people?"

"Yes, one more. Sura. He goes by his first name. The school register doesn't mention a surname either."

"Interesting, but..." GK said as he explored Sura's profile, "...he has few friends. He won't be helpful. It's astonishing that he is on social media at all after living in a place like Jomo."

"People change."

GK wondered if he should tell Kannagi about BEFOR. He was sure that she would disapprove. Precisely the same way that he disapproved of her messages to unknown people on social media, but BEFOR was different. There, his identity was a secret. Besides, he got access to some of the best brains and souls. GK tried to justify his growing addiction to BEFOR. It was not an addiction. It was only a hobby. He got information and knowledge from others. He could carry out interesting conversations.

"What are you dreaming about?" Kannagi asked. "Are you planning to write a book?" she teased.

GK lounged on his armchair with a pen in his mouth. "I might write one."

"Yes, and stock those in your dream bookstore. Dream book, dream bookstore."

GK gave a wry smile. "Everyone has aspirations, don't they?"

"Yes, I aspire to be a social worker," Kannagi replied.

GK snorted in response. "Is that why you've been at the bus stop distributing pamphlets?"

Kannagi glared at GK. "That was for my friend. She was holding an exhibition."

"Well, one can say it is a social service."

"I'll ask Tara for help. She understands me better."

Kannagi's words brought GK back to the problem at hand. "Should Tara waste so much time searching for her uncle?"

Kannagi eyed GK curiously. "What kind of a friend are you?" When GK did not respond, she continued. "Imagine being orphaned at a young age, having to take care of your grandmother as a teen, managing the household as you study, trying to make ends meet, and then learning that you have an uncle who is alive. Won't you want to meet him?"

GK shrugged. "I would be rather angry. Why would I meet someone who never bothered about me all these years? Like *my* relatives?"

Kannagi's gaze softened. "Perhaps, she is not as bitter as you."

"Yet," GK sighed. "What if her uncle does not care? What if he is dead? Or worse, what if he turns out to be a crook, a bad or immoral person?"

Kannagi shuddered. "She might get some kind of closure."

"Closure," GK repeated.

They both remained lost in their own train of thought until the doorbell jolted them out of their reverie. When GK opened the door, there was no one. An envelope lay on the floor below the door.

"Who's that?" Kannagi asked.

"Some kind of door-to-door pamphlet distribution," he said, tossing the envelope into a basket in the corner of the room. That is when the name caught his eye. The envelope addressed to him had a logo and a name in the top right corner. He rescued it from the overflowing basket and examined it. Kannagi came forward. GK hid the logo with his palm. For all the anonymity BEFOR professed, how could they send him a letter? He couldn't justify his presence on the app easily to Kannagi.

"Why don't you open it?"

"It is some kind of marketing material," GK said with a feigned nonchalance and kept the envelope in a drawer.

"Then throw it. Why keep it safe in a drawer?"

"Never mind, I'll do a bit of cleaning later."

Kannagi was unconvinced. She waited for him to leave the room, then tip-toed to the drawer, opened it noiselessly, and removed the envelope. It was light, like a marketing mailer. The name in the corner of the envelope read – BEFOR. She had not heard of this company before. Curiosity getting the better of her, she opened the envelope. A single glossy sheet fell out of it. It was a discount coupon for cameras and accessories from a store in NewTown. Kannagi knew how much GK was yearning for a good camera. "Hey, did you see this?" Kannagi asked as she went inside with the coupon in hand. GK dismissed it initially, but a few moments later, he recalled asking for good camera recommendations on BEFOR.

Could it be a mysterious benefactor from BEFOR?

He pretended to be not excited, but later that night, he dropped a few more hints in his chats on BEFOR. He chatted about stuff he wished to have but couldn't afford. Sure enough, the following day, he received another bunch of discount coupons beneath his door.

# 25

# Into the Circle

Keeping Coco at Grandpa Lal's was like babysitting two ways. Grandpa Lal loved to pamper Coco while he, in turn, kept a close eye on Grandpa Lal's movements.

Coco proved to be an alert caretaker a few months ago. Meenu was at Tara's place for an errand when Grandpa Lal had a fall. Coco ran back home, barking all the way and raising a ruckus. Meenu and Tara immediately guessed that Grandpa Lal was in trouble. They rushed back and found him unconscious. The timely intervention saved Grandpa Lal's life, as vouched by the doctor. So, when Tara decided to explore Friend Circle, she left Coco with Grandpa Lal.

"Is the mountain shaking?" Grandpa Lal asked wryly.

"Come on, Grandpa Lal. Did my grandmother come in your dreams again?" Tara guffawed at her own joke.

Grandpa Lal shook his head. "Perhaps, it's my imagination, but on some days, I feel like something is going on inside the mountain."

"You can write stories, Grandpa. Such tall tales!" She filled Coco's bowl with water and another with food. "Now stay here with Grandpa, like a good boy."

After ensuring that Grandpa Lal was snug in his armchair and Coco happy at his feet, she set out. It was a bright sunny morning, and if the weather had been any better, she would have packed a picnic basket for Coco and herself to have it by the slender and peaceful river flowing through the valley. It was a bone of contention between Jomoans and the valley-dwellers whether it was a river or a stream. Jomoans liked to believe that the diminutive cascades from their beloved mountain fed into the life-giving river. However, the valley dwellers had seen better days when the river was wider and held more fish in its belly. They considered it to be only a stream. Tara decided that one day, she would plan a picnic for GK and Kannagi by the river. She would enjoy it. It was good to have friends. Nat and Freddie left a gaping hole in her life when they closed the dog shelter. The dog shelter's occupants consumed all the love that came their way with gratitude, and Tara had plenty of love to offer. Nat and Freddie's decision to sell their place made her uneasy because of how Friend Circle was involved. Raman, dead against outsiders in Jomo, allowed an unknown organisation to set up camp in his house. The organisation's association with Raman, if only through a tenancy agreement, made them more dubitable. She made her way to the Friend Circle office with a suspicious mind, unwilling to accept anything at face value. As soon as she entered, she was greeted by the lady they met on the first day.

"Hi! Welcome back! What can we do for you?"

"I'm Tara." Tara held out her hand with a friendly smile.

"I'm Avantika." The lady shook Tara's hand warmly.

"What are your plans for the animals? I have a pet dog."

"Oh yes! I remember. Before that, I'd like to tell you about our membership benefits."

"Membership?"

"Yes, the way Friend Circle works is that you take a free membership before we help you. It's a simple process. You fill out a form. We sign an undertaking that we won't share your personal details with anyone outside the organisation. And that's it." Avantika paused to observe Tara. "Would you like to fill out a membership form?" she asked, her eyes twinkling in anticipation.

"Well, yes, but can you tell me more about your services?"

"Yes, for the pets, especially, we'll have a fun-themed park. Members can come and play around. They can meet other pet owners or other members who want to watch their pets play—"

"Meet?"

"Yes, Tara. It's up to you, of course. We believe that Friend Circle members would benefit immensely if they connected with each other and became friends. Connections and interactions could be limited to when you meet at Friend Circle. Or you may wish to trade cards or contact numbers. It's entirely up to you."

Tara stopped in her tracks as she followed Avantika to the pet park at the back. "What if I don't want to meet anyone? I only wish to ask you for help."

"Agreed. As I said, it's entirely up to you if you want to make friends or not. Regarding help, if you don't wish to share your personal details with others, we'll respect your need for privacy. Although you have to understand that we'll source help for you from other members."

Tara frowned. "What do you mean by sourcing help from others?"

"Well, we are not a governmental organization. We intend to let the members interact and get help from each other."

"What if I don't want to interact."

Avantika shrugged in response.

"Would you still help me?"

Avantika gave a noncommittal nod. She ushered Tara to the pet park. It was segregated into different areas meant for various pets. There was even a photo booth. The setup was perfect for enthusiasts like GK, who loved to click and upload pictures by the dozen. Friend Circle was cleverly catering to the needs of modern society.

Tara turned around when she heard Avantika call out to someone, "Hey! It's alright. You can meet a new friend." A sari-clad figure ran away in haste. Tara caught a glimpse of a familiar red and green sari.

"Strange lady," murmured Avantika.

"Who was that?"

"Our first member. But she is shy."

"May I ask what her name is?"

"Well..." Avantika stared at Tara. She paused before saying, "Her name is Meenu."

"Ha!" Tara exclaimed. "No wonder she ran away."

"You know her?"

Tara nodded. Meenu was supposed to be preparing lunch at Grandpa Lal's house. She must have spotted Tara and got anxious.

"In that case, you would also know she is looking for a job?"

This was news to Tara. The job search wasn't surprising. Meenu already held two, one at Grandpa Lal's house and occasionally at Tara's, but she was ambitious.

Tara turned to Avantika. "The services you provide will be for Jomoans alone, right?"

"To start with, we may soon have members from other places joining in. We would encourage visits to other sites and offices as well."

"How will that fit into our local rules? We don't allow outsiders to Jomo."

"Mr. Raman has promised us that he will persuade the Jomoans."

Tara returned home with a frown on her face. What does Raman think he is doing? On the way home, as she passed through the spot where the signal was the strongest, a frantic call from Kannagi added to the confusion of the day. "GK isn't speaking to me. He has shut himself up in his house. He won't pick up my calls or come out either."

"What happened?"

"He lost his job."

# 26

# Path Forward

It was unlike GK to ignore Kannagi even in the worst phases of their relationship. He would go out of his way to patch up. They were both under pressure from Kannagi's family. It took them a while to accept GK as their future son-in-law. Losing a job would create a furore. Kannagi's tearful call made Tara anxious, and she hurried to NewTown, as fast as possible. By the time she covered the distance on foot and by bus, it was noon.

Tara knocked thrice on the door. When there was no response, she banged on the wooden panel. A nervous Kannagi stood beside her. "I am worried about his mental state," she said while she swallowed a huge sob that gathered in her throat. Tara frowned at Kannagi. "I thought you were tougher than him." She walked around the house. A sobbing Kannagi followed. The windows were shut. There was no handle on the outside with which they could be opened. "A crowbar would've been useful, but any twig shaped like one might help," Tara muttered as she passed Kannagi. Before Kannagi's limpid eyes could get used to the plant litter in the yard, Tara found a bough and walked briskly to the window. Opening it was surprisingly easy because it was not locked. He lay on his bed, sleeping like a log. "GK!" Tara and Kannagi hollered in unison. He sat up in terror. "What? Who? Huh?"

"Idiot!" Tara shouted. "Why aren't you picking up your phone?" Kannagi yelled. GK fumbled as he groped for his phone. "Open the door. Quick!" Tara shouted as they both stomped off to the main door. GK took more time than anticipated. Tara's anger was going up by the minute. "I don't have time for this. My afternoon batch will be home soon for their classes." Kannagi looked at Tara and offered a silent apology. GK opened the door and stood aside as the two girls barged in. "What were you up to?" Kannagi asked. "First of all. How did you lose your job?" Tara asked.

"They were waiting for a reason to fire me. Being stuck in the crevice, I was obviously not present at work." GK replied with a shrug. "My phone was out of charge." Tara did not wait for more explanations. With a weary glance at GK, she went home.

GK noticed Kannagi's tear-stained cheeks for the first time. He ushered her inside. "Let's have tea. I have something to share." The tea did little to calm Kannagi's anger, but it slowed down her thoughts. She glared at GK from above the rim of her cup. "Your eyes say that you haven't slept for ages."

"I didn't sleep at all last night," GK replied. Kannagi leaned back, waiting for him to go on. "I have decided that I am going to follow my dreams."

"Meaning?"

"Meaning, I am going to open that bookstore." GK beamed despite his ragged face.

Kannagi raised an eyebrow. "Wasn't that what I was telling you all along? You had to get fired to think about it seriously?"

GK shook his head. "I've been chatting with some experts." He opened his phone and introduced Kannagi to BEFOR. The more he explained, the more suspicious Kannagi grew of the application. "Who are these experts that you chat with? They don't even have any names."

"It doesn't matter. I am getting some good advice."

"Do you tell them everything?"

"I don't share personal details, only the problem I face."

"Can I read your chats?"

"Sure," GK replied, then paused before yelling, "No! Wait! Erm… they might not like it."

"But they are nameless experts, and how would they know whether I have read your chats or not."

"Still…," he hesitated, then brightened up, "…but aren't you happy about my decision?"

"I am, but I am curious as to what or who forced you into it."

"No one forced me. I felt that it's the right decision."

Kannagi sat in deep thought for a long time. GK wondered if he committed a mistake by telling her about BEFOR. The truth was that at night after he spoke to Kannagi, GK was desperate. His conversation on BEFOR involved rants about his fiancée's family and their attitude toward him. Although he didn't mention any names, if Kannagi were to read his chats, she would immediately recognize the context. He was sure that she would take offence. She might even be hurt.

"If they are so helpful, why don't you ask them to help Tara? Why not ask them how to look for a missing relative?"

"Do you think I did not try?"

"And?"

"Not useful. First of all, we don't have any details to go on. Secondly, they told me what I already knew. Go to the police. Search on social media. Blah blah blah."

"Well, there's one update on the messages we sent. One person replied, "Hi Kannagi, will you be my friend?" Kannagi rolled her eyes as she spoke.

GK smirked. "Didn't I tell you to be careful?"

"I don't have to reply. At least we learned that someone is active."

"Who replied?"

"Sura."

"Let me handle this one," GK answered.

"Meanwhile, shall I talk to my dad about your idea to open the bookstore?" Kannagi asked excitedly. "They'll be more than happy to help you out."

GK gritted his teeth. "Not now, Kannagi."

# 27

# The Local Recruit

While GK's chats on BEFOR got longer by the day, the inventors were happy. The counter in Ronny Shikari's office ran at a frantic pace. He sat in his chair with smug contentment. His tactic worked. Maya and her team worked day and night to ensure BEFOR became a success in the Indian markets. Moreover, Jomo, a tiny dot in the political map stuffed deep into Ronny's desk, was showing progress of a different kind. The coming months will be exciting for Hunt Technologies. He had a special regional recruit to take care of business. Ronny dialled a number from his desk phone. "Munaf? How is it going with Project Hunt?"

"We are making progress, Sir."

Ronny smiled. Munaf was his loyal man. He was also his local man. So local that he refused to call him anything but Sir. "I saw your report with the tracker. Amazing work! Well done!"

"Thank you, Sir!"

"Is the FC team helping you?"

"Nothing so far, Sir. It's not their fault. It's not easy to connect offline and online. We'll reach there soon."

"All the best, Munaf. You're the pride of my team."

"Thank you, Sir."

As soon as Ronny disconnected the call, Munaf dialled a number.

"Patsy?"

"Yes, Munaf?"

"Shikari called."

"What's up?"

"Nothing, it's the usual status update."

"Was he happy?"

"Yes."

"Good, good," Patsy replied. "Let it continue this way. Have you been to Jomo yet?"

"No, Sir, I mean Patsy."

Patsy could imagine Munaf grinning at his fumble. "Ok, whenever you go, take some pictures, will you?"

"Patsy, give the Circle some time. You'll have all the pictures you wish for." Munaf said with a chuckle.

"Alright, but you take care. That Shikari is a sharp fellow. And how's your old friend doing?"

"He has no clue what has hit him. He understands nothing of the business except that the office uses his place."

Patsy roared with laughter. They ended the conversation on that highly amusing note.

Munaf leaned back in his chair as he reflected on the two conversations. About five years ago, he met Patsy running a café near a pilgrimage site. Patsy regaled the customers with his stories while his partner whipped up delicacies behind the counter. Munaf was instantly taken by the wise old entrepreneur until, one day, he asked him the secret to his passion. Patsy revealed that he was not an entrepreneur. He was a 'wandering consultant,' as he called himself, who roamed around helping others. He got free lodging and food in return. When Munaf appeared disappointed, Patsy sat with him and asked his story.

Munaf was the eldest of four siblings. The entire family depended on him to pull them up from the jaws of poverty, hungrily snapping at their heels. Munaf went to the United States for an onsite technology project, and soon his work brought him success. The client hired him and offered him a well-paid position. Everything went fine until his mother died. He returned to India for her funeral and felt the full force of forgotten history. An incident that he had buried deep inside his psyche bubbled up to the surface. When Munaf returned to America, he carried the emotional baggage of a strenuous past. After a year of unexplained aches and pains, which left him tired and unable to focus on work, he returned for a sabbatical. He planned a trip around India and met Patsy on this trip.

Patsy offered a shoulder to cry on. "Let go of the past, Munaf. It'll only tire you out. You have a bright future."

"I would have if they hadn't insulted my mother. As she lay there bereft of her breath and words, I wanted to take her to where she grew up, but how could I? The people humiliated not only my mother but my brother too. He had worked so hard to bring us all up. When I left for the States, my mother reminded me about my brother's death. Anything that involves you will have twice the consequences, she said. Why? Why should it be like that?" Munaf asked Patsy.

"Would you like to do a good turn for a community?" Patsy had asked in response

"What do you mean? Which community?"

"The same people who blamed your brother for his death."

Munaf did not return to the café for a few days. He stewed in anger at the thought of helping those people, but he remembered his mother's wise words. We are no one to punish but we are the only ones to help. If not us then who? When he met Patsy again, he was determined. "I have realised that my fight is not with the community, but with a few people, and one person in particular."

Patsy patted him in encouragement. "I can help you. I have a friend in the United States who works for a corporate firm. Apply for the role that he suggests. When you get the job, call me. I'll tell you more."

Munaf did as he was told. Later though, he harboured doubts. "Why are you helping me out?"

"That's what I do."

Munaf shook his head. "I know you are a 'wandering consultant,' but this is something different, isn't it?"

"Let's just say that we share a history." Patsy refused to divulge more.

# 28

# Outreach

GK was adamant. He didn't want to ask Kannagi's family for help. He had enough money to give the deposit for a shophouse in NewTown. All he needed was some cash to source books for his store. He didn't need any employees, at least not at the beginning. He would manage the shop on his own. Besides, he hoped that Kannagi would help. Chatting on BEFOR did not yield anything beyond discount coupons, but GK's conversation with BEFOR took a prescient turn a few days after he lost his job.

The person knew more about NewTown and Jomo than anyone he had chatted with before. "Why don't you try Friend Circle?" the person asked. GK was stunned. So far, his chats were devoid of specifics unless it was a book or a movie that they discussed. For the first time, he was given a specific recommendation. GK spent a lot of time asking the BEFOR users about Friend Circle. He chatted with many profiles, all of whom knew of Friend Circle. Irrespective of what Tara felt about the organisation, he realised they must hold some promise. Otherwise, why would so many people recommend them? So, a day after Tara visited Friend Circle, GK, too, trudged his way up the Jomo Mountain.

"Hello? May I help you?" Avantika appeared magically as GK entered the place. "Your friend visited us yesterday," she remarked on recognizing him.

GK cleared his throat. "Do you actually help with any kind of problems?"

Avantika nodded. She leaned forward and whispered. "Even medical issues. We can get you in touch with the right doctors."

GK gave a wry smile. "I don't need any medical help. Thank you."

Avantika handed out a form to GK. "You can fill out this form. You need not give any particulars but ensure that you fill this column," she said, tapping a box in the form.

Please describe your challenge—the question above the box read.

GK glanced around. A cup of coffee sat invitingly on a table. He pulled up a chair beside it and started writing.

"Please help yourself to the coffee too. I pressed it as soon as I saw you enter the office," Avantika said with a cloying smile.

GK filled out the form and inserted it into the folder placed by Avantika on the table. As soon as he finished, she appeared before him.

"Good job! Your friend did visit but did not fill out the form. I think she is still making up her mind about us. Perhaps, you'll put in a good word?"

"I will if I get the help I want," GK answered, returning the sickly-sweet smile he received from Avantika. She filed the form and invited GK to look around the premises. The interiors were uniformly furnished in the same colours as their logo—pink and yellow. The colour scheme irked GK. It was like walking through a brightly lit dollhouse. Every nook and corner had a table and a couple of chairs.

"These are our meeting spaces for members to meet and talk."

"If I didn't know any better, I might have mistaken this for a dating site," GK mumbled.

Avantika stopped in her tracks. "Sir, please hold your judgement until we work on your case."

GK shrugged in reply. "First impressions. What a customer perceives is as important as what he experiences."

Avantika bristled with emotions for a few seconds, then changed her tack. She smiled sweetly, "I'll ensure your feedback reaches our marketing department. They are responsible for all this." She waved as if trying to dissociate herself from a foolish mistake.

"What are you doing here?" GK froze as he recognized the voice. He had meant to call up Tara before visiting Jomo but forgot in his excitement.

"I could ask you the same question," GK mumbled as he turned around.

Tara remained unfazed. "I am exploring."

"Like I said, your friend is yet to fill out our form," Avantika glanced at Tara as she spoke to GK. "I assume she has a few concerns."

"I don't have any concerns," Tara said in her defence.

"In that case, would you mind filling up our form and please pay attention to a few other columns in our form?" Avantika pulled out a form and offered it to Tara. Avantika tapped her pen on one of the columns to draw Tara's attention. Areas that you can help your community with—the line stated. Tara grabbed the pen from Avantika and quickly wrote against the column—teaching and dog-walking.

GK raised an eyebrow as he read her entry. "That's all?" he whispered. "You want people to contact you for dog-walking?" he asked with a giggle.

Tara frowned as she handed over the paper to Avantika. She signalled to him to keep walking to the other end of the building. "I filled it out of politeness," she hissed.

He chuckled. "Polite, and you?"

Tara ignored his remark. "Look at this house. It's been completely transformed into an office building. And they couldn't have done the transformation in a few days or weeks. It means that Raman knew about this organisation and their plans for the office for some time now...," she paused to think, "...but he kept it under wraps. Why?"

"He didn't want Jomoans to oppose. If the Friend Circle project was stalled, he would lose a neat rental income."

A commotion from the office building distracted them. A bunch of dogs came bounding out of the house into the dog park. Behind them came a man in a T-shirt and shorts covering the distance in quick long strides. "Hey, wait!" He laughed as he called out.

Avantika followed him, panting and gasping for breath. "You are in luck, Mr. Kumar. Tara is exactly the sort of person you need."

The man slowed down and regarded Tara. "Tara?" he asked as he held out his hand.

Tara refused and glared at Avantika instead. "I thought that members could choose to not interact with others? That's what you told me, right?"

Avantika gritted her teeth. "He just walked in asking if we could find him a dog walker, and there you were."

Tara turned her attention to the dogs, who were happy to be outdoors. "Why do people keep so many dogs if they can't take care?" Tara mumbled to herself.

"Pardon me?" the man asked. When Tara ignored him and walked ahead, he caught up to walk beside her. "These dogs are not mine. They are my neighbours' dogs. They left for Dubai and will be away for three months. I tried handling them for a week, but it's been challenging."

"How did you learn about Friend Circle?" Tara went straight to the point as usual.

"Through Freddie. I live in NewTown. When I asked around, I learned about the dog shelter, but it was closed. I saw them take down the building. One of the neighbours gave me Freddie's contact. He suggested that I reach out to Friend Circle."

Tara fumed as she realised Freddie thought it better to recommend Friend Circle than call her up. She walked the dogs at the Shelter for more than five years, yet Freddie chose to recommend Friend Circle. How quickly these people had managed to gain the public's trust! "How did you come up here?" Tara flung her next question.

"I took the van."

"The van? What van?" Tara and GK exchanged surprised glances.

"Ah!" Avantika butted in. "Mr. Kumar, Tara is a Jomoan, and GK is her friend who visits the place often. So, they don't feel the need for a vehicle."

GK opened his mouth to say he would be more than happy to get a vehicle up to Jomo, but he respected the Jomoan principles. Tara spoke before he could get in a word. "Wait a minute. Do you mean to say that you have arranged a van for Friend Circle members to come up the mountain?"

Avantika replied with a smile. "Hourly shuttle service from the foothills to the Friend Circle office."

"That's why they built the road," Tara said to GK. "And Raman would have known this too," GK said in response.

"Jomo is a beautiful place," said the man as if he heard nothing of the conversation. "Since you are a local, Tara, would you mind showing me around one day? I am busy on weekdays, but Sundays are good."

Tara baulked at his presumption that she was going to show him around. GK smirked. Avantika led the man away for a secret conversation. "I wonder what that woman is telling him now." GK squinted at them and was surprised when he saw Avantika nodding at him. "She seems to be talking about us."

"This whole place is super shady," Tara remarked.

"What is their business model? How are they going to make money?" GK pondered.

Avantika returned. "Tara, Mr. Kumar asks if you could do a weekly session for his dogs, if not daily."

It was farcical to send messages through Avantika when the man was already acquainted with her. Tara strode up to him. He stood with a gentle smile, watching the dogs frolic around. "Mr. Kumar, I—"

"You can call me Balram. Kumar is my dad."

Tara stared at the dogs to avoid staring at his dimples. "Mr. Balram, I can walk your dogs on Fridays for an hour. I'll inform you about my charges."

"What about my other request, Ms. Tara?" Tara turned to him with raised eyebrows. "Showing me around Jomo?"

"I am sorry we don't entertain outsiders at Jomo. Keep yourself to Friend Circle, and do not wander around. The jungle is full of wildlife."

"But friends are allowed?" Balram asked as he glanced at GK.

"He is," she said, nodding at GK, "but he landed in trouble for wandering around. You must have watched it on the news the other day. He had to be rescued from a crevice in the hill."

"Oh! That was him! A brave man indeed," Balram raised his voice so GK could hear. "I'll wait for the day when I am allowed," he said with a chuckle. Tara could have sworn that she saw a twinkle in Balram's dark brown eyes. The eyes that she noticed only now.

The next day, Tara took Coco with her when she went to pick up Balram's dogs. They were boisterous, unruly, and equally energetic. Coco would help in guiding them. Balram was dressed in a t-shirt, shorts, and sneakers. Tara stretched out her hand for the dog leashes. To her surprise, Balram handed over one of the dogs while he held on to the other two. "I am free this evening. Would you mind if I joined you?"

"I am being paid to walk your dogs, not you."

Balram guffawed. "I promise that I'll pay your full charges as promised. As I said, I want to explore the area."

"I don't walk my dogs to Jomo. I walk them in and around NewTown."

"Why not Jomo?"

"It's usually dark when we return, and Jomo is Nanban's kingdom after dark. With four tired dogs by my side, I wouldn't want to draw his attention. They would be easy prey."

"Nanban?"

Tara narrated Nanban's story and how Jomoans have encountered him on his nightly prowls. Balram was a patient listener, and in a short while, Tara told him the story of Jomo and how it came about to be a village with no Internet.

"So, it appears that you, Tara, are at the centre of Jomo's connectionless existence," Balram observed. "So, tell me, how did you get by in those bleak times?"

Tara paused in front of a plant. "I have not seen this one before. Looks like a weed."

Balram immediately paid attention to the plant, then turned to Tara. "You didn't answer my question."

Tara took a deep breath. She did not realise how much she had spoken. No one other than GK had so far bothered to ask her how difficult her childhood was. GK was her classmate and colleague. Balram was an acquaintance she had met only once before. She threw a glance at him. He stared at her curiously. Tara turned away. "It's getting late. The dogs are tired. Do you want me to drop them off at your house, or will you take them yourself?"

Balram made an exaggerated action of checking the time. "My time's up?"

"My bus leaves in exactly five minutes from that stop," Tara said, pointing to the road.

"Ok," Balram bowed as if tipping his hat and led his dogs away.

Her phone rang. It was GK.

"Guess what? Avantika sent me a note. They have found someone interested in my bookshop."

Tara stared at Balram's receding figure. "Who is it?"

"They didn't divulge. The investor didn't want to be named."

"How does that work?"

"They'll invest via Friend Circle. Tara, I am so excited! Can we all meet for a celebration?"

"Of course. When and where?"

"Tomorrow? At your home?"

Tara rolled her eyes. "My home?"

"What better place, Tara? You have such a beautiful home."

Tara sighed. "Alright."

After the call, she scrolled through her messages. She rarely did, but the last few days had been annoying. The lawyer Thomas messaged nearly every day, asking her if they could meet. He was pushing her to decide about the estate. She could not respond without finding Nilaav. Could she ask Friend Circle for help? They seemed to have resolved GK's problem in a jiffy.

# 29

# Uninvited Guests

Tara reigned in Coco as he yapped excitedly. GK and Kannagi stood in attention outside the gate. "Don't be nervous around him. He sees you as friends. Be your natural self," Tara explained.

"Easier said than done," GK muttered under his breath. He clenched his jaw so tight that his facial muscles began to ache. Kannagi was partly amused and partly terrified by Coco. "When we have a house of our own, we shall have a puppy, too," she said to GK as she stood mesmerized by the bundle of excitement that leaped beside Tara. GK was aghast. Before he could comment, Coco yelped and jerked so hard that Tara had to let go. GK and Kannagi yelled nearly at the same pitch as they jumped aside. Coco ran past them, down the path that led to Tara's house and around a bend. GK and Kannagi let out a sigh of relief. As soon as they entered the gate, they heard Coco barking loudly. Tara raised her eyebrows. "I hope we don't have uninvited guests." She went off after Coco, but before she reached the bend, Coco came around wagging his tail. He was followed by a sheepish Balram.

"You here?"

"Can I get a glass of water? Jomo has a steep climb."

Tara clenched her teeth as anger rose to the roots of her hair, but she was not callous enough to refuse a thirsty man his water. Although, seeing Coco by Balram's side caused her to nearly say no. She felt envious. He was good with dogs. In minutes, Coco had transformed from an alert, incensed watchdog to a cute, wagging bundle of enthusiasm. Balram made all the right noises as he followed Tara into her home. He noted the quaint architecture and the simple but refined interiors. "And the view! My goodness, the view! How lucky you are, Tara!" While GK and Kannagi observed Balram with amusement, Tara was nonplussed. When GK followed her into the kitchen, she expressed her doubts about the man. "He asked me to take him around Jomo, and now he shows up here. Yesterday, he didn't let the dogs be alone with me. He followed me as I took them for a walk." GK's eyes crinkled as he tried to suppress a grin. Tara was clearly uncomfortable, and he found it funny. "It's not funny. He's acting strange. He has some ulterior motives." GK rubbed his chin thoughtfully. "What if he is interested in you. Have you thought of that possibility?" Tara glared at GK in response. When they entered the living room with the dishes and plates, they found Kannagi and Balram going through the old photographs on the wall.

"Your family?" Balram asked.

Tara nodded, and she took them through the portraits, all the while talking to Kannagi. GK nudged her. "It's painfully obvious that you are ignoring him." Tara ignored his comment as well. "By the way, how did you find your way here?" she asked pointedly, staring at Balram.

“I’m sorry to crash into your party,” he replied with a disarming smile. “This place is so beautiful, I had to explore it. Fortunately, as I made my way to Friend Circle today, I saw GK walking up the mountain with this lovely lady--”

“Kannagi.” Kannagi introduced herself.

“What a historical name!” Balram remarked. “So, I followed them. I assumed they might walk to your home since GK is your friend. Sorry for interrupting your get-together. I’ll be on my way. Do I leave the same way that I climbed?” Balram asked, turning to GK.

GK and Kannagi turned to Tara as if expecting her to say something. The dishes were set out at the table. Tara caught Balram staring at the food. “Oh, alright! Why don’t you join us for lunch? Now that you are here.” Tara hissed the invitation through her teeth.

“I was afraid you were not going to ask. So glad you did. I am famished.” Balram tucked in enthusiastically into the food at the table.

The conversation started flowing as they spoke about their childhood, schooling, and education. Balram turned out to be an erudite man. After schooling in the country’s north, he moved south with his parents, graduated, and left for the United States for higher studies. “But the homeland beckoned, so when my company offered a position in their India office, I took it up,” Balram explained in between mouthfuls. “The food is delicious,” he said with an appreciative nod.

“Half of the dishes were made by my helper.”

"It's good to have someone around. Living alone in such an isolated place is not my cup of tea."

"So, you don't like it out here? Then why are you in NewTown?" GK was curious. "Why would any organization post you at NewTown? What do they do?"

"Erm… They do market research. I am studying the market for them."

"Market for what?" GK continued.

Balram turned to Tara, ignoring GK. "Is your helper from Jomo? Does she live here with you?"

"No."

"Isn't it scary to be alone on this mountain?"

Tara scoffed. "I have Coco for protection."

Balram eyed Coco. "He's an amazing dog. Alert." Coco, lying at the door, perked up his ears and growled as if on cue. "He has noticed something now," Balram said.

Coco jumped up and started barking ferociously. "What could it be?" Tara asked, craning her neck.

"Or who could it be?" asked Balram, who had a better view of the gate. "You have a visitor, Tara."

"Why am I having so many uninvited guests?" she muttered.

Balram caught her words and flushed. "I should take your leave," he spoke to GK and Kannagi. GK motioned him to wait as Tara went to investigate the commotion by Coco. She came back with Coco firmly held by his leash. "GK, can you take him inside? Mr. Thomas is here." GK trembled at the sight of an excited Coco. Noticing him hesitate, Balram took the leash from Tara and led Coco inside.

"Mr. Thomas is my grandmother's lawyer," Tara explained to GK and Kannagi. "Mr. Thomas, these are my friends."

"Hey! Do you remember me?" GK asked Thomas. "You gave me a ride up the mountain one day."

Thomas feigned ignorance and turned to Tara. "Can I talk to you in private?"

"Whatever it is, you can say in their presence. They know everything," Tara replied.

Thomas hesitated.

"We'll step out, Tara," Kannagi suggested, pulling GK with her as she walked out of the living room.

"You haven't replied to my messages." Tara remained mute. Thomas sighed. "Listen, Tara. If you don't take any decision, sooner or later, the villagers will learn the truth."

"How?"

"There are so many ways," Thomas sneered.

"Other than my friends, only you know the truth about my inheritance."

"So, you'll have to choose between trusting your friends or trusting me," Thomas said with a smile that sent cold shivers down Tara's limbs.

"I can't take a decision until I find my uncle," Tara replied in her sternest voice.

"Well then, be prepared to face the consequences," Thomas replied with a sneer that seemed to have pasted itself on his face.

"Are you threatening me?" Tara raised her voice.

The bedroom door opened, and Balram stepped out. He stared coldly at Thomas, who was taken aback. "Oh, you have made new friends, have you?"

With his cold stare, Balram warned, "Mr. Thomas, if Tara is not comfortable with your presence, I suggest you leave."

By then, GK and Kannagi too returned. Thomas glared at all of them. With his eyes fixed on Balram, he spoke to Tara. "Be careful who you befriend, Tara. This is Thomas Uncle's advice." He left in a huff.

"Is that your uncle?" Balram asked in a puzzled tone.

"What? No!" Tara jumped at Balram's implication. "That's my grandmother's lawyer."

"And, may I ask why he was threatening you?" Balram asked as he let Coco outside the bedroom. Coco wagged his tail appreciatively. Tara shrugged. She would not share her problems with someone she had just met. Although, Balram appeared genuinely bothered.

"Alright! Shall we finish our lunch?" GK asked, eyeing his half-eaten meal. They all laughed. GK's innocent question diffused the rather tense atmosphere created by Thomas.

Tara exchanged glances with GK and Kannagi. They needed to find Nilaav as soon as possible.

Balram was, meanwhile, oblivious to the project running in their minds. He continued plying them with questions about their hobbies, jobs, and other activities. He suggested that Kannagi could join Friend Circle as an employee if she wished. "Avantika asked me if I could recommend someone to handle the office. She feels that they would need more help soon."

"Do you understand their business model?" Tara interjected before Kannagi could respond to Balram's suggestion.

"Pardon me?" Balram nearly choked on the food.

"Do you understand what Friend Circle does and how they make money?" Tara persisted with further enunciation

"I am sorry. I didn't expect such a question."

"Why?" Tara's bright eyes shone like diamonds.

Balram averted his eyes. "Hold on. Let me explain," he said as he carried his plate to the kitchen sink and returned with clean hands. He positioned himself comfortably on the couch. "When I arrived at Jomo, I was intrigued by how people could live without the internet. I expected a quaint village with no electricity or basic amenities, somewhat backward. Excuse me for my ignorance. So, with this picture in my mind, I never thought I would hear such a question from a Jomoan."

Tara frowned. She got up in a huff. GK tut-tutted. He turned to Kannagi as they took their plates inside. "Is he flirting with her?"

"What if he is?"

"I feel protective towards Tara. We are her only friends. No relatives, no family."

They were surprised to hear laughter from outside. They saw Coco and Balram on the lawn wrestle for a twig as if it was a piece of bone. Tara sat on the porch observing with a bemused half-smile.

GK whispered to Kannagi, "What do you think now?"

"He is definitely on to something," Kannagi replied with a glance at Tara.

# 30

# The Movement

Not long after the visit from Thomas, Tara received a shocking piece of news from Grandpa Lal. He was selling his house on Jomo and moving to a senior care home close to NewTown. Despite Tara's insistence on staying, Grandpa Lal was adamant. His contention was, of course, his old age and loneliness.

"You are not alone. We are here," Tara said, pointing vaguely around. Her eyes fell on Meenu. "Did she not help you, Grandpa Lal?"

Meenu wiped her brows in indignation.

Grandpa Lal smiled. "She does her best, but how long can she take care of me?"

"Where will you go?"

"Yes, she gave me a solution for that too."

"Who?"

"Their representative, a bright young lady named...," Grandpa Lal scratched his head as he tried to recollect, "Avantika, I think."

Tara was shocked. She sifted through the papers in her hand. The buyer's name was Friend Circle.

"Did they tell you what they'll do with this house?"

Grandpa Lal shrugged slowly. "Avantika told me they might have an interested buyer. The negotiations will take time. The sale will probably happen in two weeks, but I'll move into a senior care centre tomorrow. It's not far from NewTown."

"But—"

"I have made up my mind, dear child," Grandpa Lal said with a despondent stare. "I can't spend the rest of my life perched on this precarious mountain, all alone." Grandpa Lal motioned for Tara to come forward. He ran his hand over her head. "You have done more than what I deserve. You've your entire life ahead. God bless you, lovely Tara!"

"Wait for a week, Grandpa Lal, please?" Tara beseeched.

"What's going to happen in a week?"

"I've roped in my friends to find Nilaav."

"What if you don't find him?"

"I'm going to sell off a portion of my inheritance. I can take care of you, Grandpa Lal."

"What about my children?"

Tara frowned.

"You didn't think of them when you decided to sell this land or move into a senior care home. Then why are you worried now?"

"I'm doing all this with their approval."

Tara stared in astonishment. She argued, reasoned, cajoled, and nearly cried as she beseeched Grandpa Lal to not leave.

Grandpa Lal looked at Tara's earnest face. "Ok, I'll ask them for another week before I move out, and the sale can happen a week after that. Only because you said so." His wistful eyes teared up as he extended a hand of gratitude to Tara.

Tara stood up in haste. She had to meet her friends as soon as possible. If she could decide on her inheritance in a week, she could convince Grandpa Lal to stay with her. As she left with Coco by her side, she heard Grandpa Lal mumble, "Parthan was the naughty one." Of late, Grandpa Lal often mumbled, not making any sense to those around him. Perhaps, he was recounting incidents from his childhood.

Tara met GK and Kannagi the next day at NewTown. "There are two things I am worried about," Tara said as she sipped on her coffee, "My missing uncle and the growing influence of Friend Circle in the Jomoan community."

"Kannagi connected with a friend of your uncle. His name is Sura. We thought he might be helpful, but so far, I haven't received any information from him. He became a bit reticent when he realised that Kannagi was not a girl but a man." GK guffawed.

"What?!"

"I had to take over the conversation because his messages were going on the cheesy path."

Tara frowned. "At his age?"

"Seems like a lonely man," GK said empathetically. "He hasn't crossed any boundaries yet, I feel. Only a bit of sweet talk."

Kannagi cupped her mouth and leaned over to Tara, so that GK could not hear. "I think he is a bit jealous."

Tara chuckled and nodded in agreement. "So, are you still chatting as Kannagi, or as yourself?" she asked GK.

"I told him that Kannagi is my sister and that she often leaves her account open, so I replied to one of his messages by mistake."

"And now he chats with you?

"Yes, mostly about sports or movies."

"Lies, lies, and more lies," Kannagi said aloud and tut-tutted.

"Listen, I am going to tell him the truth soon," GK assured Tara with a glance at Kannagi, "but why are you so bothered about Friend Circle?"

"Well, don't you understand? The Jomoan community, which never came under the sway of fake news, fake influencers, or celebrities because we don't have the internet, is, all of a sudden, lending their ears and time to an organisation. An organisation we know nothing about."

"Who's coming under their influence? Me? Or your friends Nat and Freddie? We are not Jomoans." GK tried to provoke.

"No, it's not about you. Grandpa Lal is selling off his house and the attached land."

"Grandpa Lal? Is that his land or yours?" GK asked with an impish smile.

Tara glared at him. "It is his land. As far as I know, no one lives on our estate. So, Jomoans don't have a claim on my inheritance."

"Woah! Listen to the heiress speak!" GK shouted.

"I went through the documents that Thomas gave me. The land is on the other side of the mountain. There might be some agricultural land, I believe, but it is abandoned. The rest is a part of the jungle. I haven't explored that area so far."

"Ooh! Mysterious inheritance!" GK exclaimed again.

Tara looked around nervously. "Stop shouting."

"I don't understand your concern about Friend Circle."

"I feel they want to gain acceptance within the community and would do anything to build a friendly façade. My fear is about people like Raman. If he learns about my inheritance, he'll want to know what I intend to do with it. Or worse, he might oppose whatever plans I might have."

"What plans do you have?"

"None so far."

"Aren't you jumping several guns when you say they might oppose your plans?"

"You don't know Raman like I do," Tara pointed at GK.

"That's true, but your fears are baseless."

"You forget that Raman didn't like my uncle. Rather, when I met Nandu at his house, Raman behaved as if he hated him."

"Hated who? Nandu?"

"Nilaav, my uncle, you duffer," Tara poked GK's head, trying to jog his brain cells. Kannagi giggled as GK squirmed. "I am sorry, Kannagi, but your man needs a shakeup sometimes to make his brain work," Tara said with a grimace.

"Sometimes?" Kannagi asked with a laugh.

"Is Friend Circle capable of such a deep influence?" GK asked sceptically.

"What kind of influence?" asked a voice from behind Tara. While GK and Kannagi smiled at the owner of the voice, Tara cringed. She recognized the voice well now. By a strange quirk of fate, she met this guy every other day. GK pulled up a chair from the adjoining table and set it between himself and Tara. Balram said a quick hello to everyone at the table before sitting. "So, what kind of influence were you talking about?" he asked, turning towards GK. Tara leaned back and stared at GK, daring him to share their conversation. GK cleared his throat and, looking at Tara, said, "We were discussing Friend Circle and their growing influence."

"What about it?" Balram was genuinely curious.

"Jomo, as you are aware, is a protected community—" Tara began.

"Why? What's so special about Jomo?" Balram turned to Tara.

Tara fumbled for words. "It's a mountain, not just a village. It has a jungle. It has wildlife. It has numerous waterfalls during the monsoon." She paused. "Aren't these reasons enough to protect Jomo?"

Balram thought for a moment. "How does the presence of an organisation like Friend Circle threaten all that you mentioned?" Tara gaped. She had no answer.

Balram was right. There was no reason to suspect Friend Circle of jeopardising Jomo's ecosystem. "What you are really worried about is Jomo being discovered by others, by outsiders," Balram said with a knowing nod. "It's your home. You want to keep it for yourself. It is such a beautiful place. Why not let others enjoy its beauty too?" Balram prattled on before GK could warn him that Tara was not taking it well. Her nose bristled with anger, and GK could figure out that Balram's presumptuous accusations did nothing to improve his standing with Tara. She stood up. "I have work to do. Thanks for coming, Kannagi," she said as she turned.

"Tara, wait!" GK jumped up.

Balram sat motionless, too surprised by Tara's reaction.

"What are you doing?" GK hissed into Balram's ear as he followed Tara out of the café.

"Why is this guy around whenever we discuss important stuff?" Tara asked indignantly as GK caught up with her.

"You can't blame him this once. I invited him."

Tara stopped in her tracks. "For what?!"

"I thought you might want to expand your Circle of Friends."

# 31

# Shaky Grounds

Still miffed with GK for inviting Balram, Tara did not contact GK or Kannagi for several days. She wanted to check on the progress of their online search for Nilaav and his friends, but that would mean breaking her silence, and she was in no mood to give in. She decided to take up the search on her own. If GK and Kannagi had the internet, Tara had sturdy legs. One day, she set out in the morning after declaring a holiday for her tuition students.

Her first stop was at her old school, not the dilapidated one where Nanban had marked his territory, but the one that most children from Jomo attended at its foothills. She wasn't sure if the school existed during her uncle's youth, but she remembered her dad talking about how he walked to the quaint school building at the foothills and trudged back uphill at the end of the day. When she met the headmaster, he recognized her immediately. "Aren't you Ayyappan's daughter?" Tara nodded, overwhelmed at being identified as her father's daughter. Rarely did people mention her parents these days. When someone did, her memories filled her heart and eyes.

"I am Vasu, his classmate," the headmaster nodded with a sincere acknowledgement of Tara's loss.

Tara explained that she wanted anything connected with her uncle, Nilaav.

"I thought he was a closed chapter as far as your family is concerned."

"He was… he is," Tara swallowed a lump in her throat, "but if there was some way to confirm whether he is alive or not…."

Vasu nodded, understanding the meaning of her unsaid words perfectly. "I recollect some stories about him."

"What about the school records?"

"This school did not exist then. I doubt if many children from Jomo completed their studies."

Disappointed, Tara walked around the building, remembering her school years. In the modestly-sized playground outside the school, the children played random games while the sports teacher chit-chatted with a friend. As she strayed beyond the gate, a child came running to tell her that the headmaster had summoned her.

"Me?"

"Yes, you," the child channelled her inner disciplinarian to sound serious and important. She followed to ensure Tara went to the headmaster's room and nowhere else.

"Sir?"

"Ah, yes, Tara. I remembered something. I have heard stories about how brilliant your uncle was. He used to make weird contraptions or take things apart. Also, he would often say that he wanted to make it big in Bombay because your efforts and talent do not go waste there."

"How did you learn all this?"

"Stories that float from generation to generation. Most people remember and share only the bad stuff, his quirks, his rebellious nature, his nightly jaunts, but I try to remember the good in people," Vasu said with a smile.

Tara thanked him. As she left the room, she saw the girl who had summoned her. "What's your name?"

"Thennal."

"Lovely name. Thennal, you have a very wise headmaster. Listen to his stories and learn from them." Thennal nodded in agreement.

"She is an orphan. She stays at the orphanage," said the headmaster, who had followed Tara out of his room.

Tara looked at Thennal with renewed interest. She was about the same age as Tara when she lost her parents. The girl's eyes shone brilliance, but Tara felt the pain hiding behind those intelligent eyes. It was the bewilderment, anguish, and confusion of a child left to fend for herself in this world. Tara had suffered those emotions since childhood, but buried them deep inside her heart. If she managed to find her uncle, she would have someone to offer her solace, or so she hoped. What the headmaster shared was comforting but not helpful. A brilliant mind who wanted to make it big in Bombay. Thousands and millions of brilliant minds boarded trains and buses to Mumbai every day, hoping to make their dreams come true. How would she ever find her long-lost uncle? She did not even know his real name.

Coco, as usual, ran up to her and danced around her legs when she reached home. However, Meenu, unlike her usual self, stood on the porch with a nervous wringing of her hands.

"What happened, Meenu?"

"I'll not come to work from next week."

Tara raised a quizzical brow. "Got a better job?"

"Not yet, but I'll get it soon."

"Then why are you leaving? You can continue until you get another."

Meenu explained how it was becoming more and more difficult for her to climb up from the foothills. Since her children studied at the NewTown public school, she thought a move would make life easier besides a chance to find a new job. She suggested that her cousin could help Tara with the household. Tara shook her head. She wasn't sure if she could afford any help with how things were going, but she promised to think about it when Meenu explained her cousin's dire situation.

"Is Chellan going to stay here with your mother?"

"No, we are all moving together."

"What about your house and your land?"

"We're selling it."

Tara turned around to face Meenu, wondering if she had heard it right. "You'll sell off the land where you toiled away all these years? I don't believe it."

"None of us can toil now. We are all getting older and frailer. I have to work somewhere to send my children to the university. They said I could get a better job—" Meenu bit her tongue and stopped talking.

"Who? Who said that you could get a better job?"

"Some friends."

"Who are you selling your house to?"

"I have not found a buyer yet."

"And you plan to move to NewTown by next week?"

"Yes, Kutty."

"Is that why you asked Grandpa Lal to—" Tara stopped mid-sentence. She felt the ground beneath her move. Coco whined, growled, and cowered under the table. The shaking continued for a few seconds, and they heard vessels clatter onto the kitchen floor.

Tara and Meenu did not wait any further. They ran out. Tara pulled Coco by his leash. When they reached outside, Meenu shook Tara by her arm and pointed to the hill behind Tara's home. Rocks rolled down the slope at a frightening speed, and the trees fell with them in a cloud of dust. "Kutty! Those rocks are headed towards Grandpa Lal's house!"

They stared at the tumbling rocks in a frightened daze.

# 32

## Loss and Guilt

Jomo village congregated at the square piece of land where the food festival used to be held decades ago. Now the village gathered to grieve. The landslide occurred without warning and without any apparent reason. The sky, though dull, showed no signs of breaking down. Not a drop of water trickled from above, yet the rocks lost balance and tumbled straight to Grandpa Lal's home. They not only tumbled but trampled and pounded everything on the way. Grandpa Lal was lucky to not come in its path, but misfortune comes in many ways. A part of the roof gave away, and the house shook with the intensity of the hit. Grandpa Lal lost his balance. He hit his head against an iron bar that stuck out from the rubble. Two days in the hospital, where he was kept alive through a ventilator until his children arrived, did not help to revive his diminishing life force. The children understood as plainly as the doctor that their father's life was hanging by a thin thread. Yet, they discussed for more than a week about the next steps.

While Grandpa Lal lay in the hospital, Tara cried her heart out. She declared a holiday for her students and rarely left her house. Meenu postponed her plans to move from Jomo and stayed with Tara until late evening. Nights became intolerable for Tara. She would dream about the collapsing mountain, her grandmother's bizarre words echoing in her nightmares. Even Coco could not make her feel better. Coco reminded her that she would have lost him had she left him at Grandpa Lal's place like she usually did. It was a stroke of luck that Coco was home when the boulders crushed Grandpa Lal's home. Or perhaps, Coco would have warned Grandpa Lal or alerted the neighbours. And then, she would ponder about Grandpa Lal's misfortune. The cycle of grief, relief, and regret would begin all over again.

She would have languished at home if not for Kannagi and GK, who arrived at Jomo with clothes packed for a week and refused to leave her side. GK was working on his bookstore plans, and he trekked down and up the mountain every morning for a few hours of internet connection without complaining once. On a couple of evenings, they were joined by Balram, and Tara found his presence soothing. Balram had a subtle sense of humour which he occasionally employed to lighten up the conversations. As opposed to GK's goofiness, Balram's sedateness, under the circumstances, gave Tara the space to reflect and accept the reality of the incident. So, while Kannagi and GK tried to make the most of their days at Jomo, Balram stayed by Tara, sometimes pulling her into conversations, at times waiting silently but more often speaking to her without any expectations.

"The monsoon will be on time this year, they say. I bet the mountain gets smothered in green during the season. This year, I hope to have a place to sit and watch the rain. If you don't mind, of course," Balram said with a smile. Tara remained quiet, her thoughts flitting back to the monsoons she enjoyed the most. The rainy evenings when she would lay her head on her mother's lap and wait for the radio to be switched on. Balram continued his rambling talk about monsoons around the country and his parents' bungalow by a lake in Nainital. Tara did not stop him, realising that he did not expect her to respond. His chatter helped her forget the events of the past few days until Balram chose the wrong question to fill in the silence.

"Were you close to Grandpa Lal?"

Tara closed her eyes. She had dreaded this question since the day of the funeral. Tears streamed down her cheeks.

"I am sorry, Tara. I didn't mean to—"

Tara went inside, leaving Balram to stew in his guilt.

"What happened?" GK asked as he stomped up the steps to the porch.

"I happened to mention Grandpa Lal." Balram shook his head and opened his palms in despair. GK frowned. Kannagi, who had followed him in, reprimanded Balram. "You should have known better."

GK consoled Balram. "Not your fault. You are doing pretty well. Kannagi and I can be noisy sometimes, but you offer some calm."

Balram shrugged. "I guess it's because she doesn't have a family."

"Yes," GK added, "Grandpa Lal was close to them, and he was the one who knew about her long-lost uncle."

Balram shifted slightly in his seat. "Uncle? Tara has an uncle?"

GK had blurted out more than he should have. "Has or had, no one knows where he is," he said with a shrug. "But that is not what is bothering her." He changed the topic. "Grandpa Lal was about to sell his house and land to Friend Circle. He was planning to shift to a senior care home in NewTown."

Balram shrugged. "So?"

"Tara did not want him to leave the place. She was planning to bring him here."

"Oh!"

"And now she regrets that she did not do it sooner because Grandpa Lal would have been saved."

"Or, he would have shifted to the senior home and been safe there," Balram remarked.

Tara stepped out. She had washed her face and appeared calmer. "There is no point in discussing the past," she said in a low voice. Her friends heaved a collective sigh of relief.

# 33

# The Return

Munaf lay with his hands tucked behind his head and stared at the fan rotating morosely on the dull brown ceiling. It is not just disappointing to visit places you forever wanted to explore, only to realise that it was the most boring place ever; you feel cheated. A young Munaf would stare at the Mythili lodge on his way to school and wonder about the food they served or the type of people who stayed in the rooms above. Now that he was in Mythili, he found the food mediocre and the lodge shocking to his sensibilities. Of course, his sensibilities underwent a sea change when he travelled overseas. The lodge and restaurant were now remnants of the uninteresting, sad life that he left behind for greener shores.

Munaf was at NewTown to attend an awards ceremony. He would give out the awards and say how happy he was to represent BEFOR, an app that NewTown residents embraced with gusto within a few weeks of its launch. He was here to announce that Hunt Technologies was happy about NewTown being the forerunner in signups. Although, it was not. Ronny Shikari wanted to thank NewTown residents. Hence, the team ensured that the numbers supported NewTown's unique distinction on paper. That morning as Munaf lay on his bed, he planned to skip the oily breakfast at the restaurant and the minor detail that he belonged to NewTown. He got up with a jerk as his phone rang. Ronny Shikari was on the line.

"How's it going, Munaf?"

"Everything is fine, Sir. I have to present a few awards for community and social service. Then, in my speech, I'll thank the residents on behalf of BEFOR."

"That sounds great. Make sure they appreciate that BEFOR is sponsoring the awards."

"Of course, Sir. The banners are up around the town. Sir, may I ask you one question."

"Go on."

"Why so much focus on NewTown?"

The silence at the other end made it clear that Munaf had crossed an unstated line of corporate policy. Yet, Shikari sounded calm when he spoke. "You'll learn soon, Munaf. Until then, keep our flags flying high at NewTown."

"Sure, Sir."

As soon as Shikari disconnected, Munaf dialled a number.

"Patsy?"

"Yes, Munaf? Up so early?"

"You forgot," said Munaf with a smile. "I am in NewTown today for the award function."

"Oh yes! I forgot!"

"Shikari called. I asked him why he was focusing on NewTown."

"Oops!"

"He said that I'll learn soon."

"Hmm. Be careful, Munaf. That man is wily as a fox."

"I got it, Patsy. Wish me luck!"

"You're in your town, Munaf. You're already lucky."

Munaf chuckled in response.

"So, are you going up to Jomo?" Patsy asked.

"I know how eager you are, but I am not going today."

Munaf disconnected the call and was ready to go for the ceremony within the hour. He would be picked up by a local politician named ARN. Munaf remembered the family that ARN belonged to, one of the wealthy families of NewTown, but he didn't recognize the chap. He must be one of those who studied in the city nearest to NewTown.

The award ceremony did not go as well as he thought. ARN spoke too much. He blathered so much about BEFOR that it was difficult to say who worked for BEFOR, him or Munaf. Finally, he allowed Munaf to speak a few words after the awards were given. Munaf kept it brief. It was an hour before noon and the disinterested audience yawned away to glory. When he mentioned BEFOR, ARN began clapping, and the crowd followed. It was a thunderous applause for BEFOR. Shikari will be pleased when he watches the video. Munaf surveyed the gathering with pride. His smug smile froze when he saw a familiar face.

A face that he wanted to forget but could not. The man still walked around in a disgusting vest with his shirt open.

Munaf ended his speech and sat down, trying not to stare at the man long enough to make eye contact. Even now, he felt the man had the power to oust him from the function and NewTown. He was nervous when he stepped out of ARN's car at Mythili lodge. He turned around to check if the disgusting man was about, but he wasn't. Munaf went up to his room. It was ridiculous. Nearly two decades after the incident, the man could provoke the same fears in Munaf's heart. The fear of humiliation hung heavy in the air around him. Someone knocked on the door, and he jumped. "What? Who's there?"

"I'm sorry, Sir, but I wish to meet you. I'm a huge fan of BEFOR." Munaf opened the door. "Hi," said a young man, gasping for breath after climbing the stairs. The man held out his hand and flashed a friendly smile.

"I am GK," he said by way of introduction.

"GK?"

"Gerald Kevin is my name, but everyone calls me GK."

"What can I do for you, GK?"

GK noticed the shabby room and asked, "Sir, may I invite you to the pride of NewTown, our modest café, a few hundred metres from here?"

Munaf smiled. "Anything to get out of this dungeon." GK led the way.

"I admire BEFOR so much," GK said as soon as they finished ordering food.

Munaf observed GK with interest. "What do you do, young man?"

"I am a bookseller."

"Interesting!"

"Well, I plan to be a bookseller. I have arranged for the funds. Now it's about getting the place on lease and setting up the store. BEFOR has been a lifesaver. Your app helped me connect with like-minded individuals around the world."

Munaf coughed to hide a snicker. "How can you be so sure about people you've never met?" he asked.

GK was astonished. "Sir?"

"I mean, I represent BEFOR, so I realise how impactful it can be, but I'm trying to understand the user's perspective."

"I signed up a few days after ARN discussed it in one of his meetings."

"He holds regular meetings?"

"Yes, he's a local leader. At least, he considers himself to be one. Now people believe him."

"Fake it till you make it, huh?"

"I used to work at his uncle's textile shop... as an accountant," said GK between mouthfuls. "Then I lost my job."

"Oh?"

"It's a long story, Sir."

Munaf leaned back. "I have time."

GK narrated his unfortunate experience on top of Jomo and the following incidents without mentioning why he trekked up the hill.

"Are you saying that BEFOR helped you in that difficult state?"

"No, Sir. I was on BEFOR much before that."

Munaf waited for GK to continue. GK hesitated. "I'll just say that I had many personal issues and found the perfect solace in BEFOR."

"Be wary of the Internet, GK."

"You sound exactly like my friend, Tara."

"What does she say?"

"It's not what she says, but how she lives."

Munaf raised his eyebrows quizzically.

"She lives on Jomo, so—"

"Tara from Jomo is your friend?"

"Yes, do you know her?" GK asked in surprise.

"Someone mentioned her."

"Someone from Jomo?"

Munaf hesitated. "No, someone I met years ago."

"Who? Is he old? Can you share his details?" GK asked. Munaf stared at GK, bemused by the volley of questions. "Well, Tara is an orphan, but she is looking for...," GK stopped mid-sentence. "Never mind."

Munaf smiled. He had some news to share with his friend now. He finished his coffee and the lip-smacking breakfast. "Thanks for the invite, and let me pay," he said as he got up and left for the payment counter in a swift, seamless motion.

"No. Wait, Sir!" GK called out as he tried to catch up with Munaf.

Unseen by both Munaf and GK, Balram sat at the table behind them, pretending to read the newspaper. The open sheets hid his face, and his local attire camouflaged him among the regulars at the café. But anyone who saw his face would identify him as a nervous outsider.

# 34

# Insinuations

Balram paced around his living room. It was increasingly difficult for him to visit or meet Tara without being too obvious. She spoke and shared more often with him than before, but he had a long way to go. Munaf's appearance and his camaraderie with GK added to the challenge. Balram recalled the conversation he overheard at the café. Why did Munaf say that he knew Tara? He had to convince Tara in the coming days before anyone else could get to her, and the best place for that would be Friend Circle. He checked the time. He had an appointment with Friend Circle at six.

When Balram reached the Friend Circle office, he saw a crowd milling around the area. The number of members increased after the landslide. Friend Circle became the new sanctuary where people found solace after the disastrous incident. Many were worried whether their houses were safe. Some Jomoans found an excuse to sell their property to move further downhill. Friend Circle handled all such requests—buyers, sellers, landowners, tenants—everyone with or without a house to live in began visiting the office.

Avantika was pleased but also a tad unsettled. "This was supposed to be a centre for community welfare. Now, I feel I am running a real estate agency. People have nothing else to talk about," Avantika whispered to Balram.

"Is the dog park free?" Balram asked.

"Yes! That's one area we've developed because of Tara's dedication. Besides, she's been working in the garden as well. Tara is great with plants," Avantika beamed like a proud parent. "She resolves people's doubts about gardening and distributes saplings and seeds."

Balram entered the garden behind the Friend Circle office and saw a different Tara. Relaxed, happy, and friendly, she was in her element among the plants. Balram thought of an idea. If it worked, he would score on both fronts—professional and personal. He unleashed his dogs in the dog park, where he saw Coco sniffing around the bushes. He walked towards Tara but was stopped by GK. "Hey, Balram! Good to meet you here," GK said with a friendly thump on his back.

"Yes, it's been a while. How are you doing? Have you been coming here often?"

"Not really. Trudging up the hill is not my cup of tea. Unless Kannagi motivates me, I don't come up here. Tara seems to be doing well by herself."

Balram nodded. GK and Kannagi rarely visited, which was good for him. He chuckled to hide his thoughts. "You mean unless Kannagi forces you?"

GK gave a sheepish grin. "I can't help it, buddy. Kannagi's family has disowned me completely because of my unemployment. I am vying for a part-time job as a sales assistant at a bookstore in the city, but I am competing with fifteen other applicants. For a sales assistant job. At a bookstore in a nondescript little place fifty kilometres away from NewTown. And if I get the job, it's a two-hour commute. What do I get in return? A mere pittance."

"But you have worked in accounts before. Can't you get a better job?"

GK shrugged. "I might, but I want to work inside the store to get some experience."

"Oh yes! How about your bookstore?"

"I have a few signatures pending from the investor. So, it has got stuck for a while."

"What signatures? Oh! I almost forgot. You'll get them by tomorrow." GK stared at him in surprise. Balram coughed to hide his confusion. "Avantika told me just now."

"I spoke to her when I came in, but she didn't say anything. Strange woman."

"What has happened to him?" Balram asked, pointing to Coco. "He has lost a lot of weight, and his coat has lost its sheen."

"Hmm, well, he is a bit soiled," GK said. "As far as the weight goes, it is better this way. The dog jumps on me whenever he gets a chance. Now he can't pin me down so easily." Balram laughed uneasily. "By the way, check out my new online profile. I am building it up for my bookstore when it launches." GK shoved his phone screen under Balram's nose.

"Looks authentic," Balram nodded appreciatively.

"What do you mean? It IS genuine. I have decided on the name—GK Bookstores."

"Quite original, and I was talking about the interiors in the photo. The bookshelves, they look authentic."

Aah, well. Kannagi clicked it at her cousin's house. He has a good collection. Do you understand why GK?"

"Your name?" Balram asked hesitantly.

"Gerald and Kannagi." GK replied with a broad smile. "I am headed off to discuss my pending cheques with Avantika. See you around."

As soon as he left, Balram whipped out his phone to send a message. He then approached Tara, who was teaching a lady how to weed. "Busy?" Tara smiled as she heard his voice. It was a tired smile, but her face lit up beautifully. "The garden makes you happy, I suppose."

"I like it here."

"Hey, what's wrong with Coco?"

"You noticed? He was spoilt earlier by all the dog food from the shelter. Now he has to be happy with what I make at home," Tara said with a chuckle. "And I haven't been able to give him a good scrub lately. Dog shampoos are expensive."

"Tell me about it," Balram grimaced. "I'm waiting for my neighbours to return from their vacation. So that I can hand back their dogs. They are burning holes in my pockets."

Tara flashed a weary smile.

"Is there anything wrong, Tara?"

"What's wrong?"

"You look happy but tired."

"Nothing. A few kids dropped out of my tuition. So, it means less income. Meenu has quit. She has shifted with her family to the valley after selling their land. I don't have much help around the house now. Good, in a way, because

I couldn't afford Meenu with the kids dropping out from my tuitions."

"Why did they drop out?"

"Their families are moving to the valley. They can't come all the way to Jomo. The valley has a good network. Teachers conduct online tuitions."

"That's the normal world, Tara. Jomo is stuck in a time warp." Tara glanced up sharply. Balram bit his tongue. It did not come out the way he intended. He paused for a while before asking, "So, how are you managing the household?"

"Like I always did," Tara shrugged. She walked across the garden towards a precipice on the hill. "Except, earlier, I had Cheeru and Meenu to help me, and food was never an issue. Chellan worked the vegetable garden well and we had poultry." Balram stepped forward gingerly. Tara stood dangerously close to a drop that ended on a bunch of rocks a few metres below. Anyone who jumped would undoubtedly lose their limbs, if not their life. "We survived the pandemic. I was fifteen. We were cut off from the valley. No one would climb up to Jomo, and we never left our homes. We had no internet, which meant no constant pandemic updates and no reason to panic. Food was from our garden. There was no rice for nearly six months, but we were fine."

Balram patted Tara gently. "Shall we walk back to the garden? We are dangerously close to the edge." Tara turned around without a word. "You miss your old friends." Tara did not reply. Balram followed a few steps behind but stopped in his tracks when he heard a whisper. Was he imagining, or did Tara really say she needed to find her family? That would be a challenge for Balram, a spoke in his plans. Where did this family appear out of nowhere? There was only one way to know. He invited GK to the café in NewTown for an evening coffee.

The cafe had all kinds of patrons. Some swung by for a quick bite on their way to work, while others stayed on for a people-gazing, newspaper-reading, or self-reflection session. Some let their tea or coffee become cold as they exchanged stories. The regulars glanced at the two men sitting at the corner table. Balram and GK sat engrossed in their conversation.

"I am telling you all this only because I can see that you are genuinely interested in her," GK said. Balram did not comment. "She is a strong girl, orphaned at an early age. She has gone through a lot in life. She doesn't have any friends other than Kannagi and me. Grandpa Lal was close to her grandmother, and probably, his memories were the final thread from her childhood. When it snapped, it left her unmoored. She went through another cycle of grief."

"She also told me that her housemaid was leaving Jomo with her family."

"The two families have depended on each other since the beginning of Jomoan time."

"And she has an uncle she has never met and never knew. How is that possible?"

GK sipped his tea and grimaced over its coldness. "Her grandmother's lawyer was the one who told her."

"Who? That fibber, Thomas? He might be a good lawyer but is an equally good liar." GK looked up sharply.

It appeared that Balram was closely acquainted with him. Balram shifted in his seat uneasily as he said. "I know him from work."

"Ok," GK ordered a new cup of tea. "I can't drink it cold," he said with a smile. "So, where do you work? We have shared so much but you never mention your work."

"Well," Balram hesitated, "It's just another boring job."

"I have seen boring jobs," GK scoffed. "So, are you into sales?"

"No, I am not. I used to be in sales once upon a time. Right now, I handle operations."

"Are you a doctor?" GK asked in surprise.

Balram guffawed despite the growing uneasiness of having to talk about his work. "Not that kind of operation. The kind where you manage the day-to-day running of a company."

"Hmm," GK thought for a while and asked, "but doesn't that mean you have to be at work every day?"

"Yes," Balram replied, then realised his mistake. "I mean, I need to keep track, which I can do on my phone," he said, waving his mobile device.

"That's a good job. Does it pay well?" GK asked.

Balram hid his sneer behind his coffee cup. "It's enough for me."

"Well, if you are serious about Tara, you need to raise your income," GK said in all earnestness. "Don't think I am not aware," GK said with a nod. "You are not that good at hiding your feelings."

Balram nearly spat his coffee out. He fiddled with his phone. Messages from work kept crowding his phone screen. "So, has Tara tried to find her uncle?"

"We have been trying but not much luck."

"Can I help?"

GK leaned forward and scanned the cafe before speaking. "Tara does not want anybody to know. So, if she learns I have told you, she'll kill me. You can search discreetly if you wish, but don't tell her."

"Do you have any point where I can start?"

"I'll tell you what we know so far."

GK and Balram split their ways after a short while. Balram walked to the bus stop intending to take a bus to Jomo. Walking the dogs was no longer a valid reason to visit Friend Circle. His neighbours will arrive the day after and he'll return the dogs. He had to visit Friend Circle on some other pretext. He bought a packet of dog food and a bottle of dog shampoo for Coco. Before he could board the bus, he received a call. It was his boss.

"Any updates, Balram?"

"I'm trying."

"You've been trying for some time now."

"There are sensitive issues. I cannot be hasty."

"I heard that you're too friendly with the girl."

"I bet that fibber Thomas would have said something."

"I hired him for a reason." Balram gritted his teeth. "Have you surveyed the area yet?"

"Yes, I have, but as I said, the village has many more residents than we expected. We cannot risk so many lives."

"Make haste, Balram. I cannot wait much longer. If we can't get hold of the land, we proceed without it."

"I'll try."

There was a pause at the other end. "Why is it so noisy?"

"I'm standing by a busy road, waiting for the bus."

"The bus? I thought we gave you a car?"

Balram rolled his eyes. "I have my personal car in my garage, but I don't use it. People of Jomo don't trust others easily and, least of all, those who drive up that mountain. Besides, the men are using the jeep you gave me. They have been busy. The company vehicle serves their purpose perfectly."

"Balram, don't disappoint me. This project is time-sensitive."

"Get Thomas out of my way, and I hope Munaf doesn't spoil my plan."

There was a loud guffaw from the other end. "Munaf is there to take care of BEFOR. He won't interfere, but don't blame me if he does. He has a better work ethic than you and a better grasp of what works locally."

Balram disconnected the phone before his boss could say goodbye. The conversation riled him. This was the fifth organization he worked for, and he felt the worst. Nothing he did was enough for the boss, and without any warning, he was put into a role much below his pay grade. Although he knew the role was necessary for a project the company was undertaking, he was never clear about what was expected of him. His boss was so secretive about the project that he couldn't speak of his role in the organisation. His only incentive was the plum role as national head once the business was set in motion. Having worked consistently to climb up the corporate ladder, when his boss dangled that juicy carrot of a highly-paid position and the associated perks, Balram accepted it without qualms. Before reaching the carrot, he had to befriend a few people. The friendships served one purpose—to help him further his cause and achieve success in the mission that his boss assigned to him. However, having lost nearly all his friends to his career, he pondered if the universe would ever forgive him for making friends and abandoning them. Tara, GK, and Kannagi were all good people.

Will his life continue to be empty even after meeting such good friends?

To score some brownie points with his boss, Balram had to convince Tara to move out of Jomo, and he had to convince her as a friend. He wanted to do it the right way. His thoughts returned to his conversation with GK, and he absentmindedly whipped out a picture from his mobile phone. It was a picture of Tara that he clicked when she was working in the garden. She had an aura of contentment. He yearned for the same calmness.

Was there some truth in GK's insinuations? Was he serious about this girl?

# 35

# The Storm

The sky darkened as the bus wound its way to the foothills of Jomo. It was four in the evening, but the clouds completely shrouded the sun and sky, leaving the passengers nervous. The bus driver did not wait for his mandatory tea from the corner shop after his passengers disembarked. He turned the bus around as soon as it got empty, nearly missing the people who wanted to board. Everybody wanted to reach a safe place before the impending downpour. A storm would set back his itinerary by a day if he got stuck. In the gloomy weather, Jomo greyed out like a place of doom. Balram shuddered as he noticed the tall peaks juxtaposed against the darkening sky. He would be safe if he could reach Friend Circle before the sky collapsed. A lingering doubt about the necessity of the climb made him hesitate. A fellow passenger passing him urged him to get home as early as possible. "The Gods are angry. Can't you see?" he asked, pointing upwards.

The bus heaved away from the stop, consuming the waiting crowd like a small snake swallowing its prey. There was no turning back now. Balram had to run up as fast as he could. It started raining before he could reach the dirt road that led to the narrow tabletop where Friend Circle had its office. The scarp to the west of the tabletop sloped gently.

The men from Friend Circle had cut out the dirt path for the vehicles to drive up to the office. Balram hiked up the trail. He was nervous. Loose debris flowed down with the rainwater as he navigated tricky parts of the slope. In a few minutes, the downpour became heavier, and the visibility reduced so much that Balram could only spot his feet. The road beyond was a blur. He was drenched and had to wipe his eyes continuously to keep them open against the sharp raindrops battering him. Despite the intensifying downpour, Balram covered a lot of ground with quick strides as the slope flattened out.

On approaching the office, he heard shouts from inside. "Get out! Get out as fast as you can!" yelled someone. A hoard of people came rushing out, running helter-skelter. He caught hold of one of the Friend Circle employees.

"Why are people running?" he yelled.

The man pointed to the hill that stood like a wall to the east of the tabletop. The wall was crumbling. The rocks and boulders tumbled down the slope towards the handful of houses on the tabletop.

Tara ran out with a whimpering Coco and a terrified Avantika close behind. "Run!" she screamed as soon as she saw him.

"Where?" he asked.

"Down the slope, where else?" a horrified Tara yelled at him.

"No, wait, everybody, follow me!" Balram waved his arms to catch their attention. Some stopped for a second, but others continued to run for their lives. Balram grabbed Coco's leash and gestured to Tara and Avantika to follow. He ran into a path that cut into the steeper side of the scarp.

"Where are you going?" Tara yelled.

"To a safer place. Follow me!"

Tara ran to catch up with Balram while Avantika followed hesitantly. She was not used to the terrain. Coco whimpered as he stayed close to Balram's legs. Tara lifted him up into her arms. He had, indeed, lost a lot of weight.

The wind howled, the rain poured with a deafening roar, and the jungle rejoiced and wailed simultaneously. A scream pierced through the noisy air. It was Avantika who slipped and pushed against Tara's legs. Tara fell forward on top of poor Coco and into the mud. Balram winced as he heard Coco yelp in pain. Tara got up and regained her balance while Balram helped Avantika. Coco lay in the mud, and Tara's heart skipped a beat. When she picked him up, he whined and snuggled closer to her. He was shaken but alright.

Balram led them further down after making sure that Avantika could walk. "I am sorry for rushing you both, but the faster we reach there, the safer we will be." Behind them, they could hear shouts and raised voices.

"Perhaps, the others followed us. Should we wait?" Avantika asked hesitantly.

Balram shook his head. "They'll catch up with us. We need to get away from this storm." Soon, Balram slowed down. A metal signboard trembled in the wilderness.

Diffident black letters in yellow paint said, 'Work in progress. Trespassers prohibited.' While Avantika did not bother about the sign, Tara stared at it for a few minutes until the rain made it difficult to see her fellow hikers. Coco jumped out of her arms.

What kind of work was in progress on Jomo without the knowledge of Jomoans?

They walked further, one behind the other, as the path became narrower. Coco ran ahead as if following a scent while Balram held onto his leash. Avantika followed, lost in her thoughts, teetering at times, prompting Tara to stay close to her. She could topple any moment. "Avantika," Tara said, "I urge you to remove those heels." As soon as Tara uttered the words, Avantika's right foot slipped, kicking a flurry of pebbles into the air. Tara huffed as she supported her. Avantika whispered a quick sorry and removed her heels. Walking barefoot was more troublesome as she kept yelling and limping all the way, but at least Tara did not walk with the constant fear of seeing Avantika tumble into the jungle to the right. The more they walked, the more confident she was that they were walking straight into Nanban's region and who knew if any other animals were lurking around. She craned her neck to check if Balram was slowing down. He walked ahead at a quick but steady pace. The thought of Nanban lurking somewhere in the branches above scared Tara. She peered instinctively into the void but had to shut her eyes briefly. The rain obscured her vision as she navigated the treacherous downhill path. In a few minutes, the rain increased in intensity. "Should we take shelter somewhere?" Tara yelled to Balram.

Balram raised his hand and waved. "What does he mean?" Tara asked Avantika, who kept uttering strange words and making funny noises.

"How do I know?" Avantika asked, evidently not in a good mood. "He never tells us anything!"

"Us?"

"The Friend Circle team. He thinks he is the boss."

Tara stood frozen in the rain. "The boss?" Before Avantika could reply, Balram called out from below. "Over here!"

# 36

# Revelation

Avantika and Tara followed the path where Balram stood with Coco, pointing to a clump of trees ahead. "There's a cave here. We can take shelter." He waited for them to pass by him while Tara took the lead. She was puzzled. How does a rank outsider at Jomo know more about the mountain than her? The cave, which she did not know about, was large enough to hold the four and at least six more. Tara listened for voices above the din of the rain. "We could've brought a few others with us," she said as she rubbed her hands and legs to keep them warm. They were soaking wet. Coco was miserable.

"Where did they all go?" Balram wondered.

Avantika remained quiet. Her face was glum. She tried climbing over a cave rock to stay away from the wet floor. But not being used to any climbing endeavours, she slipped. "Ouch!"

Tara helped her stand up. "My ankle hurts!" Avantika cried. "Stay put for a while," Tara said to her calmly. But Avantika could not be consoled. "I should have taken up that opportunity in Mumbai instead of coming here to this God-forsaken place. Why did I ever agree to this?" She glared at Balram. Tara was bemused. It appeared that all of Avantika's rage was centred on Balram. "Do you have nothing to say?" Avantika asked him. He squirmed and glanced at Tara, who pretended to ignore. "We'll be out of here soon," Balram said, though his voice betrayed his lack of confidence.

"Out of this cave or out of Jomo?" Avantika asked, her eyes piercing holes into the moist cave air. She regarded Tara with scorn. "Hats off to the Jomoans! How do you live here? Why are people not ready to leave this place?"

"Avantika!" Balram raised his voice to make her stop.

"Why are you yelling at me? I'm here because of you. Had you not asked me to join your bizarre team, I would've been in my favourite city rather than this stupid jungle on the mountain."

Tara stared at Balram. He turned towards the entrance to the cave as if to leave. There was no way he could step out into the rain. "What are you talking about?" he hissed without turning around. "Oh, right! Jomoans aren't aware of your connection with Friend Circle, are they?" Avantika was not finished. She was bristling with anger. Her hurt ankle added fuel to the fire. "Listen, Tara, Friend Circle came here to persuade Jomoans to leave this mountain," she blurted. Tara raised an eyebrow and stared at Balram. He had his back towards them. "Balram is the project lead, overseeing Friend Circle's functioning. He provides the investments too."

"Investments?"

"Yes, the funds needed to buy off the land from the Jomoans. Also, other projects that we undertake to help people."

"I appreciate some of the work you do, Avantika. Like the community garden, helping people like GK with their dreams. He got the confidence to go ahead with his bookstore project only because of Friend Circle," Tara admitted.

"That money, too, came from Balram," Avantika revealed.

Balram defended himself. "It's not me. It's the company. My boss approves the investments."

"Admit it, Balram. The ultimate aim is to get the Jomoans out of here."

"But why?" Tara asked.

"Yes, why would we want to oust the people from their land?" Balram asked Avantika with a tinge of exasperation.

"Beats me," she said. "I have no answer to that, Tara, but you be careful, girl."

Tara contemplated, and then it struck her. The signboard on the way to the cave. "Balram, how did you find this cave? I was not aware of it, and I have explored every inch of the mountain."

"Even the jungle?" Balram asked.

"NO, not the jungle. Who in their right mind would walk into the jungle full of wild animals?"

"I haven't come across many," Balram said with a wry smile.

"So, have you been exploring?" He nodded in reply. "Then you might have seen the signboard we passed on our way to the cave?" Balram lost his bravado when he heard Tara's question. He gulped before he asked. "What signboard?"

"The one that said, work in progress, trespassers would be prosecuted."

"Was there one? I didn't notice."

"Really? Because the way you confidently turned from the signboard onto the path leading to the cave, anyone would think that it was a landmark."

"I was only following my instincts. I've been to the cave once before while exploring."

"You have a sharp memory. To remember a road or a landmark in the city is not difficult, but to be so familiar with the jungle, either you've spent some time in the jungle or have been on this path many times. So, what is it? Have you been in a jungle, or have you been to this place many times before?" Tara persisted.

Balram scratched his head. "I've been here once," he repeated, though his eyes betrayed the truth that his tongue wished to hide.

"Avantika, what do you know about Friend Circle?" Tara asked.

Avantika was nursing her ankle. "Well…"

"I can tell you more about Friend Circle, Tara," Balram said with a forced smile. "Let's get to a safer and dryer place after the rains stop. I can tell better stories when I am warm, well-fed, and clean." He punctuated with a forced chuckle. Tara looked at him with disdain. "Let's get out of here first, Tara. I promise I will explain their work to you."

Tara looked at Avantika, who averted her eyes. “Is he your boss?”

“No, but he thinks he is.”

“Who is your boss?” Tara addressed her question to Avantika.

“I report to the marketing head at our headquarters.”

“Headquarters?”

“California.”

“I, too, report to someone at the headquarters,” Balram said, not to be outdone. Avantika glared at him.

Tara’s suspicion grew by the second. What could bring a company headquartered in California to Jomo?

# 37

# The Calm

Tara shivered under her blanket. Her body reacted violently to being drenched for five hours. At home, she could hear the sound of the ambulances charging up the mountain. She was too tired to find out what happened to the Friend Circle's office. After she dried Coco with a towel, she changed into dry clothes and flopped onto her bed. Coco lay whining and whimpering at her feet. She didn't know if he was ill or hungry. She lay there in delirious fatigue, opening and closing her eyes at intervals. It was cold and dark. She pulled her blanket closer to her body. Something warm rubbed against her. She twisted her arm around to investigate and heard a whimper. Good old Coco. Both snuggled together for the night. She woke when she heard a commotion outside her window. She got up with a hobble and lurch to open it. It was GK. "Open the front door," he said. She trudged slowly to the front door. Kannagi stood outside with another person. They ushered Tara to her bedroom, fed her some liquids, and before she knew she was fast asleep.

"Thank you, Doctor," said GK as he handed over the doctor's bag. Coco lay on the floor, too tired to wag his tail. The doctor recommended that they take Coco to a vet. The usually alert dog was a shadow of his former self. After the doctor left, he turned to Kannagi with a sad face. "I don't know what to do with a dog. Should I carry him?"

"Why don't you call Balram? He's good with dogs."

GK ran outside and down the hill slope to a spot with a strong signal. He returned with the joyous news that Balram agreed to bring a vet.

"He's such a great guy."

"He is, and I can see that you are trying hard to convince Tara as well."

"She'll come around slowly."

By the time Balram arrived with the vet, GK and Kannagi had whipped up some food in the kitchen. They thanked the vet for making the trip up to Jomo, but one look at Balram told them that all was not well. He was too tired to drive the vet down the mountain. GK accompanied the vet instead. "Make him comfortable," he said, waving to Kannagi and pointing to Balram. However, Balram did not wait for Kannagi's hospitality. He promptly lay down on the couch in the living room. Within seconds, he was fast asleep. Kannagi sat outside on the porch and waited for GK. She jumped up as soon as he arrived to tell him about Balram's abnormal behaviour.

"What is wrong with these people?" GK asked, eyeing a limp Coco lying on the floor and an equally fatigued Balram sleeping on the couch.

After six hours, Balram sat up and opened his eyes. He stood up but swayed to the toilet instead of walking. Tara stepped out of her room in bewilderment. "How long have I been sleeping? And what's wrong with Coco?" Tara asked as she sashayed towards him.

"You both appear to have a bad hangover," GK remarked.

"Coco needs to be shown to a vet," Tara said helplessly.

"Already done. The vet has given him medicine," GK replied. Tara patted Coco on his tummy and received a meek wag of his tail in return. "He's wagging his tail. He'll be up and about soon," said Balram.

"You? What are you doing here?"

GK was aghast at Tara's contemptuous tone. "He was the one who got the vet."

"GK called me," Balram explained, though his voice betrayed his guilt.

"Get out of my house right now," Tara said calmly.

GK and Kannagi stared at Tara like she was a ghost. "What are you—?" GK began. "Isn't this my house?" Tara shot back. Her voice was steady despite her shaking legs. She held onto a chair for support.

"At least let him eat something, Tara. He is as ill as you," Kannagi reasoned.

Tara glanced at Balram. Kannagi was right. He did look ill. "Ok," Tara nodded, "but promise me you won't talk." Balram smiled wryly and pretended to zip his lips. He was happy to remain quiet and lap up the food on the table. After dinner, GK and Kannagi insisted that it was too dangerous for Balram to drive down the mountain in the rickety ambulance he borrowed from a valley resident. Tara relented. For GK, she opened up her grandmother's room while Kannagi shared her bedroom, but she did not utter a word to Balram, who snuggled up on the only comfortable sleeping place in the living room—the couch.

In the morning, both Tara and Balram were much better. Coco, too, walked around the house, albeit listlessly. When Tara stepped out of her room, Balram was already polishing off the last bit of gravy from the chicken curry. "Tasty!" he kept repeating but as soon as he saw Tara, he stood up, "I am leaving. Won't disturb you further." He quickly cleared up and said goodbye to Kannagi and GK. Tara remained mute.

"Go freshen up, Tara," said Kannagi.

"And then you will tell us what exactly happened to you," added GK.

# 38

# The Proposal

The clouds cast a shroud over the valley. A gentle breeze blew from the west, bringing intermittent rain shards. Tara, GK, and Kannagi sat silently on the porch sipping from their cups. A gloom encroached upon the mountain and their thoughts.

"I can't believe it. Balram was lying to us all this while," GK remarked in a sad voice.

"He hasn't told us the truth even now," Tara added.

"Did he refuse to answer your question, or was he giving excuses?" Kannagi asked.

"He did not utter a word. Of course, I could not force Avantika to tell me more. She was already under duress."

"She might talk if we meet her when she is in a better state," GK suggested.

"And you found nothing more about the company?" Tara asked as she shifted her leg to accommodate a sleepy Coco.

GK shook his head. "They have a rudimentary website with Friend Circle splashed all over the page. Badly designed, I would say. Like something they put together in a hurry."

"What about the company structure?" Kannagi asked.

"Nothing. Only a bland paragraph about their mission, vision, and values, which Avantika played back to us when we first met her."

GK was staring at Coco as he spoke. "Hey, Tara! I hope the vet he brought was not a fraud. Coco is absolutely out of sorts."

Tara laughed. "No, I inspected the medicine. I have seen Nat and Freddie use it at the dog shelter. I have never had to give it to Coco, though. He has always been such an active dog." She sighed as she patted Coco on his belly. He gave a thumping wag of his tail.

"Better, although lazy," GK said, nodding in approval.

"I need a steady income," Tara announced, "and I won't get one if I remain on Jomo."

"Don't tell me you plan to sell this place because that's exactly what Friend Circle wants!" Tara looked at GK sullenly. "You are the one who told us about their intentions," GK added in surprise.

"Yes, but my income is falling. What do I do?"

"What about your inheritance?"

"My uncle—"

"Nonsense! Do you know if he is alive?" GK asked. To his surprise, Tara started crying. Tears flowed incessantly, and Kannagi took her inside. She came back after accompanying Tara to her bedroom. "She is tired, GK. What are you doing?" GK remained unperturbed. "Kannagi, do you remember what that man at the Friend Circle office said when we reached there? He said that Avantika and the new girl ran down the hill with their boss."

"Yes, I remember. We thought down the hill meant Tara's house, so we came here."

"How did you know that I needed a doctor?" Tara stood at the door with clearer eyes but cheeks still stained.

"That was a coincidence," GK said, "We received messages from people asking for help to clear the rubble. We thought someone might need medical help too. I was talking to her cousin, and he's a doctor, so we brought him with us."

"That was helpful."

GK continued to ponder aloud. "So, the man working in the yard of the Friend Circle office knew that Balram was the boss," GK said, chewing his lips. "He probably knows more about the company, and might know about the work-in-progress signboard."

Kannagi asked, "Why would he tell us?" Tara sat down in the chair, too tired to think. She merely pointed a finger at her and said, "That!"

A menacing growl rose from the floor beneath their chairs, making them all jump. It was Coco. He was sprawled underneath two chairs, but his head was up and ears cocked. His eyes were set on the gate in the front. They had a visitor. Thomas strode in with a broad smile plastered on his face and a briefcase swinging from his hand.

"This is all I needed to recuperate," Tara muttered. Kannagi patted her arm reassuringly.

"So, you were in the thick of things yesterday, yes?" Thomas asked as he proceeded with a cautious eye on Coco. He continued to growl but did not get out from underneath the chairs. Tara did not offer Thomas a chair, nor did the others relinquish theirs, so he had to stand. "I heard about the disaster at Friend Circle yesterday. It is so sad. But I heard that the locals warned them. Many ran away on time."

"One boy got trapped," GK informed.

"Yes, unfortunate," Thomas said as he wrestled with his briefcase. With some effort, he extracted the documents that he was rummaging for.

"So, Tara, you are not in a comfortable position, financially—" Thomas began.

Tara interrupted, "How do you know that?"

"I was your grandmother's lawyer, and by way of inheritance, I am yours too," Thomas said with a devious smile that sent shivers down Tara's spine. "I have a proposal for you to consider. It is from a company named Hunt India. They are interested in buying your land. All of it, if you wish, or if you want to retain this house and surrounding land, they are fine with that too. Their main demand is the land towards the east of Jomo Mountain, which I am sure you have never visited, and the other areas to the north of the mountain."

"Do you have any idea how much you have inherited?" GK asked in between gasps.

Kannagi pressed Tara's shoulder and glared at GK to keep quiet.

"In return, they offer you a blank cheque. You can put in whatever figure you want or get a job if that is what you want."

There were audible gasps from Kannagi and GK when they heard Thomas. Though unimpressed with the proposition, Tara lost some of her resolve when she heard about the job. A job was what she needed. But why was this company Hunt India so eager to get hold of her land?

"Thomas Uncle, I am shaken by yesterday's events. I am unable to think clearly at this point. But you are right. I need financial help, and a full-time job would help immensely...," Thomas beamed at Tara's response, "...but I need time to think."

Thomas frowned. "Do you still carry hopes of finding your uncle? I hope not," he said, shaking his head.

Tara pondered before she spoke. "I need time until I recover fully."

"Okay. I leave on that high note. Good to meet your friends, too," Thomas said and walked away.

Then, as if he remembered something important, turned around swiftly and said, "Please do not show these documents to anyone, Tara," he said, including Kannagi and GK in a nervous swing of his eyes. "This is supposed to be a secret proposal by Hunt India. I shouldn't have said all this in front of your friends."

# 39

# The Dilemma

Coming back from Tara's home, a wrung out Balram staggered into his living room. He badly needed another nap. The conversations from the last two days played and replayed in his mind.

When GK called, he could barely walk. He sounded flummoxed by Coco's situation. Knowing that GK and Kannagi would be at Tara's, gave Balram the confidence to face her. At the cave, he couldn't offer any explanations. Tara walked off in a huff when he refused to speak about Friend Circle. What could he say? He didn't want Avantika to be a witness to anything he said. Any conversation between Tara and himself felt personal to him. Whatever he spoke could be relayed to his boss. Besides, Avantika considered him as a competition. He was acutely aware of Avantika's propensity to tattle even when he supported her up from the cave. The climb became doubly tiring because of her.

However, Balram's real competition was someone else. Munaf was also vying for the top post. Besides, the job was not what it was propounded to be. Ronny had fooled them all. He was beginning to grasp the reason behind Avantika's reluctance to work in Jomo. The job was sucking the life out of them. The mountain, the Jomoans, and his boss all loomed large on the horizon like giants coming to devour him.

He lay down for a nap, but his phone rang. His rage on being disturbed by the call was defused when he saw the number. It was his boss.

"I hope there was not much damage."

"The assessment is incomplete, but the fence is gone, and the garden is a mess."

"How about the building?"

"Not much damage. It was only debris from the nearby hill. The actual landslide happened in an uninhabited area."

"And yet, the team ran away?"

Balram fumed at the nonchalance. "What do you expect when people sense danger to their lives?"

"But you said that the actual landslide happened elsewhere."

"That was our good fortune."

"Anyway, I have some good news to share. While you were busy saving your friends, Thomas did his best. Your friend agreed to consider our proposal. So, sooner or later, the area will be under our control."

"What?"

"Why are you so surprised?"

"I requested you to keep Thomas out of this."

"He got the job done. You should be happy."

"But—"

"You get to play the good cop." Balram could sense the scorn in his voice. His fingers tightened their grip on the phone.

"But don't go above and beyond your role of a good cop to play a good Samaritan. I learned that you led some of your friends to one of the pitstops used by our men."

"Who told you?"

"So, it's true?" A chilling cackle emerged from the phone, and Balram pulled the phone away to reduce the impact on his eardrums. "I should congratulate Thomas for his credible sources. It helps to have a local connection."

Balram thrust a fist into the air and winced immediately. His shoulders were still sore. "Thomas again."

"Use him, Balram, use him well. You must learn the local dynamics if you have your eye on the big post. Don't remain a city boy. It won't help." Balram rolled his eyes. "By the way, Munaf is doing a better job as well. He has the ears of a local leader," his boss added.

"Who's that?" There was a pause at the other end. Balram thought that the line got disconnected. "Hello?"

"I'm here."

"Which local leader?"

"You should tell me, Balram. Munaf is being secretive."

Balram sneered. "I thought he was your 'loyal' man."

"He was, but now I'm not so sure."

"So, I'll keep an eye on him, while Thomas keeps an eye on me?"

The sinister cackle broke through again. After the call, Balram tossed and turned despite the physical tiredness. One call from his boss was enough to drive his sleep away. What bothered him the most was Tara's acceptance of their proposal. On the one hand, he understood that it was the right option for her, but on the other hand, he knew that it would kill her to leave Jomo.

# 40

# Corporate Cross-Connections

GK circled outside Balram's house on a cycle. As per Kannagi's suggestion, instead of barging into Balram's house, he cycled past the house and into one of the posher lanes away from the main road. Avantika lived in one of the houses on this lane. When he rang the bell, it was opened by a lady. She stared at him, expecting him to introduce himself. The cycle on which he arrived did not impress her.

"Is Avantika here?"

"Ma'am is at the office."

"Office?"

The lady nodded in response. From Tara's accounts, Avantika had sprained her ankle, so it seemed bizarre that she would trudge up the mountain in that state.

"How is she now?"

The lady's expression softened. "Not good, but she won't listen. Said she will come back for lunch."

"Come back for lunch? From her office?"

The lady studied GK suspiciously. "Who are you?"

"I've met her at her office."

The lady nodded. "Then you can meet her there."

"But have they cleaned out the debris?"

The lady realised why this man was acting so odd. "Not that office. The one nearby, she said, pointing towards the end of the lane."

GK asked in surprise. "She has an office here?" The lady shot another quizzical look and shut the door in his face. He cycled to the end of the lane and reached a junction. One road led to the town centre. The other led towards a dimly lit tree-lined path. He knew the town centre like the back of his hand but had not seen any new offices in the vicinity. He cycled away from the town centre. The wooded path narrowed into a residential lane and, after a few metres, widened into a grassy area. The place was familiar. Beyond the green patch was a house. He walked towards it but stopped a few metres away. "Nat and Freddie's dog shelter!" he exclaimed as he recollected meeting Tara and Coco at the centre. Outside the house, nearly marred by a tree, hung a board that said, "Hunt India." He called Kannagi in excitement, but the line wouldn't go through. He called Tara but heard the same beeping sound from the other end. "These Jomoans are crazy!" he said as he swiped to get his camera active. As soon as he clicked a photo of the board, he was greeted by a burly security man.

"Sir, you are not allowed to click photos of the premises," he said in a tone that reminded GK of his sports teacher at school. The voice was enough to get his knees knocking together.

"I am sorry, but the tree is so beautiful," GK said, pointing to the tree behind which the board hid shyly.

The security man scrutinized GK with some curiosity. "Do you make reels?"

GK was taken aback. "Make what?"

"Reels?"

The man's voice lost its edginess as he continued. "My grandson makes reels and uploads online," he said with a proud swish of his thumb to show how he uploads. "He'll be famous one day."

GK nodded. "How old is he?

"Thirteen." The man added wistfully, "I want to see him become famous."

"Can I meet Avantika?" GK asked, changing the subject.

"Yes, you can wait in the reception area," the man pointed to the entrance to the erstwhile dog shelter.

As soon as GK entered, Avantika came hobbling on a crutch.

"Oh, that looks bad. Tara told us that you sprained your ankle."

"It's a hairline fracture. The doctor advised me to take complete rest but work beckons."

"Hmm. I wasn't aware that Friend Circle had an office in NewTown."

"This belongs to Hunt India, our parent company. I am sorry, I can't offer to take you around like we do at Friend Circle. Here we have more corporate-y stuff," Avantika said with a wry grin.

"Tara told me some inexplicable things from your discussions in the cave. I thought she was delirious!" GK said with a chuckle.

Avantika glanced around nervously. "So, what brings you here?"

"Aah, yes! The reason for coming here is also connected with what Tara told me."

Avantika's face fell. She now rued her outburst in the cave. "About what?"

"I learned that it is Balram who arranges the investments in various projects, so I assume he is arranging the funds for my bookstore too?" Avantika nodded hesitantly. "In that case, can I speak to him directly instead of involving you in the discussion? Balram is a good friend, and I am sure he would understand me better."

Avantika drew in a deep breath and let it out slowly. She was quiet for a while, considering various possibilities, then led GK inside. "Let's talk in private." She hobbled slowly, so GK had all the time in the world to run his eyes around the space. The shelter was now a modern office space with glass-enclosed cubicles. Something he saw in a corner made him do a double take. In the far corner of the area, beyond a couple of glass walls, he saw a name embossed on one of the doors.

"Come!" said Avantika holding a door open for GK.

"Please," said GK, allowing her to enter first so he could squint through the glass walls again. Yes, he was not mistaken. He saw a familiar name on the door.

Avantika offered him a chair. "Listen, whatever I said in the cave, was supposed to be between the three of us. I didn't realise that Tara would share it with you."

GK shrugged. "Now that I know...."

Avantika opened a file. "Everything is in order in your file. Balram has done whatever he could to get you a good deal. Now it's time for you to work towards your launch. Have you fixed a date?"

GK nodded. "I have." Then he leaned forward as he asked. "So, Balram. Is he your boss or your peer?"

Avantika shut his file and sighed. "He was in the project before I joined. In fact, I was contacted by Balram with an opportunity to work for Hunt India. At that time, I think they had not conceived Friend Circle. I am not sure. I was supposed to join another project, but the day after I joined, I was asked to visit Jomo and told that my office would be on top of that excruciating mountain." Avantika gathered ire as she spoke.

"I understand. That mountain gets on my nerves, except for the picturesque locations. My followers like them," GK added with a sudden grin.

Avantika frowned. "I am a technology person. I was told that I would work on a technology project, but I ended up reporting to the marketing head at Hunt India."

"So, what is Balram?"

"Pardon?"

"What is Balram's designation?"

"He is touted to be the next business head for Hunt India, but right now, he is a regional head."

GK wanted to ask more, but someone poked their head around the door and said, "Munaf Sir asked if you would be free for a quick meeting later in the day."

Avantika nearly stood up. "Yes, sure." When the head disappeared, Avantika leaned forward as if sharing a secret. "Now, Munaf is someone who should be the head. He gets things done."

GK nodded as if he understood. "I should leave now. Good to know more about your organisation," he said, glancing around the office as he stepped out. On the way, he met the man who had poked his head into Avantika's room minutes ago. He was speaking on the phone. The name Munaf was mentioned again, and GK wondered why it sounded so familiar.

## 41

# The Treasure

GK went online to investigate Hunt India's credentials. The search led him to Hunt Technologies, a multinational corporation headquartered in the United States. It was puzzling that an organisation like Hunt India was interested in Jomo and Tara's inheritance. It was more baffling that a multinational should set up shop in a small place like NewTown and spread its presence in an inaccessible mountain village like Jomo.

His growling tummy reminded him that he had not eaten since morning, and it was well past lunchtime. He rounded the corner of the junction to his old favourite, the Corner Tea Shop. The crowd outside confirmed that it was teatime for the world, not only GK. He pedalled across the junction and parked his bicycle near the shop. A jeep passed, announcing that ARN would hold a public meeting the next day at the textile shop. He overheard someone say that the previous BEFOR session turned out to be good because there was a representative from the company itself. That's when it struck GK. Munaf was the one who had represented BEFOR the other day. The same name that he heard at Avantika's office. So, he was not mistaken when he saw the name BEFOR embellished on a glass door at the Hunt India office.

Munaf, Avantika, Balram, Friend Circle, BEFOR, Hunt India, and Hunt Technologies were mysteriously linked, and they were all in Jomo for a reason.

Since he could not connect to Tara or Kannagi's phone, he left a message. "Will come to Jomo tomorrow. Need one more day to figure out a few things." GK went straight to the hotel where he had first met Munaf, but he had vacated. He asked the manager if he knew where he might have gone. "He told me his work here is done, and he is returning to the city." GK couldn't revisit the Hunt India office to enquire about Munaf. Avantika would not entertain him.

Back at home, GK scoured the internet for Munaf. His public profile indicated that he worked for Hunt Technologies. He was last mentioned in an article about a new project five years ago. Hunt Technologies was a considerably large company, but its main business was sourcing raw materials used in the electronics industry. Why would they create an organisation like Friend Circle and set it up in Jomo? Their website did not mention Friend Circle at all. If the idea was to be socially responsible, wouldn't they have blown their trumpet, like any other corporate does? What was their mission? Too much thinking always made GK sleepy, but he had one last activity for the day.

GK logged in to BEFOR to chat. During a chat about bestsellers, he asked if the chatter knew about Hunt India and Hunt Technologies.

*ZE_3478: Yes, I know.*

GK sat up alert. *Did you know that they also ran Friend Circle?*

*ZE_3478: Yes.*

*I should have asked on BEFOR before.* GK chuckled at his clever use of words.

*ZE_3478: You can ask anything on BEFOR.*

*Is BEFOR connected to Friend Circle?*

*ZE_3478: No*

The reply appeared in milliseconds. Did he misunderstand some other name to be BEFOR? After all, he had seen the name through several glass walls. His weak eyes could have played tricks on him, but he heard Munaf's name twice at the Friend Circle.

*Do you know someone named Munaf? He works at BEFOR.*

Astonishingly, the application showed an error message, and GK got logged out automatically. The glitch was not resolved when he logged in at four am the following day. The only way to learn more about BEFOR, Munaf, and Hunt India, was to attend ARN's boring meeting.

GK arrived in time at the tent outside Radha Textiles. ARN threw his weight around. He was in a huff. The snacks were not ordered, and ARN sounded like a politician scolding his coterie. He wholeheartedly believed in the adage of fake it till you make it.

"Do you know who is attending the meeting today?" he shouted at a group of men cowering along the side lines.

GK hoped that it would be Munaf. He could talk to him about Hunt India, but to his utter surprise, it was none other than his good friend Balram. He watched with his mouth wide open as ARN introduced Balram as a senior person from BEFOR and said he was there to answer any questions the crowd might have about the chatting application. A murmur rose from the crowd and reached such a crescendo that ARN signalled his men to manage the menacing noise. It was befuddling. Were people not happy with BEFOR? ARN raised his hand and asked a person from the crowd to express their reservations. What followed was a torrent of complaints regarding the lack of control over who uses the application, its addictive nature, and the fact that they did not know who to reach out to in case they had doubts. Balram, who stepped onto the dais with his head held high, appeared flustered. Many in the crowd were belligerent enough to bash a BEFOR employee if they happened to meet one. GK gasped as he saw someone lurk behind a group of men standing at the back of the tent. It was Munaf. He sidled up to him and asked in a whisper, "Aren't you supposed to be representing BEFOR?" Munaf jumped at the question. When he saw GK, he put his finger to his lips and pointed towards the dais. Balram was about to speak. He had a confident stance but what came out of his mouth was a nervous admission of BEFOR's many failings.

Munaf shook his head slowly. "The people are going to eat him up. I can't watch this." He made his way slowly to the entrance to the tent.

GK tried to stop him. "Wait!"

Munaf turned around and gestured to GK to follow him. They walked out and into the café across the road.

"Isn't he your colleague? Shouldn't you support him?"

"Well, that's his assignment. He is eyeing the big post, and our boss wants to test him."

"But Avantika said—"

Munaf leaned forward with interest. "What did she say?"

"She mentioned that you are the real boss."

Munaf chuckled in response. "She was always at loggerheads with Balram. I am only a small fish in this big organisation. Balram is more qualified than me, but he is younger and lacks experience."

"So, you don't consider him as your competition?"

Munaf leaned forward. "Are you here to learn about your friend's career prospects?"

GK shook his head. "He was my friend, but now I am not sure."

"Why so?"

"Some events that happened...," GK began, then stopped, "...but you all work for the same organisation. We don't know who to trust. Does Thomas work for you, too?"

At the mention of Thomas, Munaf smirked. "Now I understand. Is this about Hunt India's proposal to Tara?"

"How do you know? Don't tell me you all are aware of Tara's...," GK hesitated.

"Inheritance?" Munaf added.

GK stared in stunned silence. "So, there is something shady, isn't there? The company is after the Jomoans for the land. Why?"

Munaf asked him to wait as he stepped out to make a call. GK sat dumbfounded for a few moments, then gathered his wits and followed Munaf. He stood not far from the café, engrossed in a telephone conversation. Over the din of the traffic, GK caught a few words.

"It's time, Patsy," Munaf said on the phone.

Munaf ended his call and approached GK. "Come, I have something to tell you. Rather many things."

GK sat across Munaf with a pen and notepad. "Hunt India is the subsidiary of Hunt Technologies. We specialize in raw materials for the electronics industry." GK nodded. He knew that much.

"What is needed in abundance for the electronics industry?"

GK shook his head.

"Lithium."

"Ok," said GK, unable to comprehend where the conversation was headed.

"Jomo has a hidden deposit of Lithium underneath it."

GK's eyes widened as he realised the import of what Munaf said.

"And Hunt Technologies wants to get hold of it," GK stated with disbelief.

Munaf nodded. "They have been exploring based on a hunch. A few months ago, they struck gold. Their hunch proved to be correct, but Ronny grew greedy. He wanted to explore the whole mountain area. And hence, he began his project to acquire as much land as possible."

"Is that why Friend Circle happened?"

"You have caught on quick."

"But why use such an insidious way?"

"He couldn't create too much noise. For one, the government would be alerted, and secondly, any competitors would swoop down on Jomo. He wanted to achieve as much as he could in stealth."

"The government will know at some point or the other."

Munaf scoffed. "By then he would have built enough relationships at the right places. He has recruited pawns, knights, and rooks, all the way to the kings and queens."

"Why tell me all this now? Are you trying to enlist me as well into your schemes?" GK asked, his voice quivering slightly.

Munaf smiled. "Meet me here tomorrow at the same time."

# 42

# The Plunge

The morning sun refused to show its face as Tara and Kannagi set out with a backpack each. "What a dull day!" Kannagi remarked as she peered into the sky. Tara agreed. Kannagi glanced at her sideways and asked gently, "Are you sure you want to do this? You're wobbly."

"That's because of the lack of exercise. The outdoors will do me good."

"I am worried that today is as bad as the day we had the landslide."

Tara puffed out some air. "That's why we have an emergency kit, food, extra clothes, and raincoats in our bag. I only wish I could bring Coco, but I can't manage him. He'll keep tugging at his leash. Though my boots are made for the rain, they're not good for running."

Kannagi shrugged. "We should have waited for GK."

Tara scoffed. "Haven't you seen GK climb over to my house? He'd be a bundle of nerves, not to mention out of breath!"

Kannagi surveyed the terrain. She thanked herself for remembering to wear sneakers when she joined GK at Jomo. Her parents were not keen on her stay, but they relented when she told them about Tara. There was no news from GK after a cryptic message that said—I will explain when I am there. He did not mention where he was and when he would be back. Meanwhile, Tara grew restless. Thomas's words kept ringing in her head. She had to figure out the extent of her inheritance before taking any decision she might regret later. Tara prepared for the trek but asked Kannagi to remain home with Coco if GK returned. Kannagi, however, refused to let her go alone into the jungle. Tara was exhausted after her rainy ordeal on the day of the landslide. Moreover, Kannagi presumed that the trek would be a walk around a well-maintained estate that Tara had apparently inherited. A few metres downhill, Kannagi realised how wrong she was about the walk in the park.

The land was green and fertile, but the terrain was not made for a leisurely stroll. Kannagi paused as the slope became trickier, with tiny round pebbles that became roller skates beneath their feet. One misstep could take them fast and furious into the jungle. The dense jungle covered the mountain slopes and the valley, so it was difficult to say where the valley began. One could be hurling themselves onto treetops without realising how tall they stood.

Tara scanned the map in her hand. The markings were based on what her grandmother's ancestors thought to be uninhabited but fecund land. It gave the lay of the land, as described in her grandmother's will.

"Tara, are you sure you want to do this alone?"

Tara turned to her in surprise. "Are you going back?"

Kannagi shook her head.

"Then I'm not alone. We're doing this together, aren't we?"

Kannagi nodded in confusion. As far as she was concerned, both she and Tara were alone in the jungle. She crossed herself as a mark of protection like GK often did when he had to face her family. The slope changed its gradient upwards. Kannagi panted for breath, but despite being in a recuperative phase, Tara showed no signs of struggle. As the trees around them became denser, the sky grew darker.

"Does it rain more heavily in the jungle?" Kannagi asked.

Tara stopped to think. "One would have to be moving to experience the difference, either from the village to the jungle or back. Even when we move, how do we know whether it is getting more intense? It could also be the raindrops from the leaves," Tara said, pointing to the branches above.

The trees were now so close to the path that the branches formed a tapestry with different shades of green and brown and tiny chinks randomly placed to let in the light. That morning, the chinks were ineffective in illuminating the path for them. The verdant roof became darker as they went further. The sky itself had a cloud curtain. Tara cautioned Kannagi that the next stretch was steeper and that they would be better off with a staff in their hands. She strayed into the wooded parts looking for sturdy branches that may have fallen off the trees. Kannagi had her heart in her mouth as Tara was merely a few metres away from the edge. She gasped as Tara neared the precipice. "Wait!" she yelled and scampered to where Tara stood. Unfortunately, the slope was too much for her, and she stumbled onto Tara. Their collective weight took them closer to the edge. Tara held onto a nearby tree and stopped herself from tumbling over. With one hand, she held Kannagi, who held onto dear life, clutching a thorny scrub near the tree.

"Phew!" said Tara. "Why did you do that?"

"I was afraid you might get too close to the edge and fall over."

Tara steadied herself. "Let me show you."

Kannagi asked in terror. "What? What are you doing!?"

"Come on!" urged Tara.

As Kannagi stood up shakily, Tara held her hand and led her toward the edge marked by thick roots and scrawny bushes.

"Look!" she said.

Kannagi peeped over the bushes nervously.

"See?" Tara said. "It's not really the edge yet."

Kannagi smiled with relief. "I thought that—" Before she could say, what she thought, Kannagi fell over the bushes and onto the slope beyond, rolling over the roots, dry leaves, rocks, and pebbles until she hit a wide tree trunk. She groped with her hands because she was too afraid to open her eyes. Something fell onto her arm. Her left arm hurt under the weight. It was Tara. She coughed as she spitted out mud, wood splinters, and dry leaves. She quickly heaved up to a kneeling position. Kannagi sat up against the tree trunk, nursing her arm. She grimaced. "It turned out to be dangerous after all."

"It was not until...." Tara stood up cautiously.

"Until?"

Tara's vigilant eyes roved in all directions. "Until someone pushed us."

"What? Are we in danger?" Kannagi questioned, quaking in fear.

Tara shook her head. She was not going to abandon her exploration just yet. "I might have been mistaken. These jungle floors are slippery when it rains."

A drizzle moistened their path as they walked ahead. "How far before the rain catches up?" Kannagi asked.

Tara studied the map. The tumble that they took a while ago had sullied its edges. She ran her finger along a line in the map. "This, I believe, is the edge of the forest. Beyond this is the valley. We are nearing the edge." Kannagi held the map with trembling fingers. There was fear in her eyes. The shock of the tumble remained. "Don't be scared. We turn to the north just before we reach the edge. Here." Tara traced the line upwards on the map. "As we go further north, we'll reach a stone temple."

"Temple?" Kannagi's eyes widened.

"That's what this map says. One of my ancestors built it there, I assume, to mark the northern boundary. We can then move back to the west. I know this place," Tara said, tapping at the leftmost corner of the map. "This is close to the village square where we hold meetings. So, if I go further to the east from there, we'll reach where we started." Kannagi hobbled as she walked ahead with the map in hand. She took a few steps forward, turned right, and turned the map around. "How do you make sense of this drawing?" she asked in exasperation. Tara chuckled. "I've roamed around this area as a child, but the place that I haven't been to, is here," she said, pointing to the temple icon on the map. Tara peered into the dense foliage. "That's the densest part of the jungle. That's Nanban's stronghold."

"Nanban?" Kannagi whispered, half expecting Nanban to hear.

"Let's hope we don't meet him."

"Was he the one who pushed us earlier?" Kannagi asked as she followed Tara. The drizzle quickened, and sharp slivers of water poked their skin. Tara paused. It did not help to have a terrified Kannagi for company, so she lied. "No. I don't think anyone pushed us," Tara said, wearing her raincoat, "but thanks to the tumble, we discovered that tree and got these sturdy branches," she said as she stabbed the ground with the knobbly, twisted staff. The rain increased in intensity, and the foliage carried tiny scoops of the rainwater. "How far is the temple?" Kannagi nearly yelled. The soaking forest created a din. "Doesn't matter," Tara replied without looking back. Kannagi stared at Tara in awe. Until today morning, Tara was fatigued and tired, but as soon as she decided to explore the mountain, she became a changed woman. Kannagi couldn't keep pace with her as Tara buzzed about the house, packing the essentials for the trip. With the temple close at hand, Tara displayed double the energy she had when they started. Suddenly, Tara stopped and turned towards Kannagi with a finger on her lips. Kannagi's foot froze in mid-air.

"What?" she whispered.

Tara paused and listened. The rain and the dense foliage ensconced them from all sides. A barely visible trail on the ground emerged amidst the trees. Tara turned towards Kannagi and whispered, "I heard footsteps!"

Kannagi let out a gasp. "Nanban?"

Tara smiled despite the situation. She shook her head. "Human footsteps," she said in a low voice. "I wish Coco was with us right now. He would have warned us."

Kannagi gasped. "Human? Then what is—"

Tara shushed her. She placed her palm behind her ear to convey that they should listen. Kannagi did not hear anything. Tara motioned for her to start walking. They took about twenty steps before Tara stopped again. This time there was no mistake. Kannagi, too heard footsteps and voices. Before Tara could speak, Kannagi dashed through the trees.

"No! Wait!" But Kannagi was in no mood to wait. She ran like her life depended on it. "Wait! Kannagi! Don't run! It's dangerous!"

To Tara's surprise, she heard the sound of running feet behind her. She swivelled, but the trees and the rain lashing at her face marred her vision. She turned around and gasped. Kannagi had disappeared! As she lunged forward, her feet hit a thick tree root, and she stumbled, grabbing onto thin air. In the impact of the fall, her staff flew away from her hand. She flailed her hands while the stick followed a parabolic path into the void. The voices behind her became louder. In a split-second, Tara decided it made more sense to follow Kannagi than wait for the people behind her, whoever they were, to catch up. Tara scrambled to her feet and ran toward where she thought Kannagi had disappeared. Before she could make sense of the vicious terrain, Tara lost her footing and plunged into darkness.

When light entered her eyes, her head hurt. She had fallen onto a hard rocky surface. Tara touched her forehead. It was wet and sticky. She was bleeding. She groped around with her one free hand. The other lay twisted beneath her body. Turning her head to the right, she saw a figure lying on the same rocky surface a few feet away. Her vision was hazy, but the figure appeared like Kannagi.

She heard voices approaching. Her eyes closed.

# 43

# Wild Retaliation

When Tara came to her senses, she heard two men in a heated argument. "It was you who brought these greedy men to our mountain," shouted one. The voice sounded familiar and made her nervous.

"As if you knew nothing about this. Don't bluff, Raman! I am an employee of Hunt India. But what about you?" The other voice said.

Aah, it was Raman. No doubt she felt uneasy. She tried to move her hand and heard a whine. A wet, cold tongue greeted her face as she tried to sit up. She couldn't move. Coco flopped down partly on her stomach, making her wince. She was lying on a hard, rocky surface but not where she fell. Someone had moved her to a smoother surface which was not wet. She opened her eyes slowly and turned her head to the right from where animated voices emerged.

Raman stood arguing defiantly with a man dressed in smart, formal clothes. What a contrast in appearance!

A throbbing pain in her ribs reminded Tara of her fall. "Kannagi!" she cried out. It was GK who came running to her side. "I had no clue that you were both on this expedition and without Coco. Bad plan," he said, shaking his head.

"Thank God, I found Coco. He was miserable, and I could hear him from miles away from your house. He led me here."

"Kannagi?" Tara whispered

GK pointed to a rock a few feet from Tara. "She is sleeping. I gave her a painkiller. Here's one for you too."

She searched for Raman and the other man. They had moved further into the cave and were now joined by a third man. "Who are they?" Tara asked GK, pointing feebly with her stronger arm.

"That's ARN in the blue shirt, a local leader from NewTown. With him is Munaf in the white shirt. He is from Hunt India." Tara's eyes lit up in anger. "Calm down, Tara. I learned a lot about the company and why they're here, but you should first know that further down this cave is an illegal quarry. It's run by Hunt India and falls within your estate's limits." Tara gaped in astonishment despite her bleeding forehead and painful jaw.

Suddenly, Munaf started screaming. "Don't you dare put this on me, Raman! You slandered our innocent family years ago. My brother wouldn't intentionally hurt an insect. You labelled him a murderer. Not only that, you forced our family to leave our hometown. I may not be a Jomoan, but my brother earned his living from this place. He worked hard to make you all happy, and what did he get in return?!"

GK scowled. "This argument is taking a turn for the worse."

"Who are you?" yelled Raman.

"I am Sharaf's brother. The same Sharaf who died in an accident with eight children of Jomo." Munaf walked towards

Tara. "I'm sorry, Tara. I wanted to meet you earlier, but the situation was complicated. You do remember my brother, don't you?"

Tara nodded, suddenly feeling sleepy. She managed to say, "Careful!" before closing her eyes. Munaf turned around. Raman was charging toward him with a knife. He ran out of the cave in fear. "This guy's mad. He needs to be arrested."

A manic Raman ran towards Tara instead of following Munaf. GK stood back in fear while Munaf stared at Raman from a safe distance. "I tried to push this girl off the mountain, but she survived. Not going to survive this one," he said, brandishing his knife. "Your uncle slandered my dad. My family got ostracized. You'll suffer," he said as he lunged toward her. Coco leaped on him and caught him by surprise. Munaf ran forward and struck Raman's hand. The knife fell away. Raman turned towards Munaf and charged with his bare hands. Fearing for his life, Munaf ran from the cave towards the jungle. GK held on to Coco's leash to prevent him from dashing off after Raman.

Munaf ran adrift, blinded by the rain and the dense foliage. He heard Raman yelling over the incessant radio chatter of the downpour. Throughout his argument with Raman in the cave, Munaf recollected how his family was hounded after Sharaf's accident. The fear and the humiliation felt as fresh as the muddy drops he tasted while running through the wet foliage. An errant branch lashed out at his face, and he lost his balance. Hitting the ground backward, Munaf glimpsed Raman charging toward him. Raman stopped to pick up a rock. Munaf rolled over to his side exactly when Raman dropped the rock. It missed his head by a few inches. Munaf scrambled to his feet and ran in the opposite direction. He did not wait to see if Raman followed. His body ached, and he gasped for breath. When his chest started burning, he slowed and backed up among the trees, hoping to hide.

But no one came. Instead, Munaf heard a blood-curdling scream that disrupted the precipitous symphony. He froze for a second. Then he clutched his throat, afraid that it was he who had screamed, but it was not him. It was someone else in the forest. Without waiting, Munaf ran all the way back to the cave.

# 44

# A New Partnership

Tara and Kannagi spent a month at the hospital. Both slipped in and out of consciousness, barely aware of visitors. Kannagi's parents stayed with her all the time. Tara had a stream of visitors, starting with Balram, Munaf, and an elderly person that neither Tara nor Kannagi recognized. He introduced himself as Patsy, Munaf's friend. On the second day at the hospital, Meenu visited Tara and remained with her for the whole day. "We grew up together," she told Kannagi's parents. When Tara got discharged, GK counted out the money in his account and his pockets. He had just enough to pay Tara's bills. To his surprise, the hospital notified him that they were already paid by someone who wished to remain anonymous. He didn't want Tara to worry about an unknown benefactor when she needed rest and recuperation, so he kept the incident a secret.

Tara returned to Jomo, while GK and Kannagi joined hands to set up the bookstore and their life. Back at home, Tara excused herself from her students for a week. The doctor recommended complete rest to help her recuperate. She was exhausted, but it was not the physical pain. She experienced a vague rush of emotions. Her thoughts were muddled. As she lay on the hospital bed, drifting in and out of consciousness for a few days and later sleep, her mind constantly replayed the incident in the jungle. She knew the jungle and the mountain was important for Jomo to survive. Without Jomo, would there be any Jomoans? She was a Jomoan, as was Nanban. Raman was also a Jomoan, but his idiocy and hypocrisy could have nearly wiped Jomo off the map.

Tara shuddered at the thought. Who owned the mountain? Not her. In the weeks after Grandpa Lal's death, Tara had spent considerable time speaking to the locals about gardening and farming on the treacherous terrain. They told her how getting a good yield had become increasingly difficult. The rains were washing away the soil and what remained lacked the nutrition to coax life out of seeds and saplings. The mountain needed urgent reforestation, and the land could go from bad to worse if the jungle fell into the wrong hands. As she recuperated at home, Tara's sympathies shifted from herself to the mountain. Jomo was calling. It needed help.

Coco's bark jerked her out of the reverie. An unfamiliar figure emerged at her front step. Silver-haired, with a lean, clean-shaven face and wrinkled forehead, clad in a floral-printed cotton shirt and khaki pants, the man stood tall and straight, his head only an inch below the sloping roof. His eyes wandered across the porch, grazed the framed text on the wall, which prompted a crinkling of the crow's feet around them, and came to rest on Tara's puzzled face. The gaze and the soft smile that played on his lips were familiar.

"Ye-e-s?" Tara stammered, too surprised to form questions.

"Have you decided about your estate yet?"

Surprise turned to bewilderment and anger as Tara processed the presence of this strangely familiar man on her porch, asking a question that she dreaded. "Are you from Hunt India?" Tara asked. Her voice rose in indignation.

"What did they offer you?"

"That's none of your business."

"You're right. It's your estate."

"It's not just an estate. It's the forest, the mountain, the tiny and big waterfalls, the streams, the rocks, the birds, and the animals. It is Nanban. It is Jomo. I am not going to give it up to any greedy conglomerate." Tara burst out with the vehemence that built up from weeks of brooding in isolation.

"Incredible! You sound just like my mother," the man replied with a twinkle in his eye. He pulled up a chair. "Now, my dear Tara, I have a new partnership offer for you."

Tara sat down, mesmerized by the familiar gaze.

# 45

# Reunion

On a clear day, GK and Kannagi set out with a bunch of invitation cards. “Will she come?” Kannagi asked. GK shrugged, his eyes set on the hills beyond. The weather was gorgeous, with clear blue skies, unlike the dark, gloomy weather on that fateful day when he discovered the cave deep inside the mountain. Many things changed for GK after that incident.

As soon as they all returned from the jungle, he called Avantika. “I am cancelling the deal I signed with Hunt India,” he asserted.

“Well, you can’t. The company will hold you liable now.”

“I don’t care. I’ll go to the court too. The deal is off. I’ll pay back every rupee that I spent.”

Then he spoke to Kannagi’s family and asked for a loan. They agreed on the condition that he would open a jewellery store instead of a bookstore. GK refused immediately and approached Munaf for help. He seemed like a nice guy. Munaf suggested that he could crowd-source the capital from online platforms, but the thought of going online made GK jittery. When he thought, he might have to take up his old job at the textile shop, Munaf arrived with a message from his friend, Patsy.

"Patsy is willing to invest in your bookstore, provided you let him work there."

"What?"

Munaf nodded with a grin. "That's Patsy for you."

"I'll be doubly indebted to him."

Munaf shook his head. "I don't know what financial agreement you can have with him on the payback, but this is the condition he put forth."

GK didn't have a choice. His savings dwindled by the day. He agreed to Patsy's extraordinary contract and worked towards opening the bookstore. He also took up Kannagi's suggestion to refresh his lifestyle. He began exercising daily and opted out of all online networking platforms except the one where he uploaded photographs. He finished reading Man's Search for Meaning and gained a new perspective on life. He wondered whether Viktor Frankl would have written the book had he not been in captivity.

"Aren't you capturing this gorgeous scene?" Kannagi teased GK as they paused for a moment while climbing the mountain. Climbing had become much easier for GK after he started exercising. He grinned at Kannagi. "I am happy to breathe in this fresh air. I never noticed the goodness of the air because I would be out of breath." GK shook his head. "Made a mess of my health, didn't I? I was captive in a virtual jail of my own doing."

Kannagi squeezed his hand gently. "I am worried about Tara, though."

"She needs to help herself, Kannagi. You tried to persuade her to come to NewTown, but she disagreed. You said you could lend her some money, but she refused. We ordered essentials for her, and she scolded us. What more can we do?"

"I've packed some things for her pantry," Kannagi said sheepishly.

"Is that what you are carrying in your backpack? Jesus! You're going to hear some and more from Tara." They trudged ahead in anticipation of an outburst or a lament from a lonely Tara. Instead, they got a surprise. A car was parked outside Tara's house.

"She has visitors?" GK wondered aloud. When they entered the gate, Coco rushed out. He was his usual self, healthy and active. Kannagi ruffled his hair as he jumped up to greet her. "We became friends when I stayed with Tara," Kannagi said as Coco greeted her with a yelp and a lick.

Tara was out on the porch with two other people. GK recognized one to be Thomas.

"Isn't that Patsy?" Kannagi whispered.

"Hey, Patsy! Good to meet you here!" GK shouted as they climbed up to the porch.

Thomas sighed. Tara had too many well-wishers than he thought necessary. "So, that's settled," said Thomas as he finished the dregs of his tea. He wasn't happy, but he knew he was beaten at his own game. Tara beamed as she stood beside Patsy, who patted her shoulder affectionately. GK and Kannagi exchanged glances. GK observed Patsy and Tara carefully. There was a striking resemblance. He opened his mouth in surprise. Before he could speak, a man bellowed from the gate. "Is that really you?"

Kannagi let out a gasp. "Isn't that Sura?" GK recognized the man he chatted with online, pretending to be Kannagi. Sura hobbled on a cane as he climbed up to the porch. Thomas stood up. "I'll make a move. Looks like you have a lot of visitors today," he said, nodding at Patsy. "I'll prepare the papers as soon as possible."

He walked out as Sura made it to the porch. "Nilaav! It's so good to meet you after so many years!" GK and Kannagi gaped. Patsy and Tara beamed in unison.

# 46

## Patsy's Story

"I left this place at fourteen," Patsy began his story.

Sura butted in, "I remember it well. Your mother went berserk, but your father did not even bother to lodge a police complaint."

"Raman's family could never forgive or forget me after that incident."

"Yes, he made it a point to remind me whenever he could," Tara added. "How was I responsible? The incident happened before I was born. I didn't know who Uncle Patsy was."

Patsy beamed. "Uncle Patsy. I like my new name."

"How did they name you Patsy?" GK asked.

"They didn't. They named me Parthan, though my nocturnal adventures gave me the name of Nilaav."

"So, Parthan to Nilaav to Patsy would have been an exciting journey," GK remarked, eyeing Sura as he turned toward Kannagi.

"Did you connect with me to find out more about Nilaav?" Sura asked Kannagi, who nodded shyly.

"You both could've asked me straight away. I thought some kids were playing a prank on me."

Patsy chuckled. "Let me start from the beginning. My story after I left home," Patsy glanced at everyone as if asking for permission.

"Yes, sorry. I distracted you," GK apologized.

"So, after I left Jomo, I went straight to Bombay. I started doing odd jobs – cleaning tables, washing vessels, loading, and unloading, until I came across an electrical shop and asked the shop owner for some work. He agreed. I would sweep the shop, deliver them food from a nearby hotel, and, when the owner was short of hands, help them stock the materials. Gradually, I learned about the business, and the shop owner upgraded my job to assist him while I continued my cleaning duties. My salary remained the same, but I got a place to sleep instead of the footpath."

Patsy looked around. The audience listened in rapt attention. He laughed. "Will anyone believe my rags to riches story?"

"You were always the one with tall stories," Sura remarked with a sly grin.

Patsy continued, "My habit of spinning a yarn came in handy when I began chatting with one of the customers at the electrical shop. By then, I was doing small repair work. He was amused by how quickly I could resolve his issue. I lied to him that I was an orphan. I lamented how my poverty forced me to drop out of school. While I lied, hoping he would lend me some money, he shocked me by offering to sponsor my education. Those were simpler times, and people were more gullible as well as credible. I am forever indebted to Mr. Singhal. Thanks to him, I got a degree in science from Bombay. He passed away after I joined the university, so it was tough. But I sailed through with the help of generous friends and scholarships. I joined an organisation immediately after I graduated. It was a small firm, but once more, I met a benevolent benefactor, the company's owner. He agreed to sponsor my post-graduation. I continued to work in the firm until the owner's son took over. I couldn't get along with the new management."

GK nodded. "I've been through that."

"Hence you decided to open your own business," Patsy acknowledged with a smile.

"It's a bookstore, not a business."

"Are you giving away for free?" Patsy asked sharply.

"No," said GK in a low voice.

"In that case, trust me, it's a business," Patsy said with a firm nod. "I started a business too and failed in it. Then another, which failed as well. In my fourth attempt to kickstart something, I hit the jackpot. I was sourcing raw materials for companies manufacturing electronic parts, and my first customer was a Japanese firm. That took off. I shifted my business to the United States, where I got another degree in management. My company did well. I became famous too."

GK quickly flipped out his phone. Munaf had introduced Patsy to GK as someone interested in GK's bookstore idea. GK never bothered to research his investor.

"You did not conduct any research on me, did you?" Patsy asked GK with a smile. GK shook his head sheepishly. "Bad business strategy," Patsy warned. "I, too, recruited someone without a background check. That mistake led to this fiasco we witnessed in Jomo."

"Who did you recruit?" GK asked eagerly.

"Before that, I have to tell you about my burnout. It was so severe that I couldn't get out of bed in the morning. The symptoms were drastic for someone who would go for a jog every morning before sunrise. I sought medical help. I had had enough and wanted to get away. I handed over the reins of my company to my second in command, sold off a substantial portion of my shares, divested from all my assets, donated most of it, and returned to Jomo."

"You returned to Jomo?" Tara exclaimed. "When?"

"Aah, yes!" Patsy smiled apologetically. "I never told you that part." He pointed to the framed quote hanging on the wall. "That was my handiwork."

Tara stared at Patsy in horror. GK could not control his laughter and burst out. He surmised when he calmed down. "You are the wandering mendicant whose words have been revered by Jomoans all this while. A corporate honcho dealing in cutting-edge technologies warns a village about their impending doom because of the internet, and they get off the grid. The same village that treated you with disdain when you lived here. That's sweet revenge!"

Everyone cracked up except Tara, who was in a state of shock.

"You forget, GK. It was not my letter alone that made an impact. It was that accident as well," Patsy reminded. He took out a piece of paper from his pocket. "I forgot about this," he said as he handed it to Tara. It was a black and white photograph.

"The missing piece from grandmother's family photograph!" Tara exclaimed. "How did you find this?"

"I found it lying in the mud outside the house, the day I ran away." Patsy's gaze softened. "My mother was so ashamed of me."

"Gosh! If we had this with us, we could have posted it on the internet. The search would have been so much easier," Kannagi commented quickly to change the sombre mood.

"I am wary of the internet now," GK said ruefully. "What Munaf told me about BEFOR was shocking."

"What happened?" Tara asked in alarm.

"Don't worry. No harm done except to my beliefs," GK replied. "I was so convinced that BEFOR was the best idea for humankind because it connected like-minded individuals across the globe," he said, interlocking his fingers to show how he envisioned BEFOR to work, "but," he continued after separating his hands, "Munaf told me that BEFOR was many people chatting with one algorithm or software programme. Not with each other."

"What?!" Tara and Kannagi yelled in unison. Coco got excited and started jumping up and down.

"Hush, Coco," Tara said and patted him to calm him down.

"I was like Coco when I discovered BEFOR, but Munaf shattered my excitement. Apparently, BEFOR is an intelligent algorithm that keeps learning as more and more people chat with it."

"Why would they not advertise it as an intelligent application? Why lie?"

"There comes Ronny Shikari's genius," Patsy replied on GK's behalf. "Ronny is the guy I hired from one of the leading companies in the United States. He was quick at decision-making and came with loads of experience. I handed over the reins of my company named 'Jomo Technologies' to him. Within a year, he rebranded it and gave it a new face. He had his eye on every cutting-edge technological area, but I forgot that he also had a photographic memory." Patsy took out an irregularly shaped rock from his pocket, "This was imprinted in his memory more than two decades ago."

"What is this?" Tara asked, examining the rock with interest. It had jagged edges, with white, grey, and brown streaks on a smooth surface.

Patsy leaned forward. "It's a pegmatite lithium rock." He waited for someone to nod in comprehension, but no one did. "I hope you all know that Lithium is an element that is in high demand now?" No one except GK stirred. "Lithium is used in batteries. Fifty percent of the lithium mined today goes into making lithium batteries. Lithium-ion batteries power your mobile phones, laptops, and many other devices," GK explained. "I learned it from Munaf."

Comprehension dawned on others. "Devices are obviously ubiquitous, and lithium is in high demand," Tara surmised.

"I found this rock as a young boy on one of my expeditions in the jungle. I carried it everywhere as a lucky charm. It went with me from Bombay to Poona to the United

States. When I built a home for myself, I created a special glass box to display it. Before I accorded it a special place in my home, I got it examined by a geologist. She told me what it was and its worth in the modern world."

"And you told Ronny about it?" Tara asked in exasperation.

Patsy sighed. "I was young, ambitious, and vain as a peacock. One day, when Ronny visited me, I told him about this rock."

"And that it was from Jomo?" Tara was indignant.

Patsy nodded an apology. "Little did I know that Ronny would weave an intricate web of lies, deceit, and conspiracies to get hold of more."

# 47

# The Web of Lies

The group moved into the living room when Tara announced it was time for lunch. "I tried to recreate some of the things Grandma prepared before dementia gripped her."

Patsy turned pensive as he served himself some food. "I feel guilty for not visiting you all, despite being here in India."

"How many years have you spent in India after your returned?" GK asked, staring curiously at Patsy's white hair and age-defying sturdy posture.

"Nearly twenty-two years. She must have been a baby when I visited Jomo last," Patsy replied, pointing to Tara. Everyone chewed on that piece of information for a while. "I couldn't face everyone because I literally lived the life of a mendicant for five years. I subsisted on what I earned from physical labour. One day, someone recognized me. Instead of sympathizing with me, he got into a tirade about how abstract ideas of enlightenment, detachment, and renouncement are the privilege of rich people like me." Patsy observed his audience, and though no one commented, they all agreed. "I felt ashamed of what I had done. While I renounced my duties and responsibilities and gave away most of my wealth, I still had my shares in Jomo Systems. I sold them too. Then I started investing the money in small businesses. I offered to help and mentor them as well. Usually, instead of paying me part of the profits, I ask them to give me a job, any job in their organisation. I work for them, and they pay me for it. That way, I learn about a new business and earn enough to sustain myself. When I get bored with one job, I seek the next business to mentor. It keeps me happy and satisfied. At this age, what more can I ask for?" Patsy concluded with a smile.

"How old are you?" Tara asked.

"Nearly seventy."

"So, do you invest or offer a loan?" GK asked. "What happens when you no longer work for them?"

"Don't worry, GK, I won't ask you to pay me more than what you can afford," Patsy said with a chuckle.

GK flushed in embarrassment. "I was only—"

"Listen, go home and read your contract well. I've only asked for a year's employment. Post that, I don't expect anything from you."

GK was doubtful. "But—"

"You wonder how I make money? I don't make much from my investments in these companies. I have other ways of making money. I intend to teach some to Tara. She loves Jomo and would hate it if she had to leave this place."

"It's not going to help if your money-making methods involve the internet," GK said with a grimace. "Jomo is as backward as it can get when it comes to the internet."

Patsy laughed it off. "If Munaf has his way, he might change things here at Jomo. He is the new head of Hunt

India, and he might be thinking of an internet project for Jomo—" He was interrupted by Coco, who rushed out excitedly to investigate a new arrival at the gate. It was Munaf appearing as if summoned by magic.

"I hope it is not another Hunt India scheme," Tara asked suspiciously.

"No," said Patsy. "Munaf was never happy with those schemes."

GK agreed. "Munaf was the one who led me to the illegal quarry and told me about the lithium deposits underneath Jomo."

Tara calmed a belligerent Coco. She led him into the bedroom while Munaf sat at the far end of the room, afraid to catch Coco's eye. "I came to apologise to you all. I shouldn't have let the charade by Shikari go on for so long."

"It's alright, Munaf," Patsy said gently. "You followed what I suggested."

"I was nervous the whole time. It felt like I was two-timing. On the one hand, I had to listen to Shikari as he drummed up these eccentric schemes, linking BEFOR and Friend Circle, and on the other hand, I knew that I had to listen to you because your intentions were good." Munaf now straightened up and addressed Tara. "I wish to apologise on behalf of my family. What happened to you and the other children was a mishap that should never have happened. After the incident, we were hounded by the village and had to leave."

"The village?" Patsy asked.

"No, not the village, but a few of the villagers, instigated by Raman."

"Raman was always a bad apple," Tara said. The mention of Raman sent a pall of gloom over the group.

Sura was the first to speak. "Kali would be proud of Nanban if she was alive." Patsy shook his head. "It's not good, Sura, when a leopard that has never attacked a human before mauls someone to death."

"Maybe Nanban knew Raman well," GK said with a grin. Munaf shook his head. "I wouldn't wish such death upon anyone. None of you heard him scream. I did. My heart stopped for a few seconds."

"The forest department is keeping a close watch on Nanban," Tara informed. Patsy added, "The forest officials are alert. Sometimes it is better to leave the jungle alone. I like to believe that the temple was built by my grandfather to appease the jungle spirits, as per their beliefs. Although, it's highly likely that they built it to mark their territory. My ancestors did not belong to Jomo. They came as outsiders, claimed the unfarmed land and settled here. The original Jomoans, like Cheeru's ancestors, were accommodating. They only knew to share the bounties of the forest. My ancestors had other plans." Tara shook her head in disappointment. "It's always better to leave the jungle alone," Tara stated emphatically.

"Is it a big temple?" Kannagi asked. She had been curious about it since Tara showed her the map.

"From what I remember, it was a small one made of stone slabs, inside which they used to light a lamp," Patsy replied.

"Is there no deity?"

"The jungle is the deity," Patsy said with a smile.

"I wish we had reached the temple," Kannagi said wistfully.

Tara turned to Patsy. "We nearly reached the place, but then we rolled off the slope towards the cave."

"We can go there," Patsy said with a nod, "before the forest panchayat asks us to obtain special permission."

"Forest panchayat?" Kannagi asked.

"We both decided to hand over a part of our inherited land to the village commons. The forest panchayat, part of the Jomo panchayat, will decide all matters related to the village commons. No one can sell the land or use it for agriculture or commercial purposes unless the forest panchayat approves," Patsy added.

"They won't. The forest panchayat will consist of elders and others in the village who know how important it is to prevent the exploitation of forests. Jomoans who depend on the forest for firewood, or the berries and other fruits, will be allowed, but not others," Tara explained. "I plan to stand for the Panchayat elections this year. The Jomoans know their forests the best." Patsy beamed at his niece with pride.

"So, that's why Thomas was so glum," GK said with a chuckle. "He lost a chance to make money."

"What about Shikari? What is he going to do about the lithium mine?" GK asked, turning to Munaf.

"Aah, yes! Despite all his efforts—" Munaf began.

"Wait!" Tara interjected. "No one explained to us what was the conspiracy that Shikari cooked up."

Munaf cleared his throat. "When I was entrusted with BEFOR, I was excited by the whole idea. An intelligent chatbot that could offer different levels of solace and comfort to people in need of company—that was the idea. Later I realised that BEFOR and Friend Circle was a façade to learn more about the people of Jomo and NewTown. Shikari wanted to control the largest portion of land in Jomo so that he could start the exploration project for Lithium. He had to do it without antagonizing the locals. He couldn't alert the competition and was afraid that the locals might raise environmental concerns about the project."

"But it was Friend Circle that went about acquiring people's houses and lands. How is BEFOR connected with this?" Tara could not connect the dots.

"BEFOR collected personal information and data from the folks of NewTown. It helped the company learn about local politics and social issues. People trusted the chatbot so easily," Munaf said with a smirk. "You remember how you received discount coupons from BEFOR?" he asked GK. "I was careful about not giving out personal information," GK defended himself.

"You asked BEFOR about Nilaav and Sura. Thanks to you, Patsy realised that his niece was still living here."

"How?" GK was astonished.

"I had access to the chat transcripts. When I saw the name Nilaav, I immediately notified Patsy," Munaf replied sheepishly.

"That's a blatant violation of privacy!" GK yelled.

Munaf nodded. "The company is embroiled in a lawsuit. I am sure the complainant's lawyers would reach out to all users to strengthen their case. You can add your complaints." He continued after a pause, "I might have to bear some of the consequences, too. Even if I become a witness."

"So, that's how Patsy came to Tara's rescue," GK said to puncture the uncomfortable silence after Munaf's confession.

"I sent Tara some money years ago, anonymously, hoping that she would get a good education and leave this place," Patsy said with a shake of his head. "But I stayed on," Tara said with a wry smile. "My fault. I never bothered to check on you." Patsy was apologetic.

"So, BEFOR gathered data and fed it to Friend Circle. They used that data to interact with the locals." GK surmised.

Munaf continued, "When Shikari learned that Jomo didn't have the internet, he was ecstatic and at the same time disappointed. Ecstatic because the locals would have no means to research about him or his company and disappointed because he now had to rely on something other than an app to entice the locals." Sniggers went around the room as everyone understood Shikari's shenanigans.

# 48

# Jomo Calls

At the crack of dawn, Tara approached her vegetable patch. A new batch of seeds from the agricultural department showed promise. A few peeped into the rarefied Jomo Mountain air, having broken through their skins, eager to face the morning sun. When she returned to the porch, she found Patsy up and about, doing light stretching exercises. Patsy had taken up grandma's room, and Tara felt the house put on a few years of wisdom. After Tara was orphaned, the bungalow took on the aura of a fresh-faced struggler in the world, full of determination and impulsive behaviour. Despite its dreamy post in the clouds, the house gained gravity with Patsy on the porch.

"Living in Jomo is not without risks," said Patsy as Tara brought out their morning tea. Tara nodded. Patsy was continuing their post-dinner conversation from the day before. They had talked long and deep into the night. Tara expressed her inability to imagine living anywhere other than Jomo. Patsy, though sceptical, had to relent because, in his words, "I am like a swallow. It is difficult for me to stay in one place."

"Don't malign the swallows. They migrate to survive. You are a drifter," Tara said with a grin.

Patsy chuckled. "To be called a drifter at the age of seventy is both embarrassing and inspiring." Tara reminded Patsy about their lunch invite for the day. "Yes, my new job at GK's Bookstore starts tomorrow," he said with a smile.

"I hope you'll reconsider your decision to stay at NewTown."

"I'm not as strong as you, Tara. I can't live without the internet," Patsy said with a guffaw.

They set out to honour the invite from GK and Kannagi. GK's Bookstore stood niftily at a busy main street corner. It had an enviable crowd, thanks to the newfound popularity of ARN.

Munaf had convinced ARN to visit the cave and catch the men red-handed. After he showed him the illegal exploration activities conducted by Hunt India, ARN took it upon himself to stall any further commercial presence in the jungle. The people rallied around ARN when they learned that his intentions were to get people their due while ensuring that the jungle remained protected. GK was surprised to learn that inside that bombastic narcissist, there was a heart wanting to do good. Although, some things never change.

On the day of the bookstore's inauguration, GK invited ARN to give a short speech about the importance of books, but it turned into a self-aggrandizing speech on how he saved the Jomoans from impending doom. "Had I not stopped Hunt India, they would have brought down the mountain by digging deep into its base." There were a few chuckles, but the audience tolerated his words, and some clapped. GK stood by impatiently. He was waiting for his special guest to inaugurate the bookstore. The board outside the store announcing the inauguration did not mention the chief guest's name.

"I heard that it was the founder of some start-up," Patsy whispered to Tara.

"For a bookstore? How imaginative!" Tara was unimpressed.

"Start-up founders can also be interested in books."

Tara rolled her eyes. Then quickly straightened her face. Since Patsy's arrival, she had been behaving like a teen. Throwing tantrums for trivial reasons and forcing Patsy to relent to her demands. He indulged and never said no to anything. Tara regarded her calm and poised uncle. For a moment, she glimpsed her lost childhood. She blinked rapidly to get rid of the wetness in her eyes. Patsy noticed her strained expression. He put his arms around her for a gentle pat on the shoulder. "You have grown into a wise, mature woman, my dear. The years past will give you the strength to go ahead in life. Live life on your terms. Never give up on what you love."

Tara's attention shifted to the murmuring crowd. They craned their necks as a car drew into the parking space next to the bookstore. "That's the chief guest, I presume," Patsy said to Tara, pointing to a young man dressed casually in a T-shirt and a pair of jeans.

"Has he come for a jaunt around the neighbourhood?" Tara said with a smirk, then she frowned. She recognized the man. It was Balram. "What is he doing here?"

ARN began to introduce Balram with a pompous tone. "Meet our chief guest today, Mr.—" Balram stopped him, greeted the crowd with folded hands, and proceeded to cut the ribbon. The people entered the bookstore en masse, and Patsy hurried to help GK. Many were already flipping through the books in the store. Balram hung back and approached Tara. She nodded but walked past briskly to avoid a conversation. Throughout the afternoon, she kept her distance from Balram. By evening, only a few customers remained, and Tara heaved a sigh of relief as she saw him leave.

GK, Kannagi, Patsy, and Tara teamed up at the NewTown Café to celebrate a busy afternoon of selling books. "That was a good start, I would say," Patsy said, raising his cup. "I wish many more such busy days for you, GK and Kannagi."

"So, when are you coming to Jomo with the next invitation?" Tara teased the happy couple.

"In due time," GK replied with a grin.

Patsy glanced at Tara and turned to GK. "We were astonished to see Balram cutting the ribbon today."

GK gave a quick glance at Tara and turned to Patsy. "I bet you were."

Tara could not control it anymore. "Did he talk about his role in the Hunt India conspiracy?"

GK glanced at Patsy, who cleared his throat before speaking. "He was recruited to ensure Friend Circle grew its influence in the region. His only fault was that he did not ask why they started their operations at Jomo."

"What about the men and the cave?" Tara asked in indignation. "What about the work-in-progress sign?"

"Balram didn't know about the illegal mine. He was told they were building a new operations site for Friend Circle. He even suggested a horticultural project, which he hoped that, err, you would head," GK added.

Tara laughed hysterically. "Ridiculous excuses and you fell for them?"

Patsy rose from his chair. "We'll make a move, boss. I need to wake up early for my first day at work."

GK interjected in surprise, "But—" Patsy shook his head in reply. After Tara walked away, he turned around and whispered to GK, "Tell Balram he'll have to try harder to redeem himself. She is as stubborn as my mother." When Patsy stepped out of the café, he saw Tara staring at a building across the street. JOMO Organic Solutions, said a sign at the top of the edifice.

"This is new," Tara muttered.

"Yes, it's a start-up. They deal with those new techniques of growing food." Tara raised her eyebrows in response. "You must have heard about hydroponics, aquaponics, and all those fancy terms."

"Oh!" Tara said, "but why did they name it after Jomo?

"The owner has a special liking for the place."

"Do you know him?" asked Tara as they boarded the bus to Jomo.

"Yes. I've invested in his business."

Tara reacted in a mix of reverence and suspicion. "You are so quick! Do you understand what they are up to?"

"I go with my instincts. I found the founder to be trustworthy. I am Patsy but I am no patsy," he said with a guffaw.

Tara smiled at her uncle's weak attempt to crack a joke. Then lapsed into silence until they got off the bus at the Jomo foothills. "Uncle Patsy, I can never imagine a life outside Jomo."

Patsy nodded. "You've told me before, but have you known any other place?"

Tara shook her head defiantly. "Neither do I want to know."

They climbed up the path to their house in silence. Tara was lost in her thoughts while Patsy came to grips with his diminishing lung capacity. He stopped for a bit and breathed in the mountain air. It was crisp but offered little assistance to a septuagenarian hiking a rugged slope. He gasped for breath as they trudged the path to Tara's house. "Now, do you understand why I need to stay in NewTown?"

Tara nodded sympathetically and held his arm to offer him support. "Uncle Patsy—" she began but got distracted by voices further up the mountain coming from behind her house. Coco barked excitedly from inside. She quickened her pace and opened the gate. Finding the keys, she opened the door in an awkward fumble. Coco came bounding out with a series of barks, growls, yelps, and whines. He shot straight out of the gate into the path that led further to the mountaintop. Tara could hear his barks as she walked out. Patsy stood nearby in a mix of exhaustion and confusion. Coco stopped barking, and Tara froze. A man walked down the hill with a happy Coco at his heels. It was Balram. He walked straight to Patsy after nodding at Tara. "I am sorry if I startled you. I came to Jomo with my team of botanists. They wanted to study the local flora." Balram produced a bag of dog treats from his backpack. "I got this for Coco," he said as he extended the bag to Tara. Coco circled around, wagging his tail, expecting a treat. Balram walked away to talk to his team, who wore T-shirts with JOMO Organic Solutions written on them. Coco followed him.

"For us humans, it takes ages to understand someone and, occasionally, a lifetime to forgive. Dogs aren't like that," Patsy said, nodding at Coco.

"Why don't you join us for dinner, young man?" Patsy asked Balram. Tara walked inside without a word. "I want to hear your plans for your new company," Patsy said, "and for your life," he added. His eyes twinkled with mischief.

Balram paused at the steps near the gate and turned to absorb the scene. The jungle appeared as fresh as the day he first stepped onto the mountain. The clouds drifted by with a friendly wave. The sun shone mellow on its way to the west. The birds amped up their chirpy chatters before they went quiet for the evening. A monkey screeched somewhere in the lush jungle. "For a long time, I was overwhelmed by the fear of missing out," he considered his rudderless smartphone and added with a smile, "but now Jomo calls."

**THE END**

# Acknowledgements

Eternally grateful to the Universe for the creative strength to continue writing, my twin loves, Samoj and Samidha, blessings from my parents and parents-in-law, and support from my friends and family.

I extend my heartfelt gratitude to my reading and writing communities, whose constant feedback and enthusiasm keep me going.

Special thanks and appreciation to young Saanvi Modi, who created the first drafts of the cover design with exceptional clarity and skill.

Thanks to the Notion Press team for their support.

www.ingramcontent.com/pod-product-compliance
Lightning Source LLC
LaVergne TN
LVHW041013150826
845672LV00001B/81

* 9 7 9 8 8 9 0 0 2 8 8 2 2 *